VIVIENNE

A. RAY

Vivienne
A. Ray
Copyright 2023.

ISBN: 978-1-7395723-0-3

Cover design and layout by Peter Reisner

Empty is
the sky before the sun wakes up in the morning.
The eyes of animals in cages.
> *The faces of women mourning*
> *When everything has been taken*
>> *from them.*

Me?
> *Don't ask me about empty.*

Empty is the hour before sleep
Kills you every night
Then pushes you to safety
> *Away from every kind of light.*

> *Empty is me.*

Empty is me.

Excerpt, Rod McKuen: In Someone's Shadow. 1971

1. Vivienne

It was hard to tell what was real and what wasn't anymore. Time seemed to stretch and stop, transmuting within my memories of her. I looked back ambivalently toward a cluster of blank, blurry faces and trailing tears; like cars passing on a rainy highway through a smudged window. I didn't recollect nor care for these transient people. I couldn't hear their bland voices speaking to me. They all sounded like noise in a metal tunnel. I heard nothing but the faint, dull beating of my grieving, hollowed out chest. Call me overdramatic, even melancholy. All I can say was at that point, on that day, I wanted to be in that coffin beside her.

People began to arrive and shuffle slowly along the corridors in their typical drab, black funeral attire. God, she would have absolutely hated this overly formal display. Boxy, probably borrowed, moderately expensive or cheap crinkled dark suits accompanied by old-sock-drawer ties, perhaps used previously for weddings or fancy work dinner events, maybe even a murder mystery weekend. Lacy, inky colored dresses with hems below the knees. Transparent, occasionally laddered black nylon tights. Flat, painfully boring shoes; I hardly noticed anyone in heels. No one was trying to look sexy or draw attention for this funeral, clearly.

I sat near the back of the small chapel, staring solemnly at the grand array of religious art and brightly colored stained glass that adorned the side paneling of the building, losing myself in their permanent mourning. Who created these horrifically depressing works of art? What were they trying to convey, some kind of empathy? Every human and saint in these fresco-esque paintings and glass art looked completely despondent, lonely; like they had also lost someone close to them, looking on hopelessly past me into the vast universe of an infinitely dark longing, some with tears in their eyes, missing someone or something I'd never known.

We exchanged pleasantries and stiff nods as they silently poured in; people I knew very well and others I didn't, but they knew her and maybe had worked with her, or belonged to one of her social circles, perhaps even grew up with her and remembered her before I had known and loved her. They all meandered slowly over to me one by one to tell me how incredibly sorry they were. Whether they meant it or not I couldn't really tell, and to be honest I didn't really care. I didn't even want to be here. I hated funerals. I especially hated funerals like this.

I nodded politely, mechanically, towards the people

scuttling past me like silent druids, shaking limp hands and accepting soft, half-pressed hugs against my chest when they were brave enough to come forth and touch me. My worn, scruffy face and dead eyes looked forward vacantly while I thanked them individually for attending. Some had driven across states or flown a long way to be here, after all, I should at least appreciate them for making the effort on such short notice. Why was I being so incredibly aloof, so rude? She would have loved that so many people had come to wish her a true farewell, even if I didn't feel like showing up for it.

It's not that I didn't want her to have a funeral, of course I did, I loved her desperately. She was always so good to me, so fair, kind. I guess I was just fucking angry and bothered that the old adage was coming true before me and the good ones do, indeed, get taken too soon from this earth. I didn't want to be here because being here made it concretely true that she was truly dead, that she was really gone for good. I didn't need to be hugging people and pseudo-consoling my family and friends and staring emptily at weathered, stained glass religious people crying. We should have been at home, or in the mountains, or anywhere else but here, living life to the fullest, not mourning its premature end.

Once almost everyone had arrived, they mingled nervously and located their seats in the caramel-stained pews that lined the small chapel's interior before collectively forming groups to reconnect and catch up. Flowers were loosely attached on the aisle along the edge of every peaked bench, white tea roses and rosemary bound into little gold bouquets—her favorite. The whole place smelled like a goddamn English garden mixed with frankincense; an abnormal scent for the inner suburbs of Los Angeles, where the air typically smells of choking wildfires, arrogance, career letdowns and pollution.

I noticed a few important people to her were absent, her father, most noticeably. He was a cold, self-made money man who seemed entirely impenetrable at the best of times. A poker face like you'd never seen, a stare into the center of your core like he was trying to kill your mortal soul. Every time he was around, you felt like you were being judged, sized up, mentally squashed like invasive vermin by this man's icy gaze. He was also a fully functioning alcoholic in every sense of the phrase. In typical fashion, he was unfashionably late; Probably guzzling a beer or a mini bottle of scotch in the car before eventually staggering in, red faced, puffy, ripe, and ready to dazzle us with his controversially brash, conservative opinions about politics and the current state of the failing world.

My father was here as well, in a much different facet to hers. He was a quiet, simple man, a man of few words but a loving, decent person. He owned a small landscaping company and made a modest living going house to house with his team and working on their home or business gardens. He hated being indoors. As far back as I could remember we were always outside, learning about local plants and their respective families, contraindications and poisons. This is how I fell in love with nature. She loved nature too; we were always exploring the different climates and ecosystems together and camping over the years. God, this was excruciating. I held back dry tears, rubbing my sore eyes until I saw multicolored spots before me. I hadn't been able to cry much since it happened. It was as if the tears had run out entirely, along with every other functioning liquid in my body. I felt dry in every sense of the word. My tongue scraped the roof of my mouth like gritty sandpaper against raw meat.

I could see her moving so vividly in my mind. Her long, smooth hands brushing over rugged bark and smelling the Scott's Pine tree, the one that is supposed to smell of warm vanilla. Laughing freely like a child, her thick, wavy hair blowing in the warm September wind, her face twisting into a playful dance with the world around her leading. She never cared where we were as long as we felt content, full, safe. Why the fuck was she lying here dead?

I fell in and out of daydreams and sweet memories only to snap cruelly back to the macabre, stale chapel reality playing out before me. I wanted to escape from it, to get up and drive away, and suddenly I had the desire to vomit directly onto the church floor and onto everyone around me. My stomach felt a wretched churning. A twisting deep into the pathways of my contracted intestines, working its way up to my flushed, hot, unshaven cheeks.

I slipped swiftly past family and friends who were still in the wings catching up quietly and ducked sharply for the chapel bathroom. I rushed into the stall, fell to my knees in front of the toilet, as if praying to it, and released everything

inside of me in one foul spray across the porcelain bowl.
This morning I'd only had two black coffees and a few small
sips of orange juice. I wasn't hungry for any solid food in the
slightest. I'm never hungry in the mornings, especially on
this morose Friday. The last thing I wanted to do was enjoy
breakfast without her in my life.

Upon completion of the liquid onslaught and purging
of my nervously caffeinated insides, I wiped my face quickly with a square of rough church toilet paper clinging onto
the metal roll and got up to leave, wiping the dust from my
trouser knees. God, I was a total fucking mess. She would
hate to see me like this. Just as I opened the bathroom stall to
leave, I saw my best friend, Will, standing there. I studied his
expression; it was obvious he had just heard everything and
there was no way I could lie to him about barfing all over the
chapel bathroom. He knew me too well, anyway.

"Hey, what's going on? Are you sick or something?" he
asked gingerly, putting his hand on my shoulder in a brotherly way.

"I just don't want to be here. The whole thing makes
me feel nauseous. I never thought we'd be here so soon." I
stuttered.

"Of course you didn't, V. Jesus, I mean, none of us expected to be here. No one wants to believe it when someone
die…goes. Maybe we should get out there, you know, join
everyone? I'm really shitty at consoling. I never know exactly
what to say in these situations. Come back in there with me, I
can sit with you, if you want." He gestured limply toward the

door with his long arm.

I moved brokenly toward the sink, half walking, half stumbling. He leaned over and slapped me on the back in a half hug while I studied my ragged face in the mirror. I looked awful, disheveled, blue and completely drained of life, despite being in my nicest set of clothes. Maybe because I had just chucked my insides into a church toilet, maybe because I had cruelly and suddenly lost someone I loved and admired deeply. I felt like I was looking at a skull covered in gray, scaly skin, held up by toothpicks and metal pins. A marionette of a human who once resembled me. I tried to recall how I usually looked, in my life before, when I felt alive, full of color, happy. A time when I didn't feel like a wandering skin amoeba, floating through life.

I turned on the small faucet and covered the drain, splashing some cold water onto my face and wiping my cheeks with a blue disposable paper towel. Someone had carved 'god is gay' onto the metal box that held the towels, which made me smile a little. I felt like God was dead, personally; who takes away such a beautiful person so soon? If God did exist, they certainly were a cruel asshole.

Will handed me a piece of gum in a shiny blue wrapper.

"For the bile. You don't want to smell, do you? More than you already do, I mean." I appreciated him cracking a joke. Even if it was true. I probably did smell; I could barely be bothered to shower anymore. It took a tremendous amount of effort to even convince myself to get out of bed in the morning. All I wanted to do now was sleep, to forget, to float in the blackness of the in between until the pain receded and I could see my way through the fog, finally.

I grinned wryly and accepted the gum, chewing the minty rubber square quickly to wash the taste of bitter saliva away. My throat stung from the vomit.

"Let's go back out there, alright? Come on." He put his hand on my back in that familiar, brotherly way.

"Alright, yes, okay." I sighed, defeated, and walked slowly behind him, biding my time, toward the service and into the sea of black, full of reluctance to participate in this painfully bleak day. I debated running out of the front doors and leaving, but Will walked behind me, pushing me forward from behind.

Will and I met in freshman year of high school and had been bound together since. I liked him because he never judged me, never even thought of judging me. Even in my worst moments, worst outfits, haircuts, worst days, actions, he seemed to be an infinite well of forgiveness and empathy. He was originally from Buenos Aires, Argentina, son to a wild and fiery mother and a father who seemed to have more tricks and secrets up his sleeve than a touring magician.

We never actually figured out exactly what his father did for a living. It was a constant source of excitement for us to try and guess where he was and what he was cryptically doing for work. He would hole up in his room for days at a time, hardly leaving the confines of his chamber, only to appear suddenly and leave in his car for 'work' for a week, or longer. Large wads of cash would appear next to the overflowing ashtrays and ornamental shrines to his dead relatives, but scarcely normal, day-to-day items would never be present in their home, like hand towels or forks, items most people had.

Will could have turned out to be a real fuck up, if he had let that unconventional upbringing get to him. Instead, he was probably the most evenly keeled amongst us, and he cared for me unconditionally. That was no easy feat, I could admit. I was a selfish, apathetic asshole when I wanted to be. I truly didn't deserve a friend as good as Will. The world needed people like him to lighten the rooms, make life a little smoother, lighter, more enjoyable. A human to remind us that there is indeed beauty within this dark, superficial place.

Will was that person for me. I tried to give back what he had gifted me in equal measure, but I was consistently falling short. I often felt in deficit next to him, owing credit I didn't have, nor ever would. He didn't have to try to be good, he just was. It made up the fiber of his being, the moral core of his soul. Trying to be a decent person felt like a never-ending circus act for me, a play. Surely everyone could see through the veil and any day they'd call me out on my bullshit and never speak to me again, throwing me into the pit of lost friends and shitty lovers you never care to revisit.

We made our way back into the chapel foyer and saw the cousins and aunts circling around, looking stoic and forlorn, ghostlike. Probably gossiping about the other women's outfits and their failed marriages and spoiled kids. Yet they were still managing to smile and hold court amongst everyone surrounding them, dressed in little two-piece 90's suits, simple black cotton dresses and woven hats with veils or black fabric flowers. I had always admired women, more than anything, for their ability to persistently put up with life's severe waves of exhausting pain and still move forward, still able to get up in the morning, to exist, to laugh, to persevere. Meanwhile, I was barely keeping myself together; my mental state and physical health hung by a barren thread for everyone to witness and openly gossip over.

I went back to my allotted seat in the front pew and sat down near the decorated floral altar. We were having an open casket ceremony, which was what she had wanted. She didn't want us to be afraid to see her body after her life ended. She held a very spiritual, very honest view of death. A view that death and life were so intertwined that they were almost imperceptible to us, a cycle of continuation, something we shouldn't be afraid of or run from. She would have hated having a church funeral; this was only happening due to the persistence and emphatic demands of her father, who raised her Catholic. We fought and argued bitterly over it after she was gone but he insisted that he was footing the bill for it, and it had to be in a Catholic church, no budging. Well, at least she'd be buried where she wants to be, despite the stuffy, religious prelude.

I glanced over at the open casket. People had already begun to make their way down the aisle, heads bowed, standing respectfully in front of it. Some laid flowers, or cards, others simply touched the edge of the casket and whispered words of farewell or prayers, indiscernible to anyone but them and her. I had already seen her, laying there motionless, when I had arrived. I made sure to be one of the first to see her, to really let it sink in that she was dead and gone and cut away from my life, at least physically. The morbidity of it all slightly fascinated me if I was being totally honest with myself. I had only ever attended two other funerals, and I had never actually seen a dead body before. I couldn't help but stand, transfixed, staring down at her stiff, quiet form, nestled neatly inside of her wooden rectangle.

She looked beautiful, like a fallen, slumbering angel made of hard wax. Her pale, high cheekbones looked carved from stone, flushed with a ruby tint. Her lips were the color of fallen summer cherries. Not gaudy or garish makeup by any means; the makeup artist had done some very professional work. She looked tasteful, dressed in a simple, white linen dress and covered in small white flowers. Her hands rested gently across her lifeless abdomen. I wondered, perhaps gruesomely, what she was full of. Embalming fluid? Paper tissues, cotton balls, cardboard? I recall the mortician referring to 'smoke and mirrors' to make a body look more presentable for funerals. Was she now just a preserved skin pinata full of recycled trash?

Her casket was constructed of simple wood. Pinewood, to be exact. She wanted a prolific, compostable wood that would break up within a few decades so she could truly rest beneath the earth and fertilize the forest around her. She didn't want to be bound for eternity within a cold metal box, which she believed would trap her between worlds. She wanted to become the earth, to rot entirely. We made sure to grant all of her wishes, to the great perturbation of her father, who thought she was behaving like a raging, hippie liberal. Those were his words.

"Okay, son, it's time, it's about to start," my father said to me in his quiet, collected voice, resting his rough gardener's hand on my back. I stared at him with empty, heavy eyes. "Are you going to be okay for this?" he added, looking slightly concerned.

"I'm fine. I just want to get this over with. I'm tired of being sat here, I feel like I'm just idling," I said, perhaps a little harshly, shaking my knees under my palms. My father looked at me with his kind, brown eyes. He seemed to understand my curt agitation, which I appreciated. He nodded without the need to engage in further conversation.

We leaned back in our seats and straightened up while the priest prepared his paperwork on the podium for the eulogy. I looked around at the people here, perhaps sixty, maybe seventy, sat dotted around the chapel, like a lake of dark fabric and black hats bobbing in wooden boats, scattered with spots of red lipstick and probably fake pearls. Her father had eventually stumbled in, looking and no doubt feeling rough, eventually locating his seat and sitting down in the front row. The whole place reeked of aftershave, roses and rosemary. I felt like I was going to be sick again. I sat as still as I could to avoid attention, queasily rubbing my sweaty forehead with a handkerchief.

The priest began to drone on in his boring, monotone voice, about how God always had a plan, even if we didn't understand it yet, how it was always painful to lose a loved one, to send them into the next life where they hopefully would be joined with the almighty lord and savior and bask in the glory and spoils of heaven. What the hell did he know? Had he ever lost anyone he'd loved? Did he love anyone? Was this only the first of many funerals he had scheduled today, and we were only the first to hear this incredibly dull speech that would be regurgitated to the next crying crowd with only the names and body replaced? God, please get me out of here. I stared at a long gray cobweb above the crucifix. Even Jesus himself looked bored of this dull employee working for him.

The family came next, her mother, father, and siblings all went up to say their peace and wish her farewell. It was touching to see how much people loved her. Of course they did, she was an easy person to love. They recollected fond memories and inside jokes and traits they had particularly adored in her. This made me remember my own. I didn't speak or give any kind of speech, to the dismay and disapproval of her family. I hadn't wanted to display my personal memories of her to a crowd. I wanted to keep them sacred, safe with me. I didn't feel the need or desire to say them aloud to a room of people who didn't know her the way I had.

I stared at the stone floor, legs still bouncing up and down nervously, fingers twitching against my jutting knuckles while the last of the family members said their parting words. I looked over to see the top of her forehead and nose poking out of the top of the pine box. It looked like a smooth, snowy mountaintop surrounded by dark winter trees.

After what felt like an eternity, the eulogies and speeches concluded, and the pallbearers came to carry her casket out of the chapel, the priest swinging incense back and forth in front of them. We all rose and began to follow them out slowly, some people wiping fresh tears from their faces or leaning against their partners for support, clutching handkerchiefs. Low mutterings and traditional, loud organ music filled the small room as we filed out in a solemn, silent line.

Outside, it was warm and typically sunny, the Santa Ana winds blowing in from the east, brushing heat against my skin like an open oven. The harsh afternoon sunlight shocked me out of my mourning stupor, making me squint to see where I was walking after being sat in the dark, cold chapel. It was late October, nearing Halloween, but it certainly didn't feel like autumn. In Southern California autumn doesn't really have a specific feel. It just feels warm, pleasant, easy. The only thing that makes it feel like autumn is the consumerist world around me, the world of plastic pumpkins and fake foliage. But we all knew it wasn't a real autumn. Not like it would be on the east coast, or up north. No bright red, falling leaves. No chilly, blustering air, no snow. Just tall, thin palm trees swaying in the balmy breeze, dancing carelessly in the Pacific winds.

I wondered how many caskets these palm trees had

stared down upon. How many funerals, weddings, baptisms and family fights they'd witnessed from all the way up there in the sky.

After the casket was closed and locked, she was placed in the back of the black hearse to be driven to the woods of a nearby forested canyon nestled at the foot of a local mountain range. We had purchased a small plot for her a few years back. She wanted to be buried between two tall sugar pine trees. These giants always reminded her of just how insignificant and small we were in this world. These trees survived fires, storms, seasons, drought and continued to persevere for thousands of years. This was what she desired to be nestled between on her journey to the unknown.

The burial was straightforward; they had dug the plot earlier in the day and readied it for our arrival in the afternoon. After about an hour of driving in silence, staring out of the window at the flutter of life passing around me, we finally arrived at the base. Getting up to the mountain canyon was a feat for some with only two-wheel drive or small suspension cars, through the rocky dirt roads and shoddy GPS instructions, but they got there in the end, passing beautiful, densely packed forests scenting the air with aromatic pine bark.

We gathered in a circle and said our last goodbyes, as we watched her casket being gingerly lowered into the grave made for her. It looked like a burial from medieval times, where people couldn't afford family plots in the local cemeteries or churches and ended up burying bodies where they could find open space. She was always different; knew she didn't want to be somewhere typical. I smiled again to myself, admiring her fierceness. People were probably grumbling about what a pain in the ass it was to drive up here and how she should have been buried at a normal cemetery. Fuck them, I thought. They didn't understand her. She wasn't of this world to begin with.

The final handfuls of dirt thrown on, we stared in silence for a while at the deep, dead hole in the ground, lapping up the warmth and smell of fresh pine needles and bark sap around us. Even if you didn't like nature, you should be able to appreciate that. It was goddamn gorgeous up here. I watched fluffy tailed squirrels and chipmunks eagerly running around, pouncing from log to branch and back again. Woodpeckers and blue jays flew effortlessly, making sharp chirps wherever they landed, echoing around us. The forest was totally alive, even if she no longer was.

Suddenly I wondered if any animals would attempt to dig her out of her grave. A bear, or a mountain lion perhaps? Would they smell her? Maybe the embalming fluid would put them off…

Just as I was imagining her poor body ravaged by hungry mountain lions, my dad tapped my shoulder. I looked up at him, startled away from my dark thoughts.

"It's time to go, son," he said, searching my face for signs that I was going to be okay after this.

I nodded, and proceeded to head back to the car, kicking a pinecone and spreading dust whirling into the air,

mentally preparing for the long drive down the curvy canyon roads and heading back into the bowels of the heartless,
vacuous city in which I resided, alone.

2. Vivienne

Once we reached sea level again, we drove to a small, casual restaurant with a bar and events room to the side, rented out for minor crowd events such as receptions, high school reunions and, in this case, wakes.

A long, colorful buffet was set up with an array of typical American foods; turkey finger sandwiches, cheese sandwiches, little factory-made croissants and bowls of seventies-looking fruit cocktails. Crudité, bright, neon-orange carrot sticks and fleshy, watery celery with ranch and hummus for dipping. Who actually eats this, I wondered as I scanned the room, scowling at the unattractive offering, I felt disgusted at the sight of everything.

Just as the thought entered my mind, my rotund uncle Murray barreled in and headed right over to the fruit cocktail, violently stabbing pineapple and bright melon with the spears of his plastic fork before shoveling it into his mouth, smacking his lips loudly while chewing. I grimaced, watching this grotesque scene; I guess all of that mourning makes a person hungry. I hated the sound of people eating. When you have no appetite, people eating just sounded like barbaric slapping and slurping. It made me sick.

Most people, however, went straight toward the bar. I could hear the bartender taking orders, listing off different white wines and beers on tap, single malt scotches and Mexican tequilas. Ice cubes clinked against glasses as people began to retrieve and sip their drinks, standing around, slurping thin straws, talking about what they had been up to recently, how long it'd been since they had seen one another, talking about her.

I sat in a corner booth with a tall glass of iced water resting atop a circular paper coaster, watching the neon lights of a bar sign flashing before me, dazed. It read 'Always Cold' with a nostalgic bright red, pinkish font. I fell into the rhythmic hum of the electric current charging through it. I thought of her body up there in that forest, alone. From now on her physical body would always be cold. No more comforting autumn evenings, nothing but cold, dead matter, rotting away in the dirt.

My friends meandered over and sat beside me in my booth, some more recent, some from as far back as my school days, filling up the area and squeezing me in between them. Will and his partner Agnes were there, along with some former classmates of mine who had grown up with her. We talked about our old friends whom we had lost touch with over the years, where they were working, how they were all getting along as adults. How everyone was having babies and moving out of the cities and into the suburbs. We talked about my job and what I was working on currently. I could tell they were trying to distract me, even if they understood their efforts were futile. I appreciated the sentiment; I would probably do the same if I was in their position. I sipped my iced water quietly and listened to their conversation across the table, catching full sentences occasionally between my own thoughts.

"Did you hear about Sam Sacco? She's moved to New York. Apparently she's working on like, huge sets now. Did you ever think you'd see the day? She barely made it through high school!"

"What about Felix? You know he's got four kids from three different women, right? Get that guy some condoms, am I right?"

"I never really understood what happened to her, she was trying to be a singer or something, wasn't she? God, I haven't thought about her in years…"

Will snapped me out of my mental absence and asked me if I wanted a cigarette. To my own surprise and great indifference, I did. I had never wanted a cigarette so badly in my life. He motioned for us to go outside, and we shimmied our way out of the booth and headed for the back door that led to the patio area.

Outside felt womb-like and warm again. Soothing. Like a soft blanket, sheer peacefulness compared to the ruckus of loud voices echoing in the wake. The afternoon was winding down into evening and the traffic outside had slowed a bit, before the chaos of rush hour took over and the horns began to hiss and scream down the highways. A gentle breeze was rustling around the palm trees, clapping their leaves together softly like long fingers.

Will handed me his box of cigarettes. I grabbed the tip of an orange filter and put it to my mouth, lit it, inhaled and exhaled deeply, coughing instantly which caused my throat to burn with pain. I hadn't smoked in years. I'd given it up for her because she ardently hated it and threatened me constantly. She had always given me an enormous amount of grief for smoking, ranting about how she didn't want to see me die from lung or throat cancer, how she didn't want to bury me. Now the joke was on her, considering I had to bury her first.

I had a terrible head rush instantly from the smoke and lack of food in my stomach. I could feel my veins contracting and the nicotine flooding straight to the front of my brain. It felt nice to have a distraction, a high, even in some small way, something to help me avoid the pain and confrontation of it all for as long as possible.

"So, uh, what are you going to do now, man?" Will finally asked me, breaking the silence between us.

"I'm going back to work Monday. I'm working on two projects. I'd prefer to stay distracted instead of at home, you know?" I shrugged. It was the truth. I didn't want to be home without her.

He nodded. "Yeah, yeah, I guess I would do the same thing. There's not much point sitting inside festering, is there? What are you working on now?"

"Just two more shorts. Nothing spectacular, I just want to get them edited and done with. One is about a crooked doctor, the other one's about a dysfunctional family, you know, that age-old, Hollywood-gold material." I looked at him sarcastically, rolling my eyes.

He laughed, which made me feel normal again. I was suddenly reminded that I wouldn't always walk around feeling like my ribs were broken and my mind had been scooped out of my skull.

We finished smoking and went back in to join the group, reeking of past cigarettes. Now people were heavily drinking and talking more openly, with more volume. All age groups mingled and got to know one another, occasionally coming up to me and offering tethers of support or light jokes to ease the unpleasant moribundity of the day. I recalled attempting to make my friends feel better when they were in mourning; you never really know what to say. Millions of years of death and we still don't know how to comfort one another, what the proper etiquette is when someone you love dies.

"You know we're here for you, anything you need, seriously, just give us a call, alright?" I heard, nervously, their eyes always searching my face for some kind of acceptance or reinforcement.

"Hey, man…I am so sorry you had to deal with this. You've had a shitty few years. Call me if you want to talk about anything, okay?

"If you ever want to go for a drive or dinner, just pick up the phone, I'll come right over."

"We could have coffee or something sometime, or I can send you the number of my therapist, she's really great, she's helped me a lot. I know it's a different situation, but she could really help you, too." They all started to sound the same, only the mouth saying words changed.

I appreciated this, even if I was a little sick of feeling like the center of attention. I walked over and picked up a narrow carrot stick, eating it dry. I figured I needed to eat something today or I would pass out in front of all of these people. After slowly chewing another carrot like a cow chewing cud, I walked over to the bar and ordered a whiskey, neat. I was ready to feel numb for real, even if just for an evening. I wasn't a big drinker anymore, not since my twenties.

In fact, in my life before, I was what I would deem healthy. I didn't eat red meat. I walked often and worked out semi-regularly, kept my salt and sugar intake down to a minimum and drank mostly water during the day. My only real destructive vice had been smoking, which I did religiously for over ten years, to the constant disapproval and dismay of my parents and partners. I didn't like drinking much anymore; it made my head spin. I felt discombobulated, separated from my body, like I couldn't focus. My body could no longer withstand the pelting it had taken when it was younger, when I could drink all evening without consequence. It was hard for me to grasp why so many people loved it in their later years when I could barely function after I'd had a drink at a party nowadays, but hey, to each their own. We all have that sweet, specific poison we allow to flood our bodies when we want to avoid the harshness of reality.

I was certainly starting to feel good now. I began to wonder why I hadn't returned to alcohol sooner. Three shots of whiskey in and I was talking more, laughing a little bit, even. Nodding in interest and listening to my friends, chiming in occasionally. I was ready for this day to finally be over and behind me. I felt as if I had been barely awake, stumbling around aimlessly in limbo for weeks without any reprieve. I wanted to wake up fresh tomorrow in the sunshine and feel a minute fragment of healing taking root within me, but I knew it wasn't going to occur. I knew these days would trudge on as they had before until I dealt with the pain head on, something I wasn't yet ready to face.

I decided to leave the wake, feeling fed up with the charade of being the grieving loser that people felt sorry for. I stood up from my booth, saying a loose but heartfelt farewell to my friends, hugged my family, and slinked out of the back door onto the dimly lit street. I felt like I could finally breathe. Thank God it was over. Now I could focus on being depressed, alone.

I stopped by a bright liquor store, full of fluorescence and neon, bought a pack of cheap cigarettes with a new black lighter, and walked the six blocks slowly back to my apartment, lighting up the first stick of the pack as I meandered through people and weaved between parked cars and street signs. People were sitting outside buzzing restaurants in their open-air patios, eating dinner or meeting for drinks; dressed up, laughing. First dates and established relationships or friendly chatter filling the evening air like pollen spores, making me feel just as queasy and teary eyed.

The blood-red sun was setting over the Hollywood hills as I passed buildings and lively music bars, all seemingly alive with much happier people than me, ready to start their Friday night. How fresh and new it all seemed for them, an exciting evening ahead, full of promise and hope. I felt empty, bitter, totally amputated from that sector of life. Would I ever venture out on a first date again? Butterflies flitting in my intestines, fumbling nervously for impressive conversation and peeling back layers of interest or similarities? Or would I be destined to walk these streets alone in my darkness, unable to reconcile the new and old versions of me? Was this who I was now?

Then I thought about her. I thought of what she would be doing now, what she would be thinking if it was me she was missing. Would she ignore the pain, as so many of us tended to do, or give into it entirely? Would she scream, break down, fall into a pit of despair? Perhaps she would simply move on with her life stoically. Tuck the soft memory of me away in a wooden box beneath her bed, only to be revisited on the occasional holiday and birthdays. What is the proper way to mourn someone who has died, slipped away forever? I battled with these infinite questions in my quest to reinvent myself again.

As I reached the rusted metal entrance gates of my boring, beige apartment building, I sat down on the front steps with a flat thud, hitting my tailbone against the concrete. I was feeling boozy, uncoordinated, and for once since it all happened, lonely. I never truly felt lonely in my life before. But this was different. It wasn't loneliness that came from longing, it came from loss. I lit up another cigarette and watched pedestrians passing by; occasionally exchanging glances with them if they even noticed I was sitting there in the dark, like a creep.

I didn't want to go into the apartment just yet, the small, modest one-bedroom home we had shared for years. I wasn't ready to be there on my own again. I wanted to get in my car and drive away, maybe to the woods, or some far out midwestern prairie or a desolate tropical island. To be totally alone until I was completely and utterly forgotten by the living world.

I eventually dragged myself from the stairs and made my way up to the second floor, running my hands along the tan, textured stucco walls as I went. The building was constructed in the mid-1960s and hadn't been renovated much since then. The apartments were all more or less of the same layout, with linoleum kitchen flooring and hardwood in the other rooms, a clunky, boxed metal AC unit jutting out of each apartment's windows, buzzing loudly.

Lights were on in the other apartments, and I could hear families mulling about making their dinner, smells of different foods and spices wafting through the air. It comforted me, hearing people feel alive around me. Although I still wasn't fully ready to feel comfortable or alive.

Unlocking my worn brass doorknob under the dim porchlight, I touched around sloppily against the wall for the main light switch, flicked it on and looked at the stark reality of my illuminated mess.

There were splayed clothes and cardboard boxes everywhere, belongings packed and half unpacked, dirty cups strewn around the living room and kitchen counter, used dishes piled up high in the sink, growing their own ecosystems of green mold and dust alongside the former remnants of food and stale drink within them.

I sighed, frustrated at my inability to deal with seemingly anything adult or responsible at this juncture. I couldn't bear the thought of packing up more boxes, scrubbing moldy dishes, living normally. It was almost as if my mind forbade my body from physically doing anything that was productive for me. I walked down the hall to my bathroom, kicking boxes out of the way in the hall, grunting as they slid against the wall. I turned on the pull chain light and looked at myself in the mirror again. I looked like absolute shit. Sunken, bloodshot green eyes, greasy, wavy brown hair, a patchy beard forming. I was too lazy to shave it, and I had no one to look good for anyway. I stretched and tugged at the bags under my eyes and my hollow cheeks, I was losing weight. Sick of looking at my drawn face, I turned to a more pressing matter and took a long-anticipated piss. Mostly pure whiskey at this point, no doubt.

I brushed my teeth and left the bathroom light on, disgusted at myself for being such a pitiful wreck. I didn't know how to pull myself out of this seemingly endless black hole. I tried to give myself a break; people grieve in different ways, right? Surely I was allowed days, weeks, months, even years to feel like this. It's rare that people are encouraged to feel like utter shit and even given paid time off to do it. I should have seized this moment and used it to my advantage to pursue some creative efforts. After all, I was always bogged down with work and never gave valuable time to anything or anyone else. Perhaps I should use this time to focus on what I wanted to do next, where I wanted to be and how I could better myself, how I could heal.

I walked to my messy, unkempt kitchen and looked around thoughtlessly, my lower mouth hanging open. Since I was a little drunk, I felt like I should probably eat something substantial, if only to avoid the hangover I was bound to have in the morning. My body would be screaming at me throughout the day tomorrow, my lungs sore and raw.

I raided the vintage fridge, a boxy, 80s number in a creamy pale color with wooden inlays in the handles. We—no, I—didn't have much. Stop saying 'we'. She's gone, I kept having to constantly remind myself of this. After all, we did most of the shopping together. I looked at ice cubes in their frosty, snow-capped trays. Frozen peas, fruit, a frozen bean and cheese burrito that looked frostbitten and well past its sell by date, some orange juice, four expired eggs and a head of wilting brown broccoli. I settled on the frozen burrito. This wasn't the time or the place to be picky. I would have eaten cardboard at that point.

After heating it up in the microwave, which I didn't normally use (she was against microwaves, instead opting to heat everything on the stove or in the oven), I slapped it down onto a plate, watching it fall with a dense thud. I had some salsa in my cabinet which I added to the plate and sat down in front of my television, taking care not to drop my dinner on the floor as I moved books, papers, clothes and other scattered bits out of the way in order to sit down.

Turning on the television, I flicked and scanned the evening programs until finally settling on a nature show on the National Geographic channel. It was about mushrooms and their spores have entire networks that build beneath the forest floor and communicate and connect with one another, feeding off of the decay of soil, deceased bodies and occasionally leaching life from the trees and plants themselves. My mind drifted toward her mountain grave, surrounded by trees. Were the fungal spores welcoming their new guest? Creating networks and tunnels under the earth for her? Or were they merely finding a way to extract nutrients from her decaying body to feed their own?

I couldn't bring myself to finish my uninspiring, microwaved meal. I really wasn't very hungry at all. I wrapped up the remainder in tin foil and set it back to coagulate and mold in the fridge, then I sat back down and lit a new cigarette right there in the living room, grabbing a dirty cup from the side of the counter to use as an impromptu ashtray. Fuck, she would have really abhorred this. She hated the smell of smoke in the house, on the bed sheets, on my hands and hair.

I used to have to wash my hands vigorously between cigarettes or she'd argue with me about how badly I stank. Now, here I was, smoking freely in my apartment like a defeated, lonely emperor, watching a show about fungus spores and tipping the ash into a moldy cup. I was in charge of my bad decisions in my grief state, and no one was around to stop me or tell me I couldn't do it. Perhaps there were a few advantages to losing someone you love.

I woke up a few hours later, still on the sofa. The night was black around me except for the blue and white light emanating from the television. My lower back ached from the hardback book wedged into my spine beneath me. The television host was quietly narrating the behavior and evolution of a rare species of frog in the Amazon rainforest. Groggily, I felt around for the remote and shut it off, causing the room to fall silent and dark.

I got up and stretched, hurting from the cramped position I had fallen asleep in. I took my cup of wet, smelly cigarettes to the toilet and flushed them down. The house really did stink, no wonder she had disliked it so much. Did she make me a better person? Was I always just a lazy slob who wanted to eat frozen, beige burritos and smoke cheap cigarettes inside? I mused on this theory, still half asleep, still half dead.

I washed my hands and brushed my teeth again, feeling a strong, pulsing headache coming on from lack of water, food, too much whiskey and far too many cigarettes. My

throat burned as if I'd gargled gasoline. I felt physically exhausted, yet somehow my eyes snapped wide awake, staring
into the night like a ghost with nowhere to haunt. I felt an
inexplicable heaviness within me. My mouth tasted dry and
stale, my body hurt, my heart was sore and pounding.

Walking down the hall to my empty bedroom, I tried
in vain to remake my bed from the pile of messy, crumpled
sheets and blankets atop my mattress. I straightened out my
pillows and tucked the blankets into place before crawling
in like a spider. I turned on the ceiling fan to get some air
circulating and lay in bed, staring quietly at the spotty ceiling,
thinking of nothing in particular. I watched the blades turn
and the cords shiver, listening to the chains of the light clink-
clink against the body of the fan. I heard people walking and
laughing outside of my window, having a more enjoyable
evening than I was, filling the night air with happy memories while I stewed in my sorrow within the darkness of my
lifeless apartment.

I decided to feel my way into the covers and rub my
hands over my groin, working my cock into action and tugging it awake. I needed something to put me back to sleep,
to calm me down. The only thing I could think of was this
evolutionary, primal exercise to shut me off for the rest of the
night. The only issue was I didn't know what to think about.
She was gone, the apartment heavy and rotten with palpable
emptiness. She wasn't beside me any longer, she wasn't even
close to me anymore. I tried to think about former sexual
interludes with her, even with other people, eventually com-

ing back to her. Her body, so perfect in its imperfections, the smell of her skin, like jasmine or wet soil. I rubbed harder, recalling her breath on me when we were happiest together, when we were deeply in love, when we fucked. I felt like I was going to cry, or vomit. I felt nauseated and turned on. Jacking off to a ghost. What would she say if she was here now? How would she critique this pitiful, dismal scene acted out by someone she used to respect? And when would I respect myself again, if ever?

I continued stroking harder, fixing my mental gaze on the memory of her closeness, the outline of her frame, her lips, her laugh and her hair gently touching me, eventually erupting in climax and coming all over my hand. I couldn't remember the last time I masturbated. It had been months; I hadn't felt the urge until now. Perhaps the whiskey had shaken my need to loosen up. I relaxed, letting out a soft groan, leaking milky fluid all over my dirty sheets and stomach. God damnit, I muttered to myself. The last thing I wanted to do in my sluggish state was more laundry.

I was tempted to fall asleep immediately following my woeful discharge, but I didn't want to be covered in sticky mess. I got up and walked to the bathroom, pulling toilet paper violently from its roll, wiping my hands and stomach coarsely in swift movements. It was truly a miracle I had been able to orgasm at all. Even though I had only half felt it happening, I was grateful my body allowed me this little bit of physical release. I felt wobbly and feeble standing over the toilet, as if I'd thrown off my biological balance by losing vital fluids. I knew I wasn't eating enough, and the alcohol was pumping swiftly through my blood, making my heart pulse loudly in my ears. I felt sick and dizzy again.

Back in the bedroom, I carelessly wiped away what I could from the sheets, wasting even more toilet paper, drying and patting off little dots of moisture, poorly throwing the wadded-up balls of toilet paper into my wastebasket next to the desk. I rolled my eyes and removed the duvet to re-enter the bed and lie down. Who was I becoming? I felt like I'd just jacked off in my teenage bedroom while my parents slept soundly down the hall, completely unaware of their fumbling offspring experimenting with his body.

I lay my head against the dented, dirty pillow, resting on my back, staring back up at the dimly lit, speckled ceiling and rotating fan blades, mesmerizing me in their circular pattern. After what seemed like hours, I finally lulled myself to sleep around 3 am, grasping onto my ribs in the fetal position. It was a method I'd adopted after I lost her. When I went to sleep now, my heart felt so constricted and tight, so tense and sore, that I thought someone was trying to break my rib cage, like a ghost was attacking me. I needed to physically hold myself together to stop them from pulling apart and shattering every night. To feel any sense of physical ease and to fall asleep.

3. Vivienne

I woke up diagonally. My contorted back throbbing and achy from sleeping in such an awkward position through to the morning. Slits of horizontal sunlight flashed across my face from my eastern window. My bedside clock read 11 am in bright red digits. Fuck. I didn't want to spend another Saturday doing next to nothing. In a dark, depressing, messy apartment, no less. My head was pounding, as predicted. I lay there, running over how much I'd smoked and drank, keeping an unreliable tally in my head.

I pushed the covers aside, sitting on the edge of the mattress with my feet planted firmly on the un-swept wooden floor. Observing in the stark daylight at the enormity of my sadness piled up, literally, around me. Maybe today would be the day I finally packed everything up, got rid of it all, donated it, cleaned the place up. I didn't know if I was fully mentally or physically prepared to take on that behemoth task. I sat on the edge of my bed and drank the stale, dusty water from my bedside table as I pondered what my next move would or should be.

Eventually I stood up, forcing my crooked body to move forward. Leaving my stained bed unmade and kicking boxes and overspilled clothes out of the way, I traveled down the hall to the bathroom. The hairs on my stomach were now hardened and stiff. Concrete remnants from last night's attempts to fall asleep soundly. My bowels and stomach contorted with hunger and lack of nutrients, cramping and groaning, causing me to bend over the sink and hold my abdomen in pain. I reached for the shower handle and turned it on weakly. Water began rushing from a moderately pressured nozzle, shooting arrows of warm water into the rusty tub. I still didn't want to look at myself too closely. I knew I looked awful, there was no point in salting that open wound again.

I stepped into the shower and stood beneath the metal head like a half-inflated blow-up doll, one of those bright, boneless waving numbers you see outside of used car lots. I stood hunched, letting water pour over my bony body like river water over rocks below the surface. I stared forward at the pink tiles with their little, delicately engraved white flowers. She had always loved those tiles, always talked about who may have lived in the apartment previously, what they did, who they had loved, fantasizing that great actors and actresses in the 1950s lived here before they made it big in Hollywood and moved on to reside in Beverly Hills mansions.

I washed my greasy dark hair quickly, using cheap drugstore shampoo to build a quick frothy mound. I washed the soap from my hair and body and turned the nozzle off abruptly. Everything, every movement I made, now felt like a monumental chore. I used to enjoy my morning shower, thinking up ideas and concepts, singing, hungry and excited to enter the world for the day, excited to see her and touch her and replay our dreams out loud. Now, a shower felt like an onslaught of painful little pellets, reminding me that I am barely alive and can indeed feel everything I was trying to avoid- pain, the heat and the cold. Emptiness. Loss.

I dried off briskly, throwing the towel over the shower rail and roughly putting on deodorant and combing through my wet hair, avoiding the mirror at all costs. I walked back down the cluttered hall and found some slightly less dirty clothes on the floor to put on, not caring if they matched aesthetically or smelled bad. Another thing I used to care about, taking pride in my appearance. Lately I could be wearing a paper bag for all I cared. It didn't matter, I didn't care if anyone found me attractive now that she was gone.

I searched my barren fridge for something to drink, pulling the carton of pulpy, expired orange juice out and filling up the last clean glass I had in the cabinet. I sat down at my empty dining table, across from a vacant, antique chair, sipping the juice, looking at last week's papers. I was agitated and started to zone out. Lending my concentration to the design of the old wallpaper, tapping my fingers on the surface of the dusty wooden table.

How was I supposed to spend my time now? I didn't know what to do with myself anymore. I felt antsy and restless, yet I wanted to sleep for a thousand years and forget all of this had happened, leaving me in an infinitely uncomfortable state of mental limbo. My previous morning routine of coffee and the paper with the radio on, with her, now seemed like a distant, cruel memory from someone else's beautiful life. Something I privately viewed once and could barely make out in my mind any longer. All I wanted now was to punish myself, to sit at my empty table in pain, to hear nothing but silence, not even the birds outside of my window. I didn't want to feel the sun on my skin, I didn't want to hear laughter and children playing or families enjoying their day off together. All I wanted was to sit in darkness and feel sorry for myself. To stare into the wall until the hurt had subsided and I could go back to my regular routine sans her. I wasn't entirely sure if that would ever be possible for me again.

Of course, the city felt differently than I did. People were wide awake and very much alive outside, wandering the streets casually, walking their dogs, giggling, talking loudly on their cell phones, making plans with their loved ones and meeting for brunch dates. Delighting and basking in the unmatched warmth of the California sun. Another beautiful day, they must have thought. I used to think that. Now it was just another day, like the ones that came before and were sure to follow, to dissect and wade through my drowning misery. I sat shaking my foot against the hardwood floor, looking at the filth around me, clenching my palms in the quiet daylight with my half-drunk, fermented orange juice.

I decided, after an hour or two of sitting and thinking about nothing but my own discomfort, to get up and walk

to the grocery store. I had run out of coffee the day before
and desperately wanted some caffeine to shake me out of
this deep funk I was stuck inside. I grabbed my keys from
the ceramic bowl on the counter and tied my worn tennis
shoes around my knobby feet. Just as I was about to leave, I
saw the pack of cigarettes on the coffee table, half opened
and revealing their orange legs seductively. I faintly remembered buying them from the liquor store the evening before.
I grabbed them, along with the lighter, and headed out into
the stark afternoon sunlight.

I felt like a walking zombie as I strolled brokenly down
the street. Everything looked so illuminated, so cheerful.
Almost as if it was a film set, or an acid trip. The flowers and
trees were brightly lit with vivid green, blue and red hues,
flowers opening proudly for the pollinating insects to land
and feed upon. People passing me on the street looked hopeful, well dressed and enthusiastic about their Saturday off
from work. I could only imagine what their opinion was of
my shallow frame lurching toward them. I probably looked
terrifying, trudging along the sidewalk alone.

I lit up a cigarette and inhaled, coughing a bit, feeling the fresh burn against my throat and lungs, sore from
the night before. The nicotine gave me another massive
head rush. I hadn't smoked in nearly 2 years and my throat
was harshly reminding me of that. I walked with my head
pointed down, staring at the cracks and inconsistencies of the
gray sidewalk, making an effort not to look at anyone coming
my direction, avoiding all blatant judgment and eye contact,

blowing gray clouds of smoke into the afternoon sky, adding to the mucky brown layer of persistent LA smog. I used to be more responsible than this, used to care about the world. Grief makes you incredibly selfish.

By the time I reached the grocery store, I was ready to turn around and go home again. I was tired and anxious, wondering why I had decided to leave the house at all. I was safe in my gross apartment. Now I was forced to act human around people doing normal, everyday things, it made me nauseous. I pushed myself to continue inside even though I couldn't seem to recall what it was that I actually needed to buy. I still had no appetite but felt a dull ache of hunger in the pit of my stomach which I masochistically ignored.

I meandered up and down the fluorescent aisles, passing happy families and couples buying groceries for their upcoming week. We used to shop here together, before everything was taken away from me. Blissfully unaware of anything negative or painful going on around us. Filling our carts with bright, fresh produce, pasta, and ingredients to make warming meals for one another, experimenting with recipes we had never made before. Occasionally those culinary experiments were a resounding success. Others, a bowl of overcooked, under-seasoned mush. Still, we never cared, it didn't matter. We were just happy to be cooking and eating alongside one another. Back when I still had an appetite for something besides coffee, alcohol, cigarettes and eternal sleep.

I couldn't recollect the sensation of happy hunger now. I felt like such a cliche, a heartbroken, sad man who didn't want to consume anything but pain, and guilt—and self-ishly punishing his body for it. I stared blankly at the disgusting amount of food in this overly packed grocery store, everything from cereals to canned goods, spices and fresh breads. I thought about the amount of people who were actually starving around the world, the people who didn't have a choice whether or not to go hungry or to skip meals because of their emotional state. I felt like a total asshole for not wanting to eat. But nothing appealed to me, nothing tempted me.

I found my way to the coffee and tea section, moving slowly along the freshly waxed linoleum, making a squeaking sound against the rubber of my shoes with every small step. Eventually I found the row of ground beans in bags and opted for a typical, Italian medium roast, chucking it carelessly into my mesh basket. We used to buy fancy coffee, coffee with colorful labels and interesting or exotic tasting notes.

I couldn't taste or savor anything properly now, so I didn't care. The cheap stuff would do, as long as it was caffeinated. Just as I was turning to leave the aisle, I heard a familiar voice speaking to me from over my shoulder.

"Hi, V, how are you...?" she chimed gently, her voice high and positive, lingering on the words carefully. Her face was turned into a downward frown, one of sorrow or pity, unsure how to act towards me. I recognized this face. I had witnessed a long line of these faces.

I looked down at my disheveled appearance, totally embarrassed. My hair was a wavy, wet mess. My eyes were bloodshot with deep bags below them. My cheeks were hollow with flecks of dark, unkempt beard peeking through. I looked like a rundown cowboy. I certainly felt like one. I felt like I'd survived a western shootout and now I was waiting to bleed to death in the fluorescent aisles of this phony bright Disneyland cutout grocery store.

Of course I'd run into someone I know now. You always run into people you don't want to see when you look like total shit.

"Hey, Bonnie, yeah, I'm, you know, okay, despite… everything going—"

She cut me off, putting her hand on my shoulder gingerly, with bulgingly sad eyes. She looked like a velvet painting of a doe that people sell out of their cars on Venice Beach.

"I know, I'm so sorry, I heard from Agnes. How are you holding up, you know, considering everything?" She looked at me again with wider, heavily pitying eyes. I looked at her basket; it was full of healthy, vibrantly colored fruits, vegetables and grains, and cake ingredients. Foods a hungry, mentally stable person would eat when they weren't deep in the bowels of self-loathing.

"I don't know. I'm just taking it day by day, I guess. I'm going back to work Monday, so that's something, progress."

She looked at my basket with only the bag of coffee scrunched into the corner of the mesh frame. Again, she looked at me sadly with wide, dark eyes, frowning like a mom consoling her child.

"Well, if you ever want to go for coffee, you know, to

talk, or for anything, give me a call, okay? I mean that." She put her hand on my shoulder again. I was so bored of the constant pity party. I almost wished someone else would die so they would shift their pity to their other loved ones and forget about mine. I didn't want to be viewed as ungrateful. I just wanted to be left alone.

"Thanks, Bonnie, that's really sweet of you, yeah. I'll uh, I'll let you know," I said weakly.

"It's really nice to see you, V, and I am really so sorry…" she said again in her high pitched, bubbly Californian accent, the kind where you can't tell if they're being sincere or just putting it on for the public. She turned and walked down the aisle away from me, disappearing behind the rows of perfectly stacked jars of red and blue fruit preserves.

I went to the checkout lane and stood there with my single packet of coffee. I noticed the 'Fair Trade' label and huffed audibly. When is anything ever really a fair trade? Glancing dully over the rows of brightly packaged candy and gum impulse purchases beside the register, the ones I so often pulled into my basket in my life before, it all just looked like a modern Monet of colors and wrappers, as likely for me to eat as I would a tube of actual oil paints. I looked up at the young girl ringing up my bag of coffee. She looked down, vacant and bored, absentmindedly scanning the coffee and asking me if I wanted a bag. I declined the bag and the receipt and walked the short walk back to my grimy apartment. Has she ever lost someone? I wondered.

Once I was in the door, I left my shoes on, not caring

about the standard of living I used to hold myself accountable to. Who was going to notice if I tracked in dirt anyway? Pacing back and forth around the kitchen, I tore open the bag of coffee and sloppily emptied some into my metal coffee maker, spilling grains all over the cheap Formica countertop.

"God damnit." I groaned, as I feebly swept the bean powder back into the bag with my hand.

Flipping on the gas stove and heating up the water to make my coffee, I smelled gas, flitting by my nose quickly and disappearing. Maybe I could kill myself, I thought morbidly, throwing the thought away as soon as it entered my mind. 'Man kills himself over a broken heart.' Jesus, could I be any more of a cliche? I rolled my eyes and sat down at my table.

The coffee maker hissed and bubbled, bringing me out of my melancholic thoughts. I poured the black liquid into a mug I picked up from the sink and began to drink it, scalding my tongue and throat as it burnt its way down.

"Fuck!" I shouted. Although I had to admit it felt good to feel something shocking, something real.

I spent the remainder of the afternoon aimlessly milling around my apartment, wondering what to do next, how to fill my barren expanse of time. Typically, on the weekends, I'd wash the dishes, wash the stack of laundry that had accumulated throughout the week, deep clean the sinks and sweep the floors. I was a pretty tidy person in my life before. But I just couldn't be bothered to do anything other than sit and stare at the wall, watching the light shift and change as the hours ticked by, flicking my fingers together, chain smoking.

I felt as if I was weighed down by tons of tar, the thought of washing a dish or picking up a broom too monumental, a useless task I wasn't yet willing to face. Especially when no one would be coming over, at least for a while.

Not to mention the piled-up boxes of her stuff I had to go through and carefully untangle at some point. I definitely wasn't remotely close to being ready for the emotional agony of that process. We used to go on spontaneously sweet, playful little adventures on Sundays. Flea Markets or canyon drives, stopping to explore or have impromptu picnics of fresh fruit and cheese, arranged by her, of course. Seeing late afternoon matinees of old films in the park. Things you do when you're happy in your life, or when you're in the throes of love, oblivious to everyone around you, stuck inside the little world you've built so purposefully with one another.

Evening fell once again, identical to so many before it. I forced myself to reopen a bag of half-eaten peanuts from the cabinet and shove a handful into my mouth, just enough to satiate the non-existent hunger I had, to give my body some kind of reward for staying alive. I smoked another cigarette, opening the window and blowing the smoke out into the LA air to avoid my house reeking of an ashtray and getting an unwanted visit or fine from my landlord.

I knew I was being environmentally irresponsible, self-centered and careless, but I just didn't care. Nothing mattered to me anymore. I didn't care how my body hurt or my lungs suffered. The piles of dishes and boxes stood around me like decaying statues in a desert, wanting to be paid attention to. I couldn't do anything but sit in the warm evening light and chain smoke, robotically. My poor throat, sore and raw from revisiting this horrible habit once again, like a mistress or haunting memory you can't stay away from. I knew it was bad for me, but I needed a vice, and right now I just didn't care about anything. Not my body, not my hunger, not my aching heart. I just wanted to sit and stare beyond the window and smoke and stare some more. It was the closest thing to healing I could muster. After all, everyone has their own grieving process. This was mine, I guess. I knew it wasn't the healthiest, but I was ambivalent, mentally wasted. Nothing felt like it could matter anymore, now that she was gone.

The weekend dragged on much as the weekend before had and the weekend before that. Hours upon hours stretched by like a long line of saltwater taffy, pulling toward me and sinking away from me. I sat silently, no soft music playing in the background, no tv, no radio, just with my coffee or juice, eating tiny bits of stale food, chain smoking and listening to the faint buzz of the electricity wires and chirpy conversation of the birds and the city outside.

It was Monday tomorrow. I'd been off work for two full weeks, becoming a professional at doing absolutely nothing. I was ready to go back, needed to occupy myself, to focus on something other than nothingness, than this pit I'd found myself rotting in. My phone rang all weekend, quickly filling my voicemail with apologies and well wishes and offers to talk. I ignored all of them, perhaps a little coldly. I had nothing to give back, so I didn't attempt to.

4. Vivienne

Monday morning. I woke up with a brutal punch to my brain from the foreign-yet-familiar sound of my blaring alarm. I had switched my alarm radio to a standard beeping sound a few weeks before. I wasn't ready to accidentally hear happy, loving music yet. I just wanted to be woken up by pulsed beeping, like in a hospital bed after a coma.

After showering and rifling through my closet for anything clean to wear, I settled on a striped collared shirt and some black trousers, then went into the kitchen to make some coffee and mentally prepare myself for going back to work.

As I sat there, I felt a vein of relief pulsing through me, a clarity. I couldn't sit in this stale apartment day after day anymore. I desperately needed a distraction, something to pull me out of this liminal, grey state. I poured the remainder of my black coffee down the sink, balancing the mug on top of the rest of the dirty dishes in the basin then headed out into the ever present sun, out to rejoin the world of the living.

I worked as a film editor for a small, independent

film company in West Hollywood. I'd been with the same
company for nearly eight years. Our office only consisted
of a small team of twelve, including myself. We worked on
everything from documentaries to foreign independent films
to art shorts, all on a pretty low budget, oftentimes scraping
and calling in favors or borrowing equipment from larger
studios. A far cry from the heavy-hitting, power blockbusters
that people typically think of when they picture Hollywood.
Yet I was proud of the work I did, what I could contribute to
the film world. I wanted to make a dent, a difference in some
small way, even if people found it obtuse or pretentious or
even worse, a waste of time to watch.

I'd met her at one of those art film premieres. During a
small after party, in which the studio and editorial team mingled, talking and laughing over the challenges and memories
with the film members and crew, eating standard canapes
and drinking medium weight wine. She was standing in the
corner, talking to another group of people, wearing a forest
green, slinky dress. I recall thinking that she looked like a
beautiful, smooth vine, growing against the wall, her red lips
quivered like a flower. She spoke effortlessly, with a boisterous
laugh, and moved like a smooth snake, slithering her way
to and from different groups of people. I was magnetically
drawn to her instantly.

Her laugh, her arms, the way she carried herself with
such dignity and grace. Her unshaven armpits were a faux
pas in a world where everyone looks like a rubber, slick
Barbie doll. She wasn't afraid to be where she was, of feeling

small in this horribly snobby and pretentiously surface world. By the time I was eventually introduced to her, I felt like a puddle of water next to her magnificence, melting before this goddess who could crush me in an instant if she had felt inclined to.

She had been invited by her friend who had made a small appearance in one of our films. She was always a good, supportive friend, unlike me.

"Hello, I'm Vivienne," she said, confidently holding out her smooth, adorned hand for me to shake. Two Vs, I thought. She's perfect. I wanted to know her immediately. No, I *had* to know her. Her green eyes stared back at me in a curious way, as if she may have wanted to know me, too.

"Did you enjoy the film?" I asked her, not really know-ing if I actually wanted to hear her reply. The film was tacky and horrible, I didn't want that to be her first and lasting impression of my work. I did want to hear her voice, though. It had a subtle, sugary nuance to it.

"I did. I found it…insightful," she cooed modestly, not realizing how incredibly charming she was.

"Oh, jeez. I'm glad, it's not my best work or anything," I said. My throat felt like it was closing, so I decided to be brave.

"Hey, um, do you want to go out sometime? Maybe I can take you to see a film I haven't edited, so you can critique it ruthlessly and honestly?" I added, smiling. I had no idea where this burst of confidence came from. Suddenly I felt like I had nothing to lose.

"Sure. I'd like that, but just as friends. I'm actually with someone," she said, blushing, almost as if she was more embarrassed for herself than for me.

"Oh. No, no, yeah, I totally understand. I didn't mean like, a date or anything. I'm with someone too!" I said defensively. Fuck. With someone? I had no chance in hell. I didn't expect this perfect person to be available, did I? My heart suddenly felt like it had been thrashed violently against the wall. Forgetting at that moment that I was also actually 'with someone,' and probably shouldn't be asking strangers out on dates.

I scanned the area for her date, attempting to gather a glimpse of what her type might be, instantly wondering if I was anywhere near what she found attractive. Everyone there seemed to already be coupled up. It eventually occurred to me that she was the date of her friend, the one who had invited her. I was by myself, as I usually was for film parties. I didn't bother boring my girlfriend at the time with another subpar premier, let alone dragging her down for an after party of one. If I was honest with myself, I didn't want her there with me anyways. I wasn't exactly crazy about her, as shitty as it sounds.

Vivienne wrote her number on a matchbox from the bar and slipped it into my pocket coolly before slithering away into the night with her friend. I left feeling ecstatic, electric, constantly checking my pockets to make sure I hadn't lost the matches. I had been reborn in the space of an evening, the dense fog suddenly lifting. I could see true color again.

I needed to see her again, in any context, platonic or otherwise. Her partner didn't know how lucky they were to be
with her, to be near her.

I called her a week later from my work parking lot and
arranged to see a film at an old theater downtown, followed
by an innocent, very public lunch at a small cafe. A lunch we
spent tensely trying our hardest not to flirt with one another. But I couldn't help myself, she had changed something
in me. Her presence was heady and addicting. I wanted to
know this person, to really know her, even if that meant in a
non-romantic way. I never expected what was going to unfold
over the next few years.

By the time I'd walked the twenty minutes it took to
get to my office, I had the sinking, nauseous feeling in my
stomach again. My optimistic, caffeinated confidence had
worn off quickly and I wanted to crawl back into my black
hole and go back to sleep, where the pain subsided slightly,
and blackness fell against me like a shadow. But now I was
standing here in front of my work building. I knew I had to
face it all at some point. I straightened my spine and walked
in, taking one last deep breath before opening the door.

As I entered the ground floor building, everything
appeared to be exactly the same as it had been before. Of
course it was. To me, the whole world had changed in a
matter of weeks, but in reality, life went on the same way it
always had at the office. The plants were in the same corners,
yellowing, droopy and under-watered. The brightly colored

desks were situated the way they had been since we moved into the space. I saw my coworkers with their company earphones on, heads down, concentrating, staring at their computers, utterly oblivious to my less than grand re-entrance.

When someone finally noticed me, they got up from their desk and removed their headphones, searching my face for healing, but mostly looking at my messy appearance, unable to hide their judgment within their slightly warped smile.

"V, welcome back! You look…good." His voice trailed off, looking me up and down, knowing he couldn't cover up the truth, even with a white lie.

"You don't have to lie, I know I look like shit, Jack, thanks for trying though." I said flatly.

"How are you doing? Did you have a cathartic few weeks off, at least? You know…to grieve?"

"I guess so. I'm happy to be back. I need a distraction. I needed to see something besides my four walls, you know?"

"Hey, my office is always open. Anything you need," he said with a half-smile, patting my shoulder.

"Thanks, Jack. I appreciate it." I said reflexively as I turned and walked slowly to my desk.

I watched how my colleagues looked at me with heavy eyed, sorrowful looks, most of them just nodding in acknowledgment of my return. Not many words, just simple hellos and waves. I was grateful for the break in conversation as I just wanted to get on with my day without an overwhelming sea of grief and sympathy. I felt like I was playing the same character in a film on repeat.

As I sat down in my chair, I noticed a bouquet of yellow flowers and a stack of cards on my desk. All different color-ed, pastel envelopes with different fonts spelling out my name on the front. Some thick and others thin, circular, rectangu-lar. I opened them one after the other, all of them sharing the same sentiment, telling me how sorry they were, how they were there for me. Jesus Christ, how many times will I relive this nightmare? I knew she was gone. I didn't want to be reminded of it. I just wanted to forget about it all.

I pushed the envelopes to the side, forming them in neat stacks, and turned on my desktop computer to begin work, putting my headphones on immediately, which blocked out the background noise in the office. As I edited this month's projects, I was able to lose myself a bit in the reels, forget-ting for brief moments that I was theatrically operating as a former shell of myself. Flashes of other human faces, voices, relationships and situations flooding out the despondent blankness of my own.

The day went by quickly, to my sheer relief and grate-fulness. I didn't eat lunch, but I did eat a banana from the shared office kitchen, which was stocked regularly. I mostly sat quietly at my corner desk and avoided conversation at all costs, keeping my head down and working intently on the moving screen before me.

The weeks that followed all looked the same. Going into work, barely talking, barely eating, sitting at my desk, head-phones on, avoiding the fact that people were talking about my well-being or trying to figure out a way to make me feel better. I didn't care. I was there to escape my reality through the films I edited, and I managed to, for a little while.

Evenings were always worse, however. I came home to my sloppy, unkempt apartment, ate small portions of bland food, and flopped myself onto my bed, tossing and turning before finally getting to sleep, dreaming of nothing or of everything at once, never in between. Mornings were a bitter slog of coffee, juice, staring at the cream-colored walls, noting different shades of sunlight. Keys, walk, smoke, work, repeat. I was on autopilot. Completely numb, separated from my body. I started smoking regularly, taking short breaks from the office to sit on the bench outside and puff away, looking curiously at the cars in the half-filled parking lot or driving to and from the strip malls across the street. Wondering what people were doing in there. What they were feeling, if anything? It was my feeble attempt at living a normal life after her, even if I knew this was no life.

Time dragged on, resembling the same dull pattern. Until the holidays eventually rolled around again, arriving faster than I'd ever noticed. I hadn't celebrated Thanksgiving; I had nothing to be thankful for that year and didn't want to attend any of my friends' dinners, watching everyone pity me more than they already did. The office began to decorate for the Christmas season. I was in no mood to celebrate, still, but all around me people were feeling festive and happy, and I accepted that. The halls were filled with brightly colored, shimmering tassels of tinsel, tied with boughs of mistletoe and papier-mâché ornaments. The whole office looked like a Christmas parade.

She used to decorate, too. Homemade wooden items she had painted herself in distinct patterns, collected knick-knacks from various garage sales and markets, colorful twine and pine boughs over every shelved surface. I loved how traditional she was in only this way, always feeling that people should celebrate holidays together. There was a warmth about her traditions that made me feel kinder at heart, like a child.

Although she was hardly traditional in other ways, quite the contrary. She was a wild horse. Artistic, creative and overly impulsive, sometimes to my annoyance. I was an organized person, while she was chaotic, colorful, unpredictable. One day I'd come home to a box full of kittens she'd found in an alley somewhere, the next she'd be painting boards of wood she'd picked out of a dumpster. At the time I would sigh and grunt and roll my eyes. What I wouldn't give for alley kittens or painted dumpster wood in our apartment now, accompanied by her wild laughter and stubborn eyes.

Now, I kept my head down, staring at a bright screen throughout all of December. I didn't want to decorate or join in the social gatherings. I'd started to eat a bit more, mostly out of sheer necessity to produce efficient work. I needed my brain to function in order to edit and not get fired. People didn't talk to me as much as they used to, they even stopped inviting me to social functions. I suppose they grew tired of speaking to a shadow.

December isn't very cold in LA, never snowing or falling

too far below sixty degrees at night. Despite the lack of festive weather, I reveled in the slightly cooler, darker evenings. The sky mimicked how I felt on the inside: gloomy and low.

Not wanting to go to our company's Christmas party but cringing at the thought of being alone in my apartment, I eventually forced myself to attend. Between the two, I figured one at least offered me a form of distraction and numbness, in the form of free alcohol, for an evening. This year the party was being held in a historic hotel downtown, in one of their lavish banquet rooms. The whole team, their partners, families, former clients and partnering studios were invited. It was a fancy-dress requirement, and people were excited to dress up in their party clothes. I overheard my coworkers talking about their outfits the Friday before. I wasn't excited to dress up personally, nor to spend my first Christmas without her.

That Saturday, I put on my only colorful outfit, a merlot-colored linen suit I'd purchased from a thrift store for fun a few years earlier, with a plain white collared shirt underneath and a matching wine-colored tie. On the way downtown, I stopped for a fresh pack of cigarettes, catching my glum reflection in the glass out front beneath the neon lights. I sparked one up as I walked, feeling again like a shell of myself, wondering who would be there, if anything exciting would happen, or anything awful. At least I didn't have to pay for my dinner or drinks. I was starting to spot little silver linings, even if they were buried deeply beneath heavy, consistent rain clouds.

When I arrived at the old building, the halls were bustling with shiny, happy festive people. Some I recognized as former clients and their partners, others I'd never seen before. A sea of shimmering sequins of silver, gold, red and green moved quickly, like quick fish swimming in a school past me. I picked up my invitation and name tag and found our company's banquet room. People were mingling and chatting openly on the tiled floor. An optimistic, energetic enthusiasm filled the hall. Food lined the long tables against the perimeter of the ornately decorated room, everything from shrimp to prime rib, a real opulent spread. Catering staff and chefs in white clothing darted around with trays of drinks and glinting silverware.

Almost instantly I regretted coming. I didn't want to be in a room full of happy people looking excitedly toward the future. I wanted people to feel as miserable as I did. It's ludicrous how when you're happy you want everyone else to be happy too, and when you're depressed you want everyone to share in your pain. Misery loves company and I definitely wasn't going to find it here.

"Hey, V! I didn't think you were going to make it, man!" one of my colleagues called to me as he sauntered over, dressed in a bright gold suit.

"Holy shit. Nice suit," I said, and it was true.

"Ah, do you like it? I didn't want the investors to outshine me, even though they have all the money!" He laughed, but it trailed off, as if he suddenly realized he was struggling for money.

"No, you look great. Where's the bar?" I asked bluntly.

"It's through the back, you can't miss it. Hey, drink as much as you can, tabs on us!" He patted my back.

"Thanks man, it's good to see you. Go eat some shrimp for me. Merry Christmas," I said wryly, trying to make light of the fact that I hadn't been eating much and everyone seemed to take notice, the concern and judgement flying off their parental faces whenever they saw me pass the staff room empty handed.

I walked toward the bar, observing the party unfolding around me. Smiling faces and clinking glasses were dotted around like some western disease. I ordered a whiskey on ice. The bartender was a plain looking, tall woman with a straight, expressionless face, dressed in a white shirt and black bowtie, no doubt used to working Christmas parties and catering gigs identical to this one. I wouldn't be surprised if she kicked a few of my colleagues out later tonight for being too rowdy. She looked like she didn't take any shit from anybody.

I sat on a stool at the edge of the bar and drank my whiskey alone, turning the glass in semi circles nervously. It was harsh going down, but instantly warmed my insides and I felt lighter. I was slowly loosening up, allowing myself to be in this space, with these people. After ordering another drink, I made my way back to my table with some of my other colleagues already sitting down and eating. A little girl sat beside me eating a sugar cookie shaped like a bell, covered in red icing and green sprinkles. I smiled at her, she smiled back, her cheeks and clothing covered in messy red frosting. My heart beating heavily against my chest.

She had always wanted children and I denied her that, denied myself that. I didn't want the enormous responsibility of bringing a child into this world. I was a child of divorce, my parents splitting not long after having me. Although I loved my parents, I know they struggled raising two boys, working long hours and fighting over money, something I wasn't eager to pass on to a child of my own. I also didn't want the weight of bringing a child into a world as fucked up as this one. A point of contention we so often argued about when she was here.

"The world's always been fucked up!" she'd say to me.

"Not as much as it is now, Vivienne," I'd retort.

"Don't you want to experience parenthood? To teach someone something, to have someone to take care of us when we're old, a legacy? Don't you want that…with me?"

"That's no reason to have a kid," I would say, brushing her off. I hated having the parent conversation.

"It's reason enough for me! I'd make a great mother, don't you think I'd make a great mother? I have so much to give to a child," she used to say, irate.

"It's not about that, it's about the current state of the world. I can't have a kid in this world. What about global warming, nuclear war, too many screens, drought? Do you think that's a good environment for a child?"

"It's always something with you, you're just terrified of being truly happy…"

Her voice trailed off in my head, the argument playing like a broken record, her crackling voice. Why did I deny her that? Was I a monster or was I actually denying myself the opportunity to feel happiness in a completely selfless way? Maybe I was just a selfish, introverted asshole, sadistically withholding parenthood from the woman I loved. It was all over now, anyway. I decided to stop thinking about it. I'd make a shitty parent; I knew I would. No one needed me as their father, I could barely eat or shower properly, let alone raise a child.

Forks clinked on glass and my boss rose from his seat to make a mandatory, standard toast. To us, to the company and the partners, thanking us for coming out to celebrate Christmas and the new year ahead. I looked down at my empty plate and finished the remainder of my drink. A brass band started to play soft Christmas music while people gathered on the floor to dance. I watched them ambivalently, unsure whether I wanted to stick around any longer. I decided to go outside and smoke.

When I walked through the front doors of the hotel, I saw one of my colleagues, Chris, out front smoking as well.

"Hey, man, cool party, huh?"

"Yeah, it's pretty good." How would I know? I didn't feel anything.

"Can you believe all of that food? I'm totally stuffed. I hope they fork out again next year."

"Depending on how good the films are," I said sarcastically. We both laughed a bit between inhales.

"Oh, hey, I wanted to tell you, my friend Paige saw you in there and thinks you're cute. Well, those are her words not mine. She asked if you were single. Now that Vivienne's gone, I thought, maybe…"

"I'm not interested," I said with vitriol, looking him dead in the eye.

"You're right, I totally understand…I'm sorry I brought it up, it was stupid of me. Sorry, man."

"It's fine, don't worry about it." I crushed my cigarette under my shoe and walked back in without saying any more.

I went to the bar and ordered another whiskey, feeling steadily on my way to full inebriation now. I sat back down and opted to watch the band play. I could stand music a little more now, more than the white noise and silence I had been listening to. I had missed the absence of it in the prior months. I've always loved music, especially jazz, and going without it had been rough. The band played all the usual Christmas tracks, while people slowly danced or shimmied around in their nice outfits and full bellies, happy to be here, happy to be celebrating amongst their loved ones and cow-orkers.

I watched them somnolently, wishing she was here to dance with me and eat festive food until we were sick and make hopeful toasts. She had a way of not making me feel shy or embarrassed or worried about what people thought of me. She moved like a live wire on the dance floor, sauntering and swirling along with the music. Now I sat here like a rock, unable to move or converse with the rest of them.

I saw Chris talking to a girl at the edge of the room. She had short blonde hair and a red, smooth velvet dress on. Was this the aforementioned Paige? She glanced over at me and I turned my head to the band, as if I hadn't seen her. Maybe he was telling her that I wasn't interested. I felt a slight pang of missing out. Maybe I should go over and talk to her, maybe she was nice, maybe she was what I needed to move forward. As soon as I had the thought, it escaped out of the back door of my mind, and I continued to watch people dancing.

"Hi…" a low, soft voice said to me from my right. startling me slightly. I looked over to see the blonde girl staring at me with her large brown eyes and red lipstick, matte against her curved mouth.

"Hi," I said, not really knowing what else to say. It had been years since I'd spoken to a woman romantically, let alone tried to flirt with one.

She was very pretty, in a gentle sort of way. Round cheekbones and a pronounced cupid's bow. Light makeup as opposed to the cakey plastering I'd seen around Hollywood. She had a soft demeanor, seeming graceful, kind.

"I'm Paige, Chris's friend. I work for Kolia, you know, the production music company?" She searched for recognition in my face.

"Ah yes, I hear they're a good company to work for. How long have you been with them?" I said, boring myself.

"Four years this month. Pretty cool party, eh?" She was really trying; I felt bad for not engaging more.

"Can I get you a drink?" I needed to do something be-fore I bored myself to death and died in my chair.

"Sure, uh, vodka and cranberry?"

"I'll be right back." I got up from my seat and offered her the one next to me. The little girl with the red cookie was gone.

She smiled as I walked off toward the bar, again, order-ing another whiskey for me and a vodka cranberry for Paige. It came decorated with a sugared piece of rosemary on top of the glass, which instantly made me think of Vivienne.

I walked back over and set the drinks on the table. Paige looked a little shy, but confident. We engaged in small talk about work and where she was from (Iowa) and what brought her to LA. She asked about me and my life. I didn't have the heart to tell her I felt as hollow as a bamboo cane, and she shouldn't waste any more of her time on me.

I finished my drink and said I had to go, standing up and scanning the room blankly, telling her it was nice talk-ing to her, that I was tired, and to tell Chris bye for me. She looked slightly upset, as if she didn't understand what she had said to abruptly make me leave. She said goodbye quietly as I left to get my coat and walk home.

What did I expect was going to happen? Why was I sabotaging any chance to feel real, human connection again. Vivienne was gone after all; she wasn't coming back. How do I get over her?

I walked slowly through the lamplight of the dark streets, passing sleepy office buildings and other Christmas themed parties with more jubilant, well-dressed people inside. I was empty, like I truly had nothing to give, to offer to anyone else after her. Once I reached my apartment and stumbled safely inside, I fell asleep thinking of lost opportunities, cursing myself for being so closed off to others now, punishing myself for not moving forward in any direction of my life.

I should have eaten a cookie with red frosting on it to curb the hangover I was destined to have in the morning. I wondered if Paige had gone home and slept with somebody else, somebody more interesting.

I spent Christmas day alone. Opting for a flavorless, pre-made dinner of mashed potatoes and chicken; barely managing to finish half of it. I bought myself a gift of a new pack of cigarettes and a fresh bottle of whiskey, drinking and smoking the day away to old reruns of Frasier and the Golden Girls on TV land, while so much of the world celebrated in the comforting warmth of their families. Last year we were covered in wrapping paper, delicious home cooked food and laughter. What a difference a year makes.

5. Vivienne

By the time New Year's came around, I was feeling increasingly numb and closed off. I decided, against my better judgment, to attend Will's annual New Year's Eve party. He always threw the best parties, I couldn't deny that, and I had enjoyed myself the previous years, albeit under much more positive circumstances. Medium grade champagne and well-made, home cooked food galore, lavish decorations and hordes of 'cool' artsy people Will had met from all over the place.

He had invited me coyly over the phone, even though he knew I was most likely going to decline the invitation. To mine and his surprise, I didn't. I needed another night out to forget about my crippling loneliness, even if most days all I truly wanted was to be left alone. It was a constant mental tug of war. I didn't want to lose my friends, although I had next to nothing to offer them in return. I was grateful to be invited at all, given my current state.

I arrived at his house around 10 pm, letting myself in through the front door. People were already drunk, wandering about gleefully, dressed in sparkly, gold and silver attire with shiny New Year's hats and plastic glasses on. I made my way to the open bar and poured myself a neat scotch. I saw Will making the rounds and went over to wish him well, but he saw me first and ran towards me, barreling his arms around me like a big kid pummeling his little brother.

"Happy New Year, buddy!" He grabbed me in a big bear hug, squeezing me too tight, like a father to his children. He didn't realize how big he was sometimes, and I was wasting away. I crushed and contorted under his weight.

"Yeah, yeah, Happy New Year." I patted his back, smiling coarsely, my ribs hurting.

"Come on, V! This is the time to celebrate, a new year, new you? Have some fun for fucks sake!"

"I came, didn't I? I even got dressed up, so what are you complaining about?" I said sarcastically, looking down at my simple button up shirt and black jeans.

"Well, try not to be a total downer tonight. Look at how many people are here. Mingle! Maybe you can finally cut your hair and shave again next year, huh?" He walked off laughing after tossing my hair around with his hand. I put it back in place like a little kid whose mother had just messed it up. Annoyed, I rolled my eyes and surveyed the scene with my drink firmly in hand.

Last time I was here was with her. She was ravishing. Flying around the room like a hummingbird and laughing that penetrating, unmistakable laugh. I remember her in this exact living room, drinking champagne and charming everyone with jokes and playful, flirtatious mannerisms. Fuck, this was awful. Why was I so masochistic? I should have stayed home and ordered in cheap Chinese food and watched the ball drop in Times Square with strangers who probably felt as cold and lonely as I did.

People were smoking weed and dancing to upbeat soul music, the room smelled of perfume and sweat and marijuana. I stood on the patio watching distant lights flicker. I heard the countdown coming from inside the house behind me.

"Five, four, three, two, one, HAPPY NEW YEAR!" they all screamed in unison, embracing in laughter and kissing each other. Champagne corks popped off from different corners of the room and people sang together, off key. I stood on the balcony and watched fireworks exploding into the sky from deep in the hills of Hollywood, colorful stars of red and green. I suddenly hoped their flares didn't start a fire. They had been so bad the year before. I suppose people will ignore danger for the sake of festivities.

In my own irony, I lit a cigarette and stood there for a few minutes, wondering how long this dense mental fog was going to last for. Last year I was here with the love of my life, celebrating in laughter and happiness with these same people, feeling young and hopeful and excited about the bright future ahead of us. Now I stood here sucking a cancer stick wondering why I didn't feel anything at all.

After escaping through the backyard with no one to

notice or stop me, I traveled home, dragging my feet as I moved. I tried to think about clean slates. I was thirty-four, soon to be thirty-five. Maybe this was the year I could truly move on and be more adventurous in my life, take more chances, more risks. Maybe I would be able to finally venture outside of my comfort zone and live more chaotically, less routinely, like she had.

Perhaps I should quit my job, take my retirement funds out and travel the far-reaching world, become a monk, or take peyote and find myself again. Certainly that would keep my mind off of it all. New places could keep the ghosts of my past from following me around. Everything seemed perfectly possible while simultaneously feeling entirely impossible.

I arrived back home just after 1 am and sat quietly on the sofa, still hearing cheering and laughter in the streets along with cheap, store-bought fireworks and bottles of champagne popping off. I sat alone in the soft light of my small home and pondered it all, staring into the flat outline of my beige walls. New year, new me? But nothing had shift-ed. New year, same me.

I looked over at a box. A box I hadn't been able to bring myself to open or acknowledge for months. A box amongst a pile of boxes that was rotting on the floor of my apartment. Like painfully splattered confetti, these boxes had been scat-tered around like ancient stone circles since she had gone. I didn't know what to do with them. I figured tonight was the night. It was the new year, after all. New year, new me.

I walked over and picked up the box, setting it on my

small dining table. I opened it slowly, almost afraid of what I'd see and nervous about how the contents would make me feel. I peeled back the cardboard flap cautiously, exposing the innards. It was a bag of makeup, still open, with some hair products and perfume beside it. I lifted it out gingerly, studying the capsules with liquid inside. My mind flashed to her wearing these colors, these shades, this scent. Decorating her perfect face with subtle hues of blue and pink and red.

I took the bag to the bathroom. Digging my hand around, I pulled out a lipstick with the color labeled 'hawthorn' and applied it to my lips. I was kind of tipsy and had never worn her makeup before, but it felt comforting. I inhaled, thinking of this lipstick gliding along her smooth, soft round lips, microscopic skin fragments still remaining on the stick. I glanced at myself in the mirror, shocked at how similar I looked to her. We both had dark, wavy hair, greenish hazel eyes, although hers were more forest colored, her lips fuller. I felt like I was looking at her looking back at me. It made me feel sick, and overwhelmingly sad. I missed her so much. I felt a lump in my throat as I stared at my bright hawthorn lips. I kissed the back of my hand, closing my eyes and pretending it was her. Of course it wasn't, but it felt better than nothing. I opened my eyes, glancing down at the smudged lipstick smeared over the back of my bony hand.

I ran back to the box and poured everything out of it frantically onto the wooden floor, going through all of her beauty products and skincare, applying them to my face and spraying her perfume on my neck in a frenzy. I started to cry, slowly at first, then quickly erupting into an uncontrollable sob. I cried until I felt like I had drained my whole body of water, like a tub with the plug pulled out. It was too much, holding her perfume and smelling her, without her skin to accompany it. The perfume she'd worn the entire time we'd been together.

I woke up in my bed around 10 am that morning, not recalling how I had landed there or when exactly I fell asleep. I was half naked, covered in lipstick smudges, my bedding completely disheveled. I nearly fell out getting up when I noticed a bottle on the floor. Her perfume; my whole bedroom stunk of it. Mimosa and rose. I set the bottle on my nightstand and shook my head, putting my hand on my forehead, feeling a headache pounding the back of my skull. I looked down at the rainbow of colors dotting my skin.

I walked to the bathroom, still stinking of her perfume, and relieved myself. Happy New Year. Just as I finished, I looked up to see my gaunt face covered in smeared red lipstick, staining my mouth and chin. I remembered now. I remembered the sobbing and the box and her lipstick, her makeup. What the fuck was I doing? I grabbed some toilet paper and wiped it off, embarrassed at my feeble attempts to feel closer to her.

Did I honestly think putting on her makeup and spraying on her perfume was going to bring her back?

6. Vivienne

February. My birthday month. I had been working all
of January, much as I had in the month before, taking on two
new projects, keeping my head down and barely surviving
the searing, raw pain of the holidays. Now I was back in my
quasi-comfortable headspace, alone and silent, apart from
the recurring memories and pain of her absence. The way
I preferred it, without obligations or happiness or outside
laughter. I still had her boxes strewn across the floor, which
I hadn't touched or opened, apart from my New Year's Eve
antics. I'd hidden her makeup in the back of my dresser
drawer and tucked her perfume deep under the bed where I
couldn't reach.

I was eating a little more, feeling better about not
punishing my body but still limiting how much I could
physically stomach. Small meals instead of rich, hearty ones.
Unhealthy, quick noodle and cracker jobs instead of home
cooked meals, which I usually preferred. I hadn't thought
about much else besides getting through the days and nights.

I moved robotically, without feeling or sensation.

Will had called me that sunny February morning to wish me a happy birthday. It was nice to hear from him, considering I'd stopped calling anyone on a regular basis. January was always a weird month, which let me off the hook from feeling guilty about my lack of social interaction. People seemed to go dormant and depressed after the excitement and time off from work during the holidays, the month-long hangover after starting their healthy New Years resolutions. I was used to this constant feeling of dormancy, so it didn't matter much to me. Still, I was happy to hear from him.

"How are you feeling, V? Any birthday plans? Should I even ask that?" he said, half laughing, half serious.

"I don't know, why? What did you have in mind?"

"Well, I'm glad you asked, old friend. Agnes and I want to take you out on the town. Get dressed up, make the rounds, what do you think?" He sounded excited.

I scoffed. "Hmm, I don't know, Will, I kind of just want to stay in…"

"Enough! Nonsense! I'm fucking sick of this person, V. You're coming out. You're not going to be alone on your thirty-fifth birthday! We'll meet you at eight, at Luca's. I'm not taking no for an answer this time, I'll come over there and drag you out myself."

"Alright, fine," I gave in. "But I'm not staying out too late, okay?"

"Okay, old man. See you at eight." He clicked the phone off. I sighed.

I really didn't want to go out, but I also didn't want to stay in. I was stuck in a dark purgatory of contradicting feelings. I wanted to remember a former version of myself, the person who enjoyed going out on my birthday, appreciated quality time with my closest friends and family. People wanted to take me out, to spend time with me—I should be utterly grateful that I hadn't been cut loose and abandoned after months and months of moping around and denying them my attention.

I got ready around seven and was ready to leave by 7:30. I'd washed my sheets since spraying them with her perfume and kicked her boxes to the outer perimeters of the house, out of my direct view, to be dealt with later.

I had planned to meet Will and Agnes at Luca's, an old Italian bar and eatery near the hills. He knew I loved this place because it was truly old school, like a real mob gangster meeting spot, and only old timers seemed to still come and dine here. I hated the tackiness of ultra-modern bars, roughly built, neon places with no soul, no flavor to them. They all smelled like cologne and cocaine and desperate over-networking. I was definitely born in the wrong era. Even though my companions constantly made fun of me for choosing old, dark bars. I didn't mind. I was slightly enthusiastic that they were indulging me tonight, for my birthday. A birthday without her.

Agnes was a kind woman with a gentle face and soft eyes. She and Will had been together since high school and carried with them the kind of bond that most people envy.

They were communicative and caring without being overly clingy or sappy and were always there to listen to me even when they were probably sick of hearing about it. Agnes carried herself with the kind of flowing ebullience you would expect from a Greek Goddess or some kind of hippie earth mama. Her long, curly hair bounced against her broad shoulders, her brown eyes intent, warm. Her gaze showed you that she was indeed, listening to what you had to say. I had always appreciated these serene qualities in her.

I arrived ten minutes early and found them both sitting comfortably in a dimly lit booth toward the back corner of the bar, cold drinks in hand, a vodka lime for Will and a mysterious red cocktail for Agnes. They seemed to be mulling over something only vaguely interesting, probably their monthly bills or jobs. Agnes was a middle school art teacher and Will worked for a modern interior design firm. They both possessed fabulous taste, and it exhibited in everything they did, from their home decor to the way they dressed.

They caught my eye as I sauntered clumsily over, tired and terribly hiding my disdain for celebrating my birthday this way. I appreciated their efforts, sure, but I just wanted to bathe in my own pity party in my smelly dungeon of an apartment. Although deep down I was grateful to have friends who wanted better for me.

"V, you skinny bastard, you finally made it to your own party! You look like shit! What can I get you, birthday boy?" Will said jubilantly, patting me hard on the back. He was always in such a happy fucking mood.

"Whiskey and ginger, I think. Thanks, man." I half smiled.

"Happy birthday!" Agnes stood up and wrapped her warm arms around me, holding me for a few seconds while pressing her soft, curvy body against me. It felt nice to be held, even platonically, in an alien way. "How are you getting by? How are you feeling?" she probed gently, looking into my eyes with a slightly worried frown.

"Oh, you know, work, home, whatever. I'm just trying to take it day by day, you know, trying not to die." I listened to how pathetic my voice sounded. Day by day? Who was I kidding, I was a total fucking disaster. My house was in complete disarray, my job was boring me to death, and I was probably one shitty project away from getting fired and los- ing my apartment. My life was completely empty and devoid of color and depth without her.

"That's great, that's all you can do, isn't it? Remember that grief takes time, it isn't straightforward. It's only fresh still. Remember to try to smile at the little things and see them as small triumphs. Don't beat yourself up too much, okay? Maybe you can see someone… professionally." She gave me a rub on the shoulder, looking concerned and matron-like, trying to look me in the eyes as I nodded and looked down toward the sticky, liquor-stained bar floor.

Vivienne used to tell me not to be too hard on myself. Not to take things to heart, not to let outside influences wear me down. I couldn't help letting situations affect me in a sour way, holding on to them longer than perhaps I should have.

I wondered how she put up with me and my selfish, aloof nature for so long. Especially when all the while I should have been helping her, comforting her. I was so immature, so fucking stupid.

Will handed me my drink and we talked for an hour or two about nothing special. I could tell they were asking easy questions to avoid me bailing out on them and spoiling their rare night out, occasionally laughing or joking to lighten the atmosphere while we sipped our cocktails. I hadn't eaten much during the day, as usual, and Agnes made a point of ordering plates of food for the table, which I picked at slowly.

"When are you thinking of getting back out there, like, actually getting back out there?" Will asked.

"If he's not ready, he's not ready, don't push him," Agnes said in a scolding tone, giving Will the sharp side eye. I could tell they had spoken of this subject beforehand.

"Well, he needs to do something!" Will retorted. "Do you think it's healthy that he sits at home barely eating, staring out of the window alone, doing god knows what?"

I'm not that bad, am I? I wondered. I looked back at Will.

"I'm just saying, see how you feel, go on some, like, little practice dates, just to remember what it's like to be around people besides us for a change, yeah?"

"I'll think about it," I said, anything to shut him up. I chewed on a few briny green olives and what tasted like day-old stale bread.

I had thought about it, of course I'd thought about

it. I would love nothing more than to fully move on, to feel excited and warm towards the notion of being with someone I could love again. To feel the intimacy and intricacies of a real romantic relationship outside of her. All I had left now were these tethered scraps of memories and fragments, played on a rusty reel of film filled with gaps and holes that were slowly fading by the hour. Memories I desperately clung to, obsessed over, poring over every minute detail until they seemed to fit in a wonky mosaic that no longer made any sense. I would recall foggily who said what, what I could have done to make it easier on her, how I could have been less stubborn. These memories haunted me, kept me awake at night, tortured me.

I wanted new memories now, new experiences, new love with a new person. I just didn't know if that could exist beyond her, beyond what I had already felt so perfectly and lost so abruptly. Maybe people aren't supposed to feel that kind of love twice. I didn't want to get too close to the sun when I had already been scorched.

During the height of our relationship, when we were both healthy and functional, she was so understanding, selfless and gentle toward me. A specific strain of kindness I'd never known and maybe never would know again. I found myself struck with admiration at her every gaze, her movements, her actions, words. She had stayed with me despite my firm tomb of stubborn coldness, constantly locking her out of my mind and refusing to share myself with her the way she had with me.

I was of the mind that all relationships end, regardless of their duration, and giving into them fully only makes you weak, like those pathetic people you see on the street, the floppy sugary types that 'can't live without each other,' the kind who think that film love is real love, the ones who believe in fairytales and happy endings. Vivienne knew I was an impenetrable wall and yet still she slept on the mote, for years, waiting patiently for it to open, to enter and valiantly save me from myself.

I didn't deserve her. Was she just a masochist and I was the sadist laughing down at her, torturing her for my own sick enjoyment? Now I was the one rotting here, in my grieving misery and sickness and stench, and she was long gone. The gods really are fucked.

Will slapped me on the shoulder, knocking me out of my morbid frame of thought. "Let's go to Cuzo's after this, there's a good band on. What do you think?"

"Okay," I said glumly, seeing her fruitlike face disappear from my mental view. Would I ever enjoy live music again? Everything just sounded like loud, abstract noise now. I couldn't hear melodies anymore, couldn't let my body drift away.

"Yeah, it's their classic jazz night, you'll love it. Not that shitty new stuff, they're playing the legends. Come on, get up, let's go." He pulled my arm and led me out of the booth, leaving the plates of food half full and sadly picked over. What a waste, I thought, as he dragged me toward the cash register.

After paying the bill for our drinks and meal, we walked down the road toward the tiny, hidden club. The sky overlooking the hills was a smooth, rich indigo and full of tiny sparkling lights. People were making dinner, couples were settling in for the evening, families were doing school homework. I looked up at the wave of diamond dusted hills, my eyes dancing between the inky and bright areas. I wanted to live forever in the inky areas. Beneath the eucalyptus and pine trees, until I was covered in green foliage or engulfed by wildfire.

Will and Agnes laughed together behind me. I had never noticed laughter before until it was taken away from me. The way you don't notice how much you use your hands until you injure one. All of a sudden, I felt as if I'd been robbed of this vibrant and essential emotion, crippled in a sense, not allowed to access a vital bodily function that others could easily exercise. Laughter was abruptly alien to me. I heard it, witnessed it, but it didn't register anymore. It had become a foreign language. I wondered when, or if, I'd ever really laugh again.

We arrived at Cuzo's a few minutes later and paid the ten-dollar cover charge to get in. I could hear the band playing in the background as we stood outside. They sounded decent. Will was right, they were playing classics, covering a version of Miles Davis' 'Blue in Green.'

We took our seats around a horseshoe-shaped, red tufted leather booth near the stage. Will stood up promptly to order us a round of drinks while Agnes and I watched the band, admiring the swift, talented fingers of the musicians. She looked so cheerful and light-hearted, genuinely excited to be there. Outside of the confines of her own daily routine, she looked entirely fulfilled, content. She asked me if I liked what I heard. I nodded half-heartedly, which was all I could muster.

I didn't want to hurt her feelings by saying something along the lines of, "I wish I couldn't hear anything. I wish she was here with us." I mean, the band was good, I was just a wet, pathetic straw of a man who couldn't appreciate anything or anyone beautiful in my current, apathetic, dead headspace. Despite this hollow and morose attitude, I was supremely grateful that I was here with my closest friends.

Vivienne loved birthdays. She loved all holidays, really. She enjoyed the opportunity to dress up, to turn the house into a bright parade of creative celebration, whether it was Christmas, solstices, Valentine's Day, Lunar New Year; hell, even Easter. She'd go out of her way to make each day feel uniquely special, for us to feel like excited, curious children again. She'd kept that playful, childish enthusiasm so many of us lose over the years. That hazy time when things still appeared to be made of magic and folklore. The endless nights of staying up late despite her work schedule; baking, tiptoeing around the hall and kitchen just so I'd have a special, handmade surprise and decorated apartment to wake up to.

These are the memories I took for granted the most, the memories I wanted back so I could re-do them, the memories that are fading the quickest despite my desperate attempts to keep her face with me. I can still hear her soft, sweet voice, see her lighting thirty-three candles atop a buttercream-iced cake, wax melting quickly, surrounded by colored paper streamers and sparklers, a paper crown placed playfully on my head. Gifts wrapped sweetly on the table with a long, carefully penned, handmade card from her.

"Make a wish! You must make a wish, don't pretend to or it won't come true," she'd threaten before I blew out my candles, smiling and kissing her cheeks. My only wish now was to have her near me again. I didn't have thirty-five candles or a homemade cake now. No crown, no wishes, no paper decorations, no cards. Just the absence of her and her fading voice getting more garbled in my mind.

Agnes and I sat over dim candlelight in near silence watching the band play, moving our feet and bobbing our heads. I felt slightly guilty for third wheeling this incredibly romantic date in my shabby state, glancing ambivalently around at the wide array of couples who sat attentively and happily in their seats, gazing at one another then up to the band, nursing their drinks, touching hands, kissing and smiling. So many of them were probably fresh into their new relationships, that perfect phase of majestic bliss before things inevitably go south and the romance begins to sour and morph into the boredom of the real-life mundane.

Some couples were slow dancing on the small, lacquered wooden dance floor in front of the stage, holding each other's bodies close, swaying seductively in one another's arms. In most cases, this would have been my idea of a perfectly wholesome evening. Now, on this day, my birthday, in this admittedly numb frame of mind, I could have easily been a ghost haunting the bar. I was a shapeless figure made of air, blocking out valuable dancing space. A black fly on the wall of a hip and happening place, and just as insignificant. If only I could be dead or squashed within twenty-four hours. Being a fly is underrated.

After the band finished its moody cover of Billie Holiday's 'Blue Moon', I decided to get up and get myself another drink. My body was in full blown destructive, self-medication mode; willing to accept any physical decline or disease in return for heavenly nothingness. I didn't care what I was doing to myself any longer. I wanted to dive into the depths of hollowness and feel absolutely nothing, until she was eradicated from my mind. I turned to Will and Agnes to ask if they wanted another drink, which they declined, saying adulthood and work schedules had turned them into lightweights.

I wondered if they talked about me now, how they probably said they were worried about me but couldn't find a way to bring it up. Maybe they would plan some kind of intervention and check me into a mental health facility that forced me to eat full meals and take daily psychotherapy. Their delicate, nervous stares betrayed any poker face they may have been attempting to show. I knew people were worried about me, and I didn't care.

Suit yourself, I thought, shrugging, watching them glance quickly at each other with that slightly judgmental, parental look. When you're happy in life, you're already drunk on love. But when you're fucking miserable, you need a little help to get on their level.

The band was playing an upbeat Dizzy Gillespie tune now, moving on to quicker and faster rhythms, prompting the crowd to cheer, clap and dance faster to keep up with them. I meandered over to the bartender and ordered a whiskey ginger, accidentally noticing my decrepit face and sallow frame in the mirror behind the display of brightly labeled liquor bottles. I looked like a sliver of my former self, a sketched cartoon of who I once was. Was that me? Will that always be me? Have I killed off the previously robust and interesting version of myself, the one that I actually used to somewhat enjoy living within? Would I feel like this forever, continuing to waste away until there was nothing left and my poor, unsuspecting superintendent found my slim corpse rotted on the floor of my disgusting, filthy apartment, a formerly happy man turned sad skeleton succumbing to the disease of a broken heart? Should I just go home and end it tonight? Who would notice, I wondered, as if it was an entirely original idea.

The thought had begun to creep more and more into my psyche over the past few months. Was I strong enough to commit such a selfish act? Was I brave enough to go through with it? How would I do it? Gas? Noose? Pills? Perhaps I could fill the tub with my blood so everyone could witness how I truly felt. Drained of life, of blood, of love, empty without her in my life. I knew I was too fucking vacant and weak to kill myself. Who was I kidding? I may as well be made of jelly. Plus, there was no point in dying if she wasn't around to mourn me and that's what I really wanted, in my sick, sadistic way.

As I looked blankly into the void of my narrowly dark mind, pondering my existential and pitiful philosophical self-worth, a shape suddenly appeared beside me in the mirror, to my left. An objectively pleasing and mysterious looking shape. One that I had failed to notice within the club's parameters before, not that I had been actively looking at anyone. She was murky and obscure, her dark hair blending into the array of clear and green bottles. However, I could tell she was physically attractive. I pried my gaze away from the mirror and looked to my left to see a woman, about my age, stood achingly close to my body, closer than anyone other than friends or family have stood in a while. So close I could feel the heat emanating from her smooth, freckled arm. I tensed up reflexively. I hadn't been this close to a woman I'd found attractive since Vivienne and I instantly felt limp and, surprisingly, nervous. I was like a schoolboy who didn't know how to act around their elementary school recess crush.

The bartender handed me my drink, and I reached for my wallet to pay, fully intending to turn around swiftly and never see this mysterious woman again. Just as I laid my cash tip on the bar and turned my back, she spoke, shocking me out of my timid bashfulness.

"So, you like jazz, huh?" a small but confident voice arose from her silky, toned throat.

"Yeah, um,"—I cleared my throat—"yes, I do, I always have," I managed to croak out shyly, unable to look her directly in the eye. Instead, I looked at a brown water stain in the ceiling. Fuck.

"I'm Jan, like January, and you are…?" She gave me a flirtatious look, kind eyed, playful, holding her hand out for me to shake, putting her thick, wavy hair behind her ears with her opposite hand. She was wearing bent brass earrings, hammered into the shape of Matisse-esque flowers. I focused on them for a while before reminding myself that I was indeed engaging in conversation with a live, human person. I needed to remember how to do this. Vivienne had made it all so easy, so natural. But I wasn't Vivienne. I'm a fucking wreck.

"I'm Venn," I finally blurted out quietly.

"Nice to meet you, Ben!" she nearly shouted in my ear. Her breath was hot on my face, a strange feeling. The band was loud now, and people were dancing like crazy, like a scene from the beatnik sixties.

"No, Venn, like the Venn diagram!" I shouted back, embarrassed that my parents had chosen that for me, something I had always been made fun of for while growing up.

"Oh, Venn! What a cool name, I've never heard of that before," she said with a cocked head. Apparently, my name was good for something, even if it was embarrassing. "Do you want to dance with me?" she went on, sipping her Shirley Temple cocktail and stirring the maraschino cherry around the bottom of the glass, almost seductively, stabbing her straw into the ice and looking back at me with curious eyes.

"God, uh, I don't know, I haven't really danced in a long time… not since…"

"Oh, come on! It will be fun. Here, let me take this." She snatched my drink away from my hand and set it on a nearby table, atop a round, thick coaster. Then she reached for my tightly clenched fist, smoothing her hand around my pale, nervous knuckles. I tried to relax and relinquish control of my body, letting her soft, small hand hold onto mine, guiding me toward the floor. I didn't know what to do. Was I doing something wrong? I still loved Vivienne. Holding another woman's hand suddenly washed me over with burning guilt.

She practically elbowed her way through the crowd and began her own personal rendition of a modern jazz dance. She was taller than average, about 5'9, with thick dark hair and green-blue eyes, like an algae bloom in late spring. Her curvaceous body resembled that of the Birth of Venus, with her wavy hair falling wild and loose around her heart shaped face. She didn't seem to have any reservations about dancing with total strangers, which led me to question if she came here often, dancing with anyone who would be willing. I admired that kind of confidence.

That was something I'd also admired in Vivienne. She was always excited and willing to dance erratically and expressively, completely unaware and unbothered of who may be watching or judging her. She would float and move like a dandelion seed, flawlessly graceful, feet tapping and arms swaying like a Shiva. I, on the other hand, was extremely shy toward any kind of public dancing, something she always openly disliked about me.

In order to really dance, I needed to be hideously drunk, unable to care about my surroundings or the searing eyes of onlookers. I always cared about how others saw me, a stark difference between Vivienne and me. Once I arrived at the stage of drunkenness where I felt comfortable dancing, a blobby, dad-like sway would ensue, no doubt embarrassing Vivienne as much as myself. Why was she with me for so long? She could have dated some sexually appealing dancing fool, cutting it up with her on the floor like John Travolta in Saturday Night Fever. Why did she love me so much, despite my horrendously painful display of faults?

In Jan's case, I was already slightly tipsy, to my content, and had nothing to lose at this juncture, in this tiny jazz club. I didn't care if people were judging me because I was in a state of total nonchalance about my appearance, my body and my mental wellbeing. I didn't care if I was Fred Astaire or an earthworm at this point. I was mostly concerned with the idea of another person touching or being near me who wasn't my darling Vivienne. I hadn't felt another human body against mine in what felt like an eternity. I was out of practice and totally alone in this new feeling, with this new person.

Jan began to move and sway in a cool, collected way, upturning her arms and kicking her legs like a tantric dancer, almost as if mixing modern dance with a hint of traditional swing. I stood still, watching her movements, fascinated, like an anthropologist observing a human mating ritual, in shock that this beautiful creature had chosen a near cadaver to join her in this vivid display of music and culture. I attempted to emulate her contemporary moves, to my failure. Still, I managed to sway and swing roughly to the upbeat music, watching her smile and twist around with every change in tone and rhythm.

I had to admit it felt good to allow myself to be free, even in this minuscule and fragmented way. It felt like progress. I had been so incredibly uptight, so deep within myself for what seemed like so long, I'd forgotten how good it felt to just let my body move and fully feel something awake inside of me, like someone had come in and turned a light on in a vacation home, typically left empty and dark for months. I was grateful to Jan for selecting *me* to dance with. After all, she had no idea just how empty I truly was, how devoid I had been over the last year. I suddenly wondered what her story was, where she came from, who she had loved, if anyone. Was she here mourning a loss as well, dancing and drinking to cure the pain?

I glanced over the crowd toward the red table where Agnes and Will were sitting contently beside their nearly empty drinks. They both stared at me moving like a writhing slug and Jan dancing like a swan, completely surprised and transfixed, almost rudely gawking at us. Will was smiling a sly smile, staring into my eyes, as if to say to me telepathically 'finally.' I smiled back half-heartedly, resigned to what little movement I could offer, and continued looking at Jan in her full, glorious form.

As I danced, I contemplated how long it had been since I'd appreciated the company of another human. I had cut myself off completely for over a year, punished myself into believing I was merely unlovable. I had accepted that I was flawed, probably too flawed, too much work, at least romantically. Even being my friend or acquaintance at this point was hard work. A pesky perturbation of a man who didn't need to bother taking up valuable time in the pursuit of love or friendship. A waste of a perfectly decent evening, bad company, dead conversation.

What does a human being really have to achieve to receive love? Is there a mental and physical checklist, a degree of accomplishments and self-evaluation to further our prospects and combined goals, or are we just mammals drawn together for propagation, fucking each other in order to procreate and eradicate the terminal disease of loneliness? Or perhaps to stamp out crippling solitude by allowing our flaws to be an amalgamation of characteristics in which we can relate to others with similar flaws, who also wish to not be alone in this life? Do we need to truly experience loneliness in order to appreciate truly unconditional love? And if you do find true love, how do you know it's true love and not just a figment of your imagination, what you expected love to look and feel like?

I hadn't ever really minded being alone, I enjoyed my own company. Before I met Vivienne I had always lived on my own, except for intermittent partners. I worked long hours so I could afford the comfort of living within my own, sacred domain of comfort. Without the distraction or annoyance that roommates could bring into a shared living space. I appreciated coming home to a house exactly as I'd left it. To my own food in the refrigerator, listening to my own music and radio programs loudly, walking around naked without the worry of offending someone who didn't agree with my specific approach to life.

Once Vivienne and I had decided to move in together a few years ago, my perspective changed seemingly overnight. I finally allowed another human into my private, personal space, my cave of solitude penetrated by this perfect human of light and creativity. She floated into my apartment and exorcised the demons of my domestic darkness, filling every nook and cranny with a kind and patient touch.

I hadn't realized living with another human could be so easy, so carefree, so good. My previous partners had made me feel trapped in a phony, routinely domestic hell. She made me see the world in this bright, extraordinary way, almost resembling a fantasy. I had always resided in a world of black and white, but she filled my life, my home, our home, with the most incredible brightness. She always danced to our records and the radio, barefoot, gliding her imperfect, dirty feet along the floorboards with ease, like a water glider on a Minnesota lake in summer.

My ribs hurt again. Fuck. I miss you so much, Vivienne, I want to see your dirty feet dancing in our home. I want to be near you again, smell your sweat, your hair, your floral breath...

As I watched Jan glide her own feet across the dance floor, I tried to come back into my body and leave the stabbing memories hidden in my head. I need to just be present in this moment of sudden positivity and welcome change. I needed to find a way to stop revisiting these feelings, these old, slipping memories. To move forward in any slight, significant way. I physically attempted to shake myself off these memories by shaking my shaggy hair, which only added to the illusion that I was really dancing, or trying to.

Jan came over and pulled my clammy hands open, holding them up with hers and suggesting we engage in a sort of mirrored movement together. I followed her guidance in a futile, infantile way but she didn't seem to mind. Her red lipstick separated to reveal a beaming smile. This made me smile in return and we continued to dance slowly, palm to palm.

"You're getting there, kind of...You don't dance much, do you?" she joked, making me twirl her around in a delicate circle while she held tightly onto my hand.

"It's been a while, I admit," I had to nearly scream back over the loud music.

"That's okay, I'll teach you, just move along with me!" she yelled back, laughing an ebullient, playful laugh. Her smile waxed and waned as she moved and glanced over her shoulder seductively at me. I was confused as to what this sweet, exciting woman saw in me. Didn't she see what I was seeing? I decided not to question it or push my luck.

So that's what we did for the next two hours. I stood, semi-rigid, trying to move and dance as much as a rooted tree stump could, while Jan fluttered and moved like a butterfly all over that tiny dance floor. We drank intermittently when we became sweaty and parched, becoming increasingly more drunk in the process.

The alcohol helped my glued feet move a little more, which I was grateful for. Despite my awkward demeanor and desperately shoddy dance skills, Jan remained interested in me throughout the evening, and for the first time in a long time, to my surprise, I felt somewhat interested back. I felt as if my dead body had been jolted back to life with a female defibrillator, just for the briefest moment. In this little dark club, with this vibrant woman, I felt something turning, growing warm from the winter frost I'd grown so accustomed to.

After a while of watching us and smiling in our direction excitedly, Will and Agnes eventually grew bored, perhaps even a hint of jealousy creeping over their well-meaning smiles. They had been together for so long, and although they were always thought of by our friendship group as the ideal couple, the perfect unit, the welded team devoid of drama or destructive behavior, they were still human, and humans always recall fondly that electricity that emits when you've just met someone new and interesting. The mystery is rampant, the elusive curtain of wonderment that befalls two individuals trying to figure out one another. That is, before the inevitable realization that they are boring or awful and you decide to part ways for good, their memory fading into the wind and the electricity fizzling into ash. I would never feel the electricity I felt from Vivienne, but like any addict, I was willing to get my fix from a cut, substituted version, no matter how long it lasted.

Will strode over and mouthed that they were going to go, giving me a sly little wink after patting me on the back. He introduced himself to Jan and they exchanged a brief handshake. Agnes leaned in and gave me a kiss on the cheek, told me to have a great—emphasis on great—evening, and like a breeze, they were gone out of my eyeline. The club was still semi-full of people dancing wildly, some who had perhaps known one another for years, others who had possibly only met this evening, like me and Jan, curiously open to where the night could take them.

I was, to my delight, experiencing the early stages of romantic electricity. For once I felt less like a zombified, walking skin sack and more like a real, flesh-and-blood human. Feeling this body dance against me warmed me, emotionally and physically, opening me up to the most minute possibility of affection again for the first time in what seemed like forever. I didn't want to get used to it. I knew I was broken, and I didn't want to lead anyone on, especially myself. My heart had been stolen a long time ago and now could only be occupied in its absence through short bursts of stand ins, but never claimed. Not the way she had.

Once the band began to wind down and play their last

song, covering 'Chitlins Con Carne' by Kenny Burrell, we swayed and moved closer than we had before, moving our feet together in little semi-circles on the small dance floor. Jan allowed my hands to gently explore her lower back while she placed hers on my shoulders, flirting with her mannerisms and smiling that shy, downward smile of someone who may really be attracted to you. I'd forgotten how enchanting it could feel to allow yourself to open up to someone new, even in this small, insignificant way. Something as trivial as an innocent dance in a small jazz bar, made me feel like a brand-new human, at least for a little while. Distraction was the newest drug and I needed more of it.

Once the band finished, the violently bright lights were raised to kick everyone out. We found ourselves awkwardly standing around, staring at the wet dance floor, looking at each other with uncertain, coy eyes, questioning what to do next. We moved to the bar to finish our drinks, both unsure as to how to proceed to the next chapter of the evening. Jan's body language was telling me she wanted to stay and talk to me longer, or at least get to know me more. I obliged, as I wanted to eke out this feeling for as long as possible. Anything was preferable to moping around my apartment getting wasted in the circles of my deserted mind.

I sipped my drink nervously, darting my eyes toward her then away, tapping my glass with my fingers. I felt as if I was doing something elicit, cheating on the love of my life with this new person. As if at any moment Vivienne was going to briskly walk in and catch me with her, tugging me away and arguing with me in the dark street, screaming, asking me why I had wronged her in this cruel way, claiming I never loved her. She would never know how much I loved her.

That moment never came, of course. I stood there as I had before, sipping my drink and staring at my glass, watching the ice cubes melt, debating what my next move was going to be. Should I be polite, thank her, and just walk away now? After all, I'd had a more exciting night than I'd had in ages. I looked away in thought. Jan finally broke the silence with her kind, sweet voice.

"So, where are you from?" she asked, seemingly genuinely interested.

"Not far from here, where all the old orange groves used to be before they bulldozed them over. It's alright. Where are you from?" I asked back. Was this a date? Am I on a date now?

"I'm from Texas, San Antonio, see?" She proudly pointed down to her feet. I hadn't noticed in the darkness and flurry of the dance floor that she was wearing bright red cowboy boots with little white stars stitched into them, half covering a tattoo of the state of Texas. She reminded me of Sissy from Urban Cowboy, but I was no Bud. I wasn't even the antagonist. I was just the dead, curled up worm in the bottom of the tequila bottle, waiting to be chewed up and swallowed.

"Texas, wow, that's cool. I've never been there, although I've wanted to. Home of the old American West. What brought you out here?" I prodded. I didn't really want to visit Texas. In fact, the thought of visiting Texas scared the shit out of me. I envisioned my body lying in the vast plains riddled with hundreds of bullet holes.

"I'm trying to be an actor, aren't they all?" She pretended to dip a cowboy hat like they did in old fashioned westerns. I realized then that she didn't have a heavy Texan accent. Or really any discernible accent. Perhaps she was working hard in vocal lessons to blanch it out, for feature films. I always found it kind of sad when people pushed their past away to pursue a career. I suppose that's the reality of making it in Hollywood.

"What do you do?" she continued, sucking the dregs of her drink loudly through the straw.

"I work on films, independent and small productions mostly. I'm an editor, it's pretty boring..." God, I bored myself. At any moment this poor, sweet, tortured Texan queen was going to find a real desperado to ride on out of here with, leaving me behind in her dust.

"That's so awesome! Anything I've heard of? Hey, maybe you could introduce me? No pressure, though," she said excitedly, followed by a look of embarrassment, knowing she'd leaped too quickly at the word 'films.'

"Trust me, these aren't really the kinds of films you'd be interested in, but sure, okay, maybe I could..." I trailed off, wondering if I was making a false promise.

She finished her drink and began to draw circles with

her finger on the bar. She was looking around for answers. I knew this was that part of the night where you talk about going home together. I hadn't played this role in so long; I didn't want to fuck it up and frighten her off.

I hadn't slept with anyone since Vivienne, didn't even know if I could manage it.

Jan spoke up first, to my great relief and satisfaction. "Do you live around here?" She was beginning to look a little antsy.

"Yeah, uh, not too far, maybe a fifteen-minute walk," I said, in a matter-of-fact tone. I felt like I was totally fucking this up. I studied her face for signs or obvious cracks in my behavior, attempting to seem casually light and carefree.

"Well…do you want to go to your place? Maybe we can stop and get some food first? I'm starving from all that dancing, aren't you?" she said, her voice as kind and soft as an angel. A hungry angel.

"Yeah, sure. Yes, that would be nice, let's do it." I sounded like I was convincing myself more than her. I wasn't hungry at all, of course. I'd nearly forgotten what an appetite was, I'd suppressed mine for so long. At this point I would have eaten gutter leaves if it meant pushing away the darkness and forgetting about her for a little longer. I was grateful that Jan wanted to do anything with me at this point.

I paid for the drinks on my tab and motioned for Jan to follow me through the front exit onto the street. She picked up her purse and sweater and followed me out, her curly hair bouncing lightly with every step.

As we walked down the boulevard toward the street food joints, the sky was midnight black, illuminated by the vast array of neon signs and headlights passing through the busy, noisy streets, full of club goers and bar patrons. We continued to ask each other simple questions while we strolled. The type of questions you ask when you're meeting for the first time, about our families, our interests, our dislikes. I enjoyed her company immensely. I felt at ease, like I could breathe. This kind Texan had seen something worth getting to know in me, and for that I felt beholden to her.

We stopped at a street vendor cooking tacos and ordered some food. Jan quickly covered her offering with various hot sauces and salsas. You could tell she was from Texas. I was impressed and turned on. It always bothered me when people didn't top their food with hot condiments. I felt they only improved the dishes.

Sitting on a curb in the parking lot, I watched Jan eating happily while I sat looking down at my small, pathetic plate of two flat tacos. In my life before, I could have easily demolished twenty of these delicious rounds. Now, with my sorry two, I felt a pang of guilt and sadness. I wished I could jumpstart my appetite again and truly savor food the way I used to. I glanced over to see Jan finishing her meal with shiny salsa running down her fingers. She licked it off and smiled toward me, a satisfied glimmer washing over her face.

"Aren't you hungry?" she said, frowning, looking at my untouched meal.

"It's not that, I just haven't been able to eat properly for a while…"

"Oh, no! Were you sick or something? I always lose my appetite when I'm sick," she said. God, I wish I had just been sick.

"No, well, kind of like being sick. I lost my partner a while ago. I haven't been able to really eat well since losing her."

"Oh my god, I am so sorry!" she said, grabbing me in a hug, wiping her greasy salsa covered hands on my shirt and back, rubbing and patting me furiously like a deeply concerned parent.

"It's okay, really…it's just something I guess I'm still working on getting over. I hope I can eat normally again someday. I used to really love food and cooking. Now I feel like I'm just eating to survive, like it's a chore, does that make sense?"

"I can't even imagine. I lost my grandmother and cried for like a whole month. I wouldn't be able to eat either. I'm so sorry." She looked down at her red boots, clicking them quietly together like Dorothy in The Wizard of Oz. I wondered if she was thinking of her hometown in Texas. It must be so different out here for her, as if being a woman in this fucked up world wasn't hard enough.

I decided to stop being a downer. My mind was always selfishly occupied with the loss of Vivienne, and I was happy to be on a mental vacation at this moment with this refreshing and considerate woman. The last thing I wanted to do was dive right back into that pool of cerebral darkness. I already lived there full time—I wanted to stretch this feeling out for as long as possible.

I ate one of my tacos slowly and offered my remaining taco to Jan, which she accepted, still looking at me with wide, sad eyes. Great, now I was 'that guy.' The one people feel sorry for and feel like they need to approach with caution. I was so tired of people treating me like a mourning loser.

"Do you still want to come over?" I asked, genuinely unsure as to how she was feeling now. Maybe she didn't want to coddle a guy who had recently lost his partner. This was supposed to be a light, exciting evening, not some morose, comedown buzzkill.

"Yeah, of course I do. Should we walk?" she said encouragingly.

"Sure, it's not far at all. Are you okay with those?" I pointed to the cowboy boots.

"I was born in boots, honey," she said in a strong, fake Texan accent. We both laughed a bit. God, it felt good to laugh. It felt like I had just been punched with a new emotion deep within my guts.

So, we walked. Strolling along the dark, swaying palm trees, neon lights and dirty streets. We continued to ask each other light, easy questions and poked fun at the responses. I lit a cigarette and smoked it as Jan told me her roommate had moved here from rural Illinois to make it as a singer and was constantly bothering her by incessantly breaking out into cheesy top 40s pop songs. We joked and talked, and it felt easy. Before I realized it, we had arrived at the gates of my apartment building. I nervously inserted my key in the gate and turned to Jan, looking at her standing under the lamp-light like a saint.

"This is me," I said, waiting for her to back out. Surely, she had figured me out by now. But she didn't. Instead, she nodded and lifted her eyes excitedly.

I walked up the stairs in front of her, cursing myself for not deep cleaning my apartment this morning. It was still full of her boxes, her things. What would Jan think of those? Would she pity me, or find me totally creepy for keeping them around? Perhaps she would feel compassion and elicit some degree of further affection toward me. Looking down onto Jans' kind, patient visage, I was distracted. Maybe I was just buying time. But I couldn't stand at my front door forever, she'd think I was some kind of psycho. Finally, I fumbled around in my trouser pockets for my set of keys and slowly inserted them into the brass lock and opened the door, ready for my mess to unfold before her.

I flicked the light switch on and illuminated the innards of my pathetic space. I hadn't had company over for so long, I'd forgotten how to act, how to host, the rules for having people over. I felt like I had amnesia, entering a fugue state of total societal blankness.

Jan seemed blissfully unaware of the mental somersaults going on inside my head. Be calm. She has no idea what has gone on for you this year. Remember how to act, breathe. She's here, isn't she? I must be doing something correctly. Maybe her kink is depressed, sickly looking guys in mourning? We all have one.

"Do you want something to drink? I have, uh, orange juice, coffee, water, whiskey?" I said, nervously looking around my empty kitchen.

"I'll have what you're having," she said confidently, a small smile breaking across her kind face. Whiskey it is.

"Okay, cool, let me see here…" I fumbled around boyishly in my empty cabinets looking for glasses and a bottle. God, I hope she couldn't see how tragically vacant everything in my apartment looked. She would assume I was a total creep, one of those people who uses dummy apartments to get their victims inside and eventually kill them. I used my body to shield my movements so she couldn't see what a sorry excuse of a human I was. I still wanted to have some kind of sexual appeal, even if I was extremely rusty. I glanced over to see Jan flicking through my coffee table books—mid-century architecture and structures—seeming amused by what she saw.

I poured us two small glasses of cheap whiskey. It was all we could have anyway, as I was now fresh out of whiskey.

I carried the two tumblers over to where Jan was sitting and sat nervously on the sofa beside her, trying not to sit too close, handing her one of the glasses.

"Thank you, Venn, cheers. And, hey, happy birthday!" she said, raising a glass for me to clink.

"Cheers. Thanks a lot for coming over." Is that a weird thing to say? Be cool. God, I sounded like a total fucking weirdo.

We sat silently for a few minutes, sipping our drinks and listening to the cacophony of noise in the city around us. I was waiting for her to make some kind of a move, but we continued to sit politely, hands in laps, sipping our drinks. Perhaps I should have made a move. Should I ask her first? Do people still find that tacky, or was that the right thing to do? I certainly didn't want to force myself upon her.

She was starting to look a little bit bored, which instantly scared me. She exhaled deeply and flicked her forefinger against her thumb in an obvious, direct way. I panicked. I didn't want her to leave now. After all, this was the first person I've had in my house romantically since Vivienne. I needed to remember how to be human and function socially again, despite the massive absence in my heart.

7. Vivienne

The first time I kissed Vivienne was…wrong. Everything about it was wrong. The place, the timing, the way we went about committing the act. We were in love before we had even gotten to know one another properly. She made me terribly sick with nerves, exhilaration and raw lust. I tried to talk myself out of meeting her again for hours before I decided to go through with it. I told myself it was wrong, that I wasn't a cheater, I couldn't go through with it. But I ignored my conscience, we both did, and it was the darkest shade of perfection I could ever experience. Every time I closed my eyes, I wanted to taste her in my mind. I couldn't control my growing obsession towards her.

We met for the second time in a part of the city we knew none of our friends or colleagues would ever be seen in, an area our partners at the time wouldn't be caught dead in either. It was a dive bar full of old, forgotten ex actors and bad screenplay writers, the kind who wrote D-list films and now drank booze for a living on the little royalties they earned. A real old man's place, not hip or cool in any sense of the word, not even ironically. Dark, tucked away, hidden—totally safe for wannabe cheaters and people looking to fuck up their average, unfulfilled relationships.

I showed up first. Fidgeting nervously whilst peeling the paper from my Coors light coaster and debating whether I should make a run for it and forget this stupid fantasy entirely. Maybe I *was* good and decent, maybe I wouldn't go through with it after all. Still, I didn't want to stand her up, that would be bad practice and rude on my part. Not to mention I had already lied to my girlfriend in order to be here, telling her I was meeting my boss for lunch, in order to avoid any unwanted phone calls. However, the thought of meeting someone in a romantic, illicit way to potentially engage in any form of adultery still didn't sit right with me.

I thought back on the moments I'd talked my friends out of cheating on their partners, giving parental, objective advice. "It's not worth it, don't do it. Just end it and make everyone's lives easier," I'd say confidently from my high horse. Now here I was, in a dark, dingy bar in Silverlake, about to meet up with someone who could end my own solid enough relationship and harnessed the powerful capacity to completely fuck me over. Someone I couldn't not meet with; I was utterly addicted to everything about her from the moment I met her. I needed to meet her again, I was submissively drawn to her.

When we'd arranged this clandestine meet up a few

weeks prior, it had all seemed so innocent. A few quick phone calls, lightly flirting with one another under the pretense of being kind, or friendly, but we both knew what we were doing. I would step outside, telling my girlfriend I was going for a walk to the store—no, she didn't need to come, I'd say, I'd be right back, asking if she needed anything, just to make myself look better, like I was being the dutiful partner. It was a real piece of shit move. Then I'd leave her sitting on the sofa or at the dining table looking completely unaware of what I was actually doing, painting her nails a new shade of beige and watching crap reality TV, the kind where tacky scripts play out and the women fight over the asshole person that they are both involved with.

My girlfriend and I had never questioned one another before, we never had to. We both lived a quiet, routine existence, never too exciting or interesting. Our sex life was painfully bland and borderline boring, but despite that, we were close friends. The most difficult part about it all was knowing she loved me more than I could ever love her. She wasn't a bad person, far from it. She was just simple, naively kind, and uninspiring. Staying with her could have been incredibly easy, despite the lack of spark or any real attraction towards her. We could have had one of those relationships where people stay together for sheer companionship and disregard the fact that the sexual or romantic aspect fails to ever enter the partnership.

We had been together for a few years by the time I'd met Vivienne. Suddenly the thought of quietly spending my days with her seemed utterly and completely silly. Why would I continue to trudge along in a partially happy relationship when I could explore one with someone who made me feel the most alive? Sneaking out to call her, to arrange these drinks, to hear her honey voice, her laugh. This is when I realized, fully, how infidelity really happens. People escaping reality for a fantasy, but not just a fantasy, a fantasy that could turn into their reality. I wanted my fantasy to be my reality. I was sick of my real life. I wanted her.

She arrived twenty minutes late. This initially annoyed me, as I'm always early to meet people, especially when it's something important to me. Did she not deem this important? Did she know what we were doing here? Maybe I had gotten it all wrong, I thought. Misinterpreted her tone. Did she just want to be friends who met for innocent cocktails in dark bars?

I find lateness an inexcusable lack of respect for the other party, unless you have a damn good reason, like a car accident or a traffic ticket. I later found out that she had been debating whether she would meet me, pacing around her apartment, anxiously stepping in and out of her front door, talking herself out of coming, crossing that invisible boundary into the land of no return.

Vivienne had been in a similar relationship for over three years. Nearly mirroring my own, she lived a simple, safe and unremarkable life with her partner. They watched films and ate takeout food together, laughed as friends do, had straightforward, comfortable, albeit not exciting sex. She had wanted more out of it for a long time, even if she didn't want to admit it aloud. She knew how safe it was being with him, a software developer with a significant income. He had told her she didn't even have to work, if she didn't want to. Of course, she continued working, believing that she needed to retain at least a fraction of financial independence in case, for some miraculous reason, he left her. She knew if anyone left, it would be her. He was too robotic, monotonous, sedentary, in every sense of the word.

She would beg him to go outside with her, to travel, going as far as planning surprise trips to remote cabins just to get him away from the desk and his work, much to his dismay. He was safe for her in a way no other partner had been. He provided honesty and stability to a stale degree, virtually too lazy and simple-minded to go looking for anything else.

It's not that she wanted to hurt him, she wasn't a cruel person by nature, but she knew they were wrong for each other. He was the antithesis of everything she was and wanted to be. Vivienne found herself itching for change, aching for her old, adventurously wild lovers and former flings that had filled her with excitement and passion.

She met with me for the same reason I met her, we both emitted the secret, dangerous pheromones that only humans caught within the same predicament can detect. Two complacently unhappy people were searching for something different, something more. Even if it was wrong. When I turned and finally saw her coming towards me within the safety of our illicit place, I felt relief washing over me in the place of guilt. My eyes burned with a torrent of fire and passion for this person I hardly knew, and suddenly it was clear that I didn't give a fuck about anything but her. My relationship, my job, my life could disappear, and I wouldn't flinch. I wanted to stare at her face until I perished, feeding on her utter electric emissions, her smell, her laughter, her voice.

"Do you want to watch a movie or something?" Jan asked me, ripping me away from the thought of Vivienne in that far away bar.

"Yeah, we can, if you'd like. What kind of films do you watch?" I asked, absent. I could still smell her perfume in my mind.

"Ah! I know better than to answer that to someone who works on films, you'll just judge my taste!" She laughed playfully.

"I like all kinds of films, I'm just as trashy as I am classic, I swear." It was the truth.

"Do you have any old-timey films here?"

"I think so, I can have a look if you—"

As I attempted to finish the sentence, she did it. Her lips were on mine. Another person's lips were on mine. My eyes were open, still looking toward the shelves where I kept my films and records, frozen in my response. Now, in an abrupt instant this brave woman had decided to take her chances on the empty man and kiss me. I was being too analytical. I snapped into the present and remembered that kissing, good kissing anyway, involved two people's mouths moving in unison. I moved the back of my hand up to her hot face and tried to kiss her back, feeling her lips, her tongue, her teeth against mine. I clutched the back of her neck, pushing her closer to me.

I compared her lips, her smell, the taste of her saliva to Vivienne's. It was kind of the same, if I really squinted and breathed less and didn't think about it too hard. Her lips were similar but somehow different. She moved quicker, harder, pressing her hands against my neck and holding my cheeks with her soft palms. I exhaled, drowsy and dizzy at this new feeling, this new person. Kissing was indeed like riding a bike, a different model of bike, but a bike no less. I remembered what I was doing as we continued to suck each other's lips rhythmically. I moved my hand down her clavicle to her beating chest.

"Take me to your bedroom," she whispered between kisses. Her Texan accent oozed a little.

"Okay," was all I could muster between breaths.

We parted lips eventually and I looked at her for the first time in twenty minutes. Our hair was tossed and messed up like protein waves, her red lipstick smeared artistically around her mouth, her lips shining with my spit. She was a beautiful, Texan mess.

I grabbed her hand and tugged her down the hall, kicking stray cardboard boxes out of the way, not bothering to turn on any lights. If I turned on a light now, she might run for the hills after noticing the disheveled, shocking atmosphere of the place, definitely not sexy. She pushed me against the wall near the bathroom, kissing my neck and rubbing her hands along my stomach, outlining the shape of my growing erection, sucking my neck. I broke the moment and pulled her to my bedroom, kicking off my shoes and hearing them hit the wall before landing on the floor.

She pushed me onto the bed and climbed on top of me, straddling me with her legs on either side of my chest. We continued to kiss and feel each other's bodies, sloppily exploring this unknown, somewhat unfamiliar territory. I felt good, different. I felt drunk, but excited. Was this, okay? Am I allowed to feel this, this soon? I needed to get out of my head and focus.

"Please fuck me," she begged in a seductively direct way.

I took off her shirt in one swift movement and she proceeded to remove her bra, tossing it carelessly onto the floor beside the bed. I ran my fingers over her breasts. Slightly bigger than Vivienne's, smaller nipples, different firmness. Different, but beautiful. I was getting too caught up in comparing features when she reached for my pants and started to fumble open my buckle, ripping it off in one quick swoop.

I took my boxers off, and in the sienna light of the bedroom noticed the protrusion from my naked body. I was genuinely turned on with another person for the first time in over a year. Was it her or was it the thought of her? Was I imagining her or was I hoping Jan would be as desirable as Vivienne was?

She grabbed my face and pulled my body on top of hers. I fell on top of her clumsily, my body weight causing her to fall back, but she didn't seem to notice – or care.

"Fuck me, please," she said again. My head was spinning with confusion and something resembling carnal lust.

I finally gathered my thoughts and continued to kiss her back, making my way down to her chest and sucking her skin between my teeth, biting her nipples and ribs and smelling her sweat. I entered her, which caused us both to gasp like virgins. I automatically began to fuck her in a slow rhythm, as if some primal urge had taken over and evolution suddenly reminded me how to copulate.

We continued to roll around the bed and kiss, and I could feel her flexing, pushing me in, scratching my skin and back with her colorful red nails. She moaned into my mouth, causing me to inhale her peaty whiskey breath.

At that moment I knew exactly what I wanted. What I wanted and what I desperately needed.

"Hit me," I said breathlessly. I was out of shape, in sex and in life. I needed to eat more before drinking and having sex.

"What?" she said, stopping instantly and looking at my face, squinting in the weak light of the streetlamp outside. She was studying my face, wondering, clearly, if I was joking.

"Fucking hit me, hit me across the face," I said, commanding her.

"I don't know how to do that…" she said timidly. Her mouth curled up in fear.

"Just pretend you hate me and hit me." I was still inside of her. I needed to punish myself for doing this to Vivienne. I wanted to feel the real, honest pain and ramifications of my actions.

"Venn, I don't think I can…" Her voice went quiet.

"Just fucking hit me!" I screamed back at her.

Then I felt it, a lightning fast fist to my nose. Fuck. Ouch, what the hell was I doing? A moment ago, I was enjoying some perfectly decent consensual sex and now I was yelling for this kind, innocent woman to hit me?

I put my hand on my face where she had struck me. Suddenly I felt a wave of electricity, felt alive again. I smiled in the dark.

"Do it again," I said calmly.

"No." She was resolute. And she was not smiling.

"Do it again, please, please, Jan, I need to feel something. I am begging you."

"Fuck you, no!" She moved me away from her, which caused our bodies to separate from their seal, and began to fumble around for her clothes in the darkness.

"What, wait, where are you going?" I didn't want her to leave.

"I'm leaving, this is too weird, what happened to you?"

"Jan, wait, don't…I, I just haven't felt anything in a long time, and I wanted to feel something, I can't really explain it, I just got lost in the feeling. Haven't you ever…?"

"I don't even want to hear it, I should have never come over, this was just too fucking weird. Your nose is bleeding, by the way," she said without looking at me. She was almost fully dressed now and getting up to find her shoes on the floor. My mouth tasted like metal and blood and my room smelled like sweet sex gone horribly sour.

"Can we talk about this or maybe, like, start over again?" I pleaded, grabbing her shoulder.

"Don't call me, okay? Ever." She shrugged me off violently, finished pulling her boots on and headed toward the front door, picking up her bag on the way. I heard the door slam with a heaviness and defeating permanence I wasn't expecting to feel tonight.

I *knew* I was going to fuck this up.

I sat there, stunned by my coarse actions. I wiped my nose on my hands and stared at the blood in the low light. I had just told a woman to hit me so I could feel something, to be punished for not having her in my life. Was I ever going to experience normality again? A normal sex life, a normal date, a normal relationship?

I grabbed my pillow and screamed into it. Smearing fresh blood over my white sheets and duvet. My bed still smelled like Jan. Her insides, her sweat, her perfume. How things could suddenly change so drastically in an instant confounded me. One moment I was inside a beautiful, charismatic woman, feeling alive and awake again. Now I was alone in darkness covered in my own blood after begging her to punch me.

"Fuck you, Vivienne, for taking away my ability to be vulnerable and independent again. Fuck you for always punishing me. Let me live a normal life, let me be happy again, I'm begging you!" I thought angrily, biting my lip in frustration for still being so committed to her. I screamed into my pillow, mixing fresh blood with dry tears, seeing her face shining down on me in my mind. She would find this whole evening utterly pitiful and fiercely unattractive.

8. Vivienne

I woke up around noon feeling surprisingly achy and
sore, and for a moment I hadn't the slightest idea where that
pain could be stemming from. Then, all at once, my brain
was flooded with fresh cerebral consciousness, and I remembered every glorious and despicable event from the night
before. The bar, the boots, the blood. Her lips on mine, her
fist against my face, her slamming the door and walking away
into the early morning light, never to be seen or heard from
again. I'd really fucked that situation up royally.

My first attempt at a typical, normal dating life and I'd
asked her to hit me? What was wrong with me? I'd never
been that masochistic before. Vivienne had transformed me
into a sick version of myself I'd never explored or known
about until now. I lay there thinking of Jan, wondering how
she was feeling this morning, if she arrived home safely,
if I had scared her. Would I be a new topic in her therapy
sessions now? Had I emotionally scarred her for life, or was

I just a funny LA tale she would laugh about with her Texan friends? I sincerely hoped for the latter.

I pushed the bloody sheets away from me and sat up. My head was throbbing. The dull, unmistakable ache of a bad hangover mixed with bad decisions. I looked down and my chest was covered in crusted, brown blood, intermingled with chest hair. I ran my hands over it. Had I bled for her, or for me? Was I purposely sabotaging any situation that could ultimately lead to happiness beyond Vivienne? My sheets were covered in scattered dried blood droplets. Another thing I didn't want to have to force myself to do today: laundry. I groaned and forced myself to move forward, collecting my ruined sheets up in a bundle and chucking them into my laundry basket to be dealt with later.

I walked naked to the bathroom and looked at the damage to my facade in the mirror. I had dried blood all over my face and the shadow of a dark, half circle shiner forming underneath my eye. When I was drunk, I guess I couldn't tell how hard Jan had physically struck me. Those Texans know how to hit a target, that's for sure. I examined the bruising, and for a second, thought I looked kind of cool. Rugged, maybe even tough, when I knew that couldn't be further from the truth. I was weak, pathetic, broken, and bruised. Literally and metaphorically.

I shrugged it off. One stupid night, a stupid thing, a one-off weird event. It was my first time back out there and my big birthday and the first time I had slept with a woman since Vivienne. Something awful was bound to occur and I couldn't beat myself up over it. Move on. She's gone, get the fuck over her, before more women beat you up, before you beat yourself up more than you already do, I scolded myself.

I stepped into the shower and watched the brown blood particles circle and disappear down the drain. I dozed off beneath the water, thinking about how kind Jan had been to me, how considerate she was, before I asked her to punch me and she rightfully ran off, like you should from a psychotic masochist. I laughed at this body I was currently inhabiting. I didn't know this person, but I had to admit, it was kind of funny. I wouldn't tell anyone what had happened, of course.

When Will called the next day for an update on the evening after he and Agnes had departed, I told him I had walked Jan home and that was it. I didn't need him cutting me off now, he was all I had left.

As I got dressed, I realized I felt something new twisting within me. A pang of hunger. I was somewhat hungry for the first time in over a year. The mental pain of loss and the new, physical pain of being socked squarely in the face had given me some appetite. I relished this feeling, the connection of the brain and stomach, wanting me to feed it. I put my pants on and skipped down to the kitchen to hunt for some food.

As I should have expected, I didn't have much, barely anything, really, to eat. I had only been eating small, bland meals to get me through the identical days and I certainly hadn't gone out of my way to buy anything special. I sighed when I found some old oats in a bag and ran a jar of crystallized honey under the faucet to soften it and sweeten my oatmeal. By the time I was ready to eat, I realized I hadn't thought about Vivienne all morning, and it scared me. I couldn't lose her, no matter how desperately I wanted to move on. I wasn't ready to let go of her, not yet.

I barely ate six bites of my oatmeal before I felt full and sick again. My head was pounding, which I cruelly ignored and masked with caffeine and aspirin. I glanced over at my coffee table. Two watery, beige drinks sat in each other's company; one glass rimmed with smeared, bright red lipstick. I laughed openly to myself, at myself. I really knew how to ruin a perfectly good evening.

The first time I slept with Vivienne sexually was like a religious epiphany. We had been sneaking around together for almost a year, but we hadn't slept together. We'd been lying, hiding, deceiving our respective partners into believing we were doing something innocent, like getting gasoline for the car or going to the grocery store. A yoga class, a record shop, a late work meeting. They all began to blend together in a messy painting of her and I, fucking everyone over in order to spend time together in secret. I started to put my phone face down when I was in the house with my girlfriend, who failed to notice this new cheating technique and continued to love me unconditionally throughout the year I was stepping out on her. I'm not saying this was acceptable behavior by any means, but I was too weak to hurt her, to leave. Although my heart was with Vivienne, she had been my partner and friend for years and I was wary of hurting her feelings. Even if by doing so I was prolonging her suffering. It was completely selfish of me.

"You just need to break up with her if you don't love her," Will would say to me, sternly.

"It's not that, I just don't know if I'm attracted to her romantically, you know?" I'd confess, feeling guilty.

"Do us all, especially her, a favor and end it. You're just going to end up hurting her more, man, and you know it. She wants to have kids. She's already in her thirties, don't do that to her. It's wrong."

I knew he was right; he was always right. Even when I hated his obnoxiously saintly advice and common sense, I knew he was right. But he didn't know about Vivienne. No one did. No one could know. I just needed to find a way to end my stale relationship somewhat smoothly, take on all the blame and grief from my friends, and casually slip away with the love of my life. The woman who made me insane. The person who made my current relationship feel like a total sham. I didn't want to do the wrong thing, but I didn't want to break my partner's heart, so I continued to see Vivienne in the shadows. We continued to cheat but not fuck, and I continued to fall irreparably deeper in love by the second.

We'd meet in secret everywhere. In an underpopulated cafe on the other side of town. The dark Chinese karaoke bar where she'd order the same thing every single time (sweet and sour tofu with Chow Mein, extra broccoli on the side) and I would sit there wondering how this absolute epitome of perfection in human form chose me to spend her days sneaking around with, risking her own safe, easy, vanilla relationship. She would walk her friends' dogs for free and we'd meet in the park like old friends, sitting on wooden benches and talking for hours about our relationships, our plans, what we could do if we were together, what we should do.

The first time I felt her body was in a dark theater that played old cartoons on a Monday. The perfect hiding place for sneaky, life-ruining adulterers. We started off innocently enough, watching those classic cartoons and smiling coyly in the dark at one another, reminiscing and bathing in our childhood nostalgia. I looked over and grabbed her curled up hand, so in love with her that it made me feel sick and debilitated to be near her skin. She responded by placing my hand up her thighs and near her crotch over her sheer, navy blue tights. My whole body tensed up as if I'd never felt another human body before, as if an angel was allowing me to touch their celestial body before God. I nearly crumbled entirely then and there, with the classic cartoons laughing at me, giggling and bulging in their comical fury. Meanwhile I was dying over and over only to be resurrected again in full health. But we exercised restraint, we went no further than that, that day, at least.

Then there was the time we were almost caught. This was a very bad time for us. Vivienne was taking care of one of her friend's dogs (to keep up the charade, but really, she was an animal lover so she would have done it regardless) and invited me up to her apartment, which I'd never seen until then, nor had I planned to. We had been so careful up until this point and I thought we were going to continue being careful until we both figured out how to painlessly end our other relationships and be together once and for all.

Vivienne lived in an old high rise downtown and her apartment was eleven floors up with an old Otis caged elevator moving sluggishly between the floors, occasionally getting stuck. It resembled something from a Hitchcock film, kind of spooky, kind of old, oddly beautiful. It was full of dark corners crawling with fading color. Old floral wallpaper and bright green, 1970s plants in large planters. I had walked by it previously and kicked the ground, wondering what she was doing up there. Was she cooking him dinner? Fucking him? Did she make him feel as good as she made me feel or was I just completely delusional?

Maybe I was just some kind of strange game to her, I would think as I casually strolled by, casting my gaze bitterly north of the building. I didn't even know what her boyfriend looked like, what he did for his job. He could have been anyone I walked by on the street. Maybe I passed him daily and didn't even realize it. He didn't know me, and I didn't know him, we were just two sorry saps in love with the same remarkable human. In a way I felt kind of bad for the guy; he was probably just as limp as I was around her. She had this mystical power of making a person feel helplessly hungry and entirely full at the same time, as if they were always thirsting for her, unsatiated. The only difference between me and him, really, was that she didn't love him the way she loved me. At least that's what I liked to tell myself, that I was different, that what *we* had was different.

This time, however, I didn't just nonchalantly stroll past the apartment building peering in like I had before. This time, I went in. I rode the old elevator up with Vivienne and her friend's sweet but yappy little blonde dog, and wondered, floor by floor, if we were crossing a terrible line. I had never been to her house, her boyfriend's house. I didn't know if I was ready to see how she lived with him, how they made their house a home together, his things, their things. I didn't want to see pictures of them together on the fridge or the sheets of the bed they fucked on, but I was desperate to spend any time with her, and she assured me she wasn't in love with him anymore. We couldn't go to my house, certainly, and we'd exhausted so many of our usual hiding spots that people would be starting to catch on and someone would eventually find out, so I gave in. I decided to trust her and followed her up.

When we arrived at her door I took a deep breath, literally crossing a boundary, a threshold that felt wrong. Entering someone else's domain, someone else's home. Vivienne put her keys down in the kitchen and fed the dog while I sheepishly looked around the place, craning my neck around walls and up shelves. It was a nice penthouse-like apartment with a great view of the hills and a wrap-around balcony. Much nicer than my apartment, which instantly stung me with jealousy. Would I be able to take care of her financially the way he had? Would she miss this lavish lifestyle and come running back to him once she grew tired and bored of our physical rendezvous together? Perhaps this was a strange cuckold fantasy, and I was just the loser who fell for it all, any moment he was going to jump out of a side closet and they're both going to laugh at me and explain their sick game and how easily I fell for the charade. But it didn't happen.

The apartment was big for the city, but it was kind of shabby and run down upon closer inspection. Built in the 1930s, there was a corner fireplace which was clearly never used, as Southern California is rarely cold enough to enjoy a roaring fire. Shelves were full of a vast array of colorful books, records and magazines, many of them clearly belonging to him. I knew he collected films and books. Still, he had great taste, which also bothered me intensely. I suddenly felt totally unoriginal; we liked the same authors, same films, the same music. I wanted to be seen as totally unique, cool to her. It was clear to me now that Vivienne had a distinct type. I stared at the floor and sighed deeply.

All at once my self-esteem plummeted. I walked back toward their bedroom but prohibited myself from going in. That was a boundary I refused to cross. I was already a cheater, a trespasser, an actor in my other life. There was no way I was going to sit on the bed he she fucked him on, the bed in which she allowed her sacred body to be entered by him. I felt like I was going to be sick on their brightly polished wooden floor.

"Are you okay?" Vivienne asked, concerned. Holding my hand in that perfect, gentle way.

"I feel weird here, I don't know. It's all his things, your shared bed, your life with him…" I felt disgusted in myself. I knew I shouldn't be here, but I couldn't resist her.

"Don't think about it like that, there's no love here, at least not from me. We're just like roommates, friends with benefits. You know how it is." She smiled weakly, an attempt to stroke my ego and deflect my feelings of stinging jealousy.

"I know, it's just, I feel bad for him, too. I would hate to be him right now." I looked down, imagining how horrible it would feel to be in his shoes. He was probably at work currently; totally unaware of his partner in his house, leaning against the walls they decorated together, with me.

She stopped my train of thought and kissed me firmly. I fell for it. I kissed her against the wall of her and his apartment and for a while I didn't notice or care that it wasn't our place. All that mattered was that it was our place right now, and I was with her.

Every time we kissed, we would feel each other's bodies achingly, like a blood frenzy, never actually engaging in any physical sex acts beyond kissing. No, we knew that was crossing the line pre-breakup. We had longed for one another in a way that made me feel like I was going to physically implode. It was never the sneaking around that turned us on either, it was just her, the way we fit together, the way she tasted. I wanted to overdose on her and die entwined within her. Everything about her turned me into a boneless servant, a slobbering dog, a perfectly willing, submissive slave.

How do you relinquish that kind of physical intoxication after you've experienced it?

Just then, with my knuckles around her neck pushing against the door frame of their shared apartment, mixed with the smell of their bodies, I heard a beeping coming from the other side of the thin plaster wall. The unmistakable beep beep beep of that old fucking Otis elevator trudging slowly, wheezing its way up the floors. Vivienne lived on the last floor, so I recognized immediately that this wasn't going to bode well for me, or for her. I had heard the elevator before her and by the time she had realized what was going on and snapped out of her haze what could potentially blow up in our lustful, cheating faces, it was too late.

She opened the door and pushed me forcibly out into the hallway like bad milk, wiping the lipstick from her beautiful, messy face and combing quickly through her long hair with her fingernails. Just as the elevator opened and a man about my age stepped out onto the patterned carpet floor. He looked normal, a little shorter than I was, a typical tenant coming home from work, blissfully unaware of any negative rift in his romantic life. I realized then I was, indeed, an evil person.

Without hesitation, like a total dipshit, I ran to the end of the hall and flung open the latched door leading to the stairs and fire escape, looking back just in time to catch him asking her who the fuck I was, demanding to know why I was in their house. I heard them arguing loudly as I ran down the

stairs, like I was escaping a burning building. Who knows, it
might be a burning building later tonight, I'd thought. I had
felt horrible abandoning her like that. Should I have pretended to be just a friend? An old high school acquaintance she
merely bumped into. Had running away instantly tattooed a
bright red 'guilty' sign across my forehead?

That was the first time he had seen my face, seen us
together. Was this it? Was this the end of our relationship
or the beginning of the end of theirs? She had smoothed it
over easily enough with him, she told me later. The way she
always did, with that milky conviction and undeniable, cloy-
ingly sweet charm of hers. She told him matter-of-factly that
I was indeed just a friend she'd run into on the street and had
invited me up for coffee and a catch up. Even though he saw
me bolt down the stairs with his own eyes, he believed her. In
his own empty way, he didn't care if she was fucking someone else, so long as she came crawling back to him at the end
of it all. I really felt for the guy. He was just as spineless as I
was around her.

Vivienne never actually met my girlfriend formally, however. At least, not when we were seeing each other in secret.
She had eventually come to my apartment when my girlfriend was away on business or in another state for her family
trips. She had seen how we lived together, remarked on
how boring it all was (to my annoyance. Was she calling me
boring?), how the house felt completely devoid of love and
sexual energy, before violently pushing me to the floor and
kissing me senselessly, softening the blow of insults. We slept

on the floor in the living room and talked into the night for hours. It was perfect, in the worst possible way. Perfect until she saw me and my partner at a film convention together.

Vivienne had attended with her partner; I had gone with mine. Something we failed to mention to one another as we'd never run into each other in the city before. Without thinking, I studiously ignored her, subtly attempting to turn my girlfriend's gaze toward something, anything else to distract her from seeing my other sacred and culturally taboo relationship. Vivienne, being her impulsive and occasionally chaotic self, yelled in my direction, "Hey, Venn!" which caused both my girlfriend and I to turn instantly and look at her perfect face dead on.

My eyes nearly bulged out of my head when I witnessed my two secret worlds colliding. Shit, shit, shit, this was not supposed to happen. I clenched my teeth and waited for impact. I looked at her boyfriend, a normal guy with straight, dirty brown hair, black framed hipster glasses and slightly too-tight black jeans, looking boredly at me like she did this sort of thing all the time. She probably did, she was an incredibly charming, unintentional flirt with an abundance of male friends in her harem. I was just another weak fly caught in her silky, alluring web.

My partner looked at me gratingly, demanding to know who she was and why she was yelling my name so comfortably. Sensing some kind of connection that I was desperately trying to avoid. She cocked her head left and right, clearly wondering why she hadn't met this person before. I denied all of it, said she was calling someone else's name, (Ben, surely?) and that I didn't know that person, even though the words alone pained me to say. How could you possibly deny knowing Vivienne after meeting her? She was like a permanent internal vital organ, a scar that would never fade. We walked on without incident, my partner and I, and the tense and terrifying moment faded from memory, at least for my girlfriend. It was burned in mine as the moment that almost completely revealed us. I made sure we communicated any further future plans that may involve us accidentally running into one another.

Vivienne told me later in our relationship that she had gone into the parking lot of the convention center and kicked herself with jealousy over this perversely bland woman who seemed to have a specific hold on me. She couldn't understand why of all the fascinating and beautiful women in the world, I was with her, and why I couldn't just end it and be with her. But I couldn't. The truth was I felt like I owed my partner something. She had tenaciously pursued me and even though I wasn't fully attracted to her, I had loved her as a person and truly enjoyed our friendship.

She had moved across the country to be with me, and I was too much of a coward to break her heart, even if she didn't have mine. It was true, she wanted children and constantly nagged me about getting married.
I didn't want that, didn't want any future where we ended up together, but I didn't know how to end it. So, the vicious cycle continued, and I continued to feel more and more like

a total piece of shit.

Vivienne must have felt the same way, at least to some degree, because she didn't end her relationship either. So, for a year after that first meeting at that dark bar, we met, talked, fondled and kissed for hours, eventually forcing ourselves to separate and go back home to our monotonous, safe relationships. Staying up late secretly conversing, hiding messages, sneaking out, over and over on repeat. Both of us were too frozen in false comfort and security to make the first painful, vulnerable move.

Occasionally, when we ran out of places to meet, we would volunteer to house sit for friends or—even rarer—buy a hotel room for the day. Just to have somewhere we could simply be together, without prying eyes or fear of getting caught in our encroachingly small perimeters. It's amazing how much you sincerely value your alone time with someone when you aren't allowed to be seen in public together for fear of it getting back to your partner and ruining the content little world you've built.

In this instance, burned in my mind forever, we decided to rent a room in a building we had walked past on a late summer day. We were sweltering hot, dehydrated, sick for one another, and had run out of places to hide. So, we waltzed into that old hotel, and I casually paid for the room on a card my partner never looked at: my company business card. I signed the standard paperwork whilst Vivienne and I played honeymooners the whole evening, despite wearing casual clothes and having no luggage, the staff eyeing us suspiciously. I knew they'd seen this a million times. Hotels are fabulous at keeping the secrets of the underground.

We drank cheap Prosecco and licked each other's skin in the balmy afternoon light. It was the first time I saw her fully naked, and I nearly passed out. She was everything I'd ever wanted, everything I was attracted to. She held me in the palm of her glorious hand. Vivienne was no model or superstar, she wasn't the idea of societal perfection by any means, in fact she was riddled with flaws, but to me, she was perfection embodied. She danced around the room naked beside me and we fell on the bed, kissing and holding each other tightly. Then she begged me to go down on her.

This was our first foray into the world of being actual, real-life physical cheaters. She held her ankle out of the open window frame with me nuzzled between her legs as the LA breeze blew the drapes over her soft thighs. She screamed and quivered against me, and I came alongside her. We both swiftly showered without soap to not attract an unknown, unfamiliar smell and throw off our partners or raise suspicions. We left the room drunk and dizzy on each other and held each other forlornly for an hour in the hallway before returning home to our partners. My lips were swollen and aching, but my heart was full. This was when I knew I was in deep shit.

I came home to my girlfriend that evening as I had for years, watching TV, doing her nails, looking up at me as if it was just any other day.

But this day, everything had changed in my mind. I instantly felt like a malicious, evil monster and went to the bedroom to lie down. This was the beginning of the end. The first end.

9. Vivienne

I needed to get away from the city. I needed to leave. I decided my mind was too cloudy and useless to attempt any further professional work at the office. People had noticed my lack of concentration and began to comment on my slow work pace and shoddy performance. I called my boss and asked politely for a week off, to clear my head, citing that I wasn't feeling all too well in my grief and asked sweetly if I could work from home, even though I hated working from home. Prone to constant distraction and pacing, procrastination always seemed to creep in like bindweed and prevent me from flourishing, whereas the office space was like a prison cell, forcing me to move forward, adhering to a rigid timeline devoid of outside temptation.

To my surprise and relief, she agreed to the week off on the stipulation that I finish some editorial work that evening before I left on my trip. It amazed me how well the grief card worked. She would have never agreed to let me go before. I wasn't sure exactly where I was going to go, just that I needed to get the hell out of this city for a while and out of my stuffy apartment that reeked of her ghost. I saw her everywhere and I was sick of it. I wanted to see new faces, new roads, new distractions.

I stopped by the office for an hour and pretended to professionally obtain the equipment I needed for my big week off, pulling and tugging at various headphones, thumb drives and chords, chucking them into a canvas bag. As I turned to exit the building, I noticed the seething, envious faces of my robotic colleagues burning a hole in my skull. I bet they wished for someone to die at that very moment so they too could escape their lives for a while. Although I wouldn't wish that on anyone, and I knew I couldn't get away with the grief excuse indefinitely.

As I walked away from the building, I suddenly felt both restless and tired, as if all my acting and putting on a happy face had finally slid off and my body had caught up with me. A severe absence of laughter, nutrition and an overindulgence in booze and cigarettes wasn't exactly helping, either. I didn't know where to begin. I hadn't been on a proper vacation in over a year. The last time I left town for more than a day, I was with Vivienne. We visited the towering and majestic Redwoods in Northern California, staring up in awe at the ancient giants, running and falling in the mossy undergrowth as we gazed up, my hands pressed into her soil-drenched clothing and skin, her hair muddy and tangled in my fingers. It hadn't been that long, but to me it seemed like a lifetime ago.

I passed a small, tan stucco strip mall with a variety of shops toting different services, from acrylic nails to health foods and color photocopies for ten cents apiece. As I lit a cigarette on the corner, I stopped to admire a giant, thin-smooth cactus jutting forward in one of the windows of a faded pink donut shop and realized that was exactly where I needed to go: the desert. I needed to be in the middle of fucking nowhere, where all that really mattered was sheer survival. A place where the sun would blind my eyes and burn my skin, a sort of elemental baptism of fire to remove her from my mind and heart. A place I could bleach her out of my memory and finally begin to move forward.

She was too fresh here, too present. She still stained and scented all that resided within my fiber. I needed to be exactly where she wasn't, where we didn't share happy memories, where she never existed, at least not to me. Out of sight, out of mind. Only here she was out of sight permanently, and forever living in my mind.

The sun was setting on Sunset Boulevard. It was a typical Tuesday feel; not much seemed to be happening as far as restaurants or nightlife were concerned, many of the restaurants were still closed or prepping dishes before dinner service later in the evening. This was a quiet time in an otherwise noisy city. People meandered home from work in the lingering heat of the evening, lost in their thoughts, or in their phones. Cars drove slowly; sludging up and down the worn pavement, honking, crying, singing, staring at the stoplights absently.

I passed by a restaurant I had purposefully avoided in every way for over a year, a restaurant we comfortably sat in secrecy and in love for so long. Moon Garden, the Chinese karaoke dungeon of adultery and hidden memories. I stopped and pivoted to face it for the first time since I had lost her. It looked exactly as it always had. The over exaggerated English Chinese character font, the kind you see in old Kung Fu films, lit up in a bright vermilion. Dim, cloudy windows gave way to soft silhouettes having an early dinner inside. I couldn't make out any faces, only shapes moving. It wasn't a particularly crowded or popular place; the kind of eatery where you consume decent food and feel satisfied, but never blown away. A small family joint that held its weight in charm and kitsch. It was dated, sure, but it was special, despite not topping the Michelin Guide any time soon.

That was why we had always loved this place; we could hide in plain sight and feel lost in time together. I clenched my teeth as snapshots of her laughing came to mind, her holding chopsticks incorrectly, eating food that was too hot for her pink tongue. Her front tooth, a little crooked against the other ones, her messy dining demeanor and overly theatrical outfits. Her snapping open the fortune cookie like a kid and reading my fortune as if it was written in my destiny to be true. Me, staring at her, disgustingly in love regardless of her faux pas. I felt a wave of heat and ice fall over my skin as I stood in that parking lot staring at the now tainted, pain-filled restaurant.

Then, just as I turned around and walk home, my body surprised me and headed not away from the front door of the restaurant, but toward it, as if being pushed by some ethereal force from behind. I decided to go in, despite my head pounding against my eye sockets in disagreement. I knew what being here would do to my psyche, I knew how seeing her departed essence here would make me feel, but my masochistic side needed to do this, like ripping off an incredibly painful, strongly attached band-aid, like ripping off my skin. So, I walked through the front door.

Everything looked exactly the same as it always had. Big-eyed, multicolored orange and black fish swam serenely in a brightly lit, foggy fish tank surrounded by fake neon aquatic plants and a streamline of infinite bubbles rising from a plastic treasure box. Bamboo plants and red lanterns lined the reception and hosts' desks, surrounded by squat Buddhas and gold coins. The glossy, plastic covered menus, the same as they ever were. The familiar smell of sizzling Szechuan and peppercorns wafting enticingly from the kitchen. A member of the family who owned the restaurant, a familiar older woman in her sixties, bustled around collecting glasses and menus from tables, while her daughter took orders and delivered them to the kitchen.

"Hey, long time no see!" she said once she recognized me, with a kind smile. She approached me and gave me a friendly pat on the shoulder. She was wearing a light cream button up shirt, with sensible slip-on shoes, the kind with extra grip you see older ladies wearing. Her hair fell across her face in short, playful wisps of black and gray, held back by colorful clips.

It suddenly occurred to me how much I missed this place. Finding new places to eat when you're avoiding your old favorites really wears on you, especially when you don't have an appetite. I felt like I was back in a comfortable, welcoming environment, even if a significant element of the dining experience was now absent.

"Yeah, I know, it's been forever, how are you? How's business been?" I said, as cheerfully as I could muster.

"It's good, everything has been good! Happy New Year to you also. Where is your pretty wife?" She looked to the left of me as if suddenly she would appear from the ether beside me. This stung me sharply, like a wasp sting, and I flinched, closing my eyes. Most people in my life knew not to ask about her anymore.

Obviously, this was going to happen at some point, and I couldn't fault her innocent query. Naturally she expected her to be with me. She always was, until now.

"Oh, well… she's not here today, it's just me," was all I could manage.

"Tell her I said hello, okay?" She pointed her finger and smiled, as if she held me to this promise sternly.

"Of course, I will," I said, looking at the floor, then half smiling at her. What was I doing here? I really was addicted to the pain.

"Now let's get you a table, you are looking so skinny!

Trying to lose weight?" She pinched my cheek like a grandmother at Thanksgiving dinner.

"No, well, not really, I guess I..." She started to walk toward the green leather booths in the back, near the kitchen.
I knew exactly too well where she was heading and suddenly
felt that sick pit in my stomach pulling my intestines again.
I sighed, staring at the floor as I made my way behind her,
afraid to look up.

"Here we go, your favorite booth!" she said cheerfully,
laying one lonely plastic-coated menu down onto the table
for me and scooping up the opposite glass and cutlery. It was
our booth. The booth we always dined in, laughed in, hid
in when we came here. The shabby green booth in the back
corner by the evening karaoke set up, near the altar of Bud-
dha and big bamboo plant. The kind of booth you can duck
and hide in if —God forbid— anyone you knew came in to
eat or collect their takeout order.

At first, we sat there because it was the most inconspic-
uous booth, a hidden corner within our hidden world. After
we had allowed ourselves to be together in the open, we
continued to frequent the restaurant and always sat in 'our'
booth, for old time's sake. Almost as an homage to how far
we had come, together. I looked down at the glass tabletop,
the same small dents and scratches carved into its surface, the
same view from the window, how can everything be exactly
the same when everything was now so different, I wondered
as I picked my nails nervously under the table.

The owner came and poured me a glass of ice water.

I wasn't particularly hungry, as usual, but I was starting to mentally wade into the pool of familiar pain in an attempt to desensitize myself to the frigid temperature of my surroundings. It's going to be okay, you're okay, I told myself, rather unconvincingly. One emotional band-aid at a time.

The light in a room changes when you've lost someone. You tend to notice every small detail or lack of detail when you're searching for anything else to think about. Colors you missed before, even if those colors no longer bear brilliance or feel nostalgic. You see everything plainly for what it is, for what it always was, without the tinted lenses and aura that used to glow around it. As I looked around now, it just looked like any typical, slightly aging Chinese restaurant. One of millions across the country. It no longer looked like a womb of secrecy, a portal of magic delicacies and tastes, everything looked dull, sober. I looked across the booth at the empty seat opposite me and tapped my foot uncontrollably beneath the table, staring at her absent outline. Remembering her back leaning casually against the tufts.

"Can I get you something? Your usual?" a voice snapped me out of my train of thought and my empty stare.

"Hi, oh, let me have a look here…" I said, looking blankly at the menu. I, we, had always ordered the same items. We didn't even need a menu anymore. We shared the same dishes, fed each other, dropping chilies and cashews and laughing.

"I'll just have the 'Jewel of the Garden'," I said, pointing to the first thing I saw on the menu.

"Are you sure? No sweet and sour tofu with broccoli, Chow Mein?" She raised her eyebrow, looking me in the eye quizzically. Calling my bluff.

"You know what, yeah, I'll have the sweet and sour tofu, with Chow Mein, no broccoli this time, please. Thank you, Li." I smiled at her as she took the menu away. She smiled back in a caring, concerned mother sort of way. She could tell something had changed.

I didn't know how I was going to consume that quantity of food, but I figured I could take the leftovers to go. When we dined here before, we never had any leftovers. We always finished every last thing on our plates. I guess that tends to happen when you're hungry in love, you're hungry everywhere else as well.

I stared despondently out of the window at the passing cars on the road and the various people walking past the restaurant window, wondering from time to time if any of them had recently lost someone close to them. Were they wandering the city aimlessly, trying to escape their reeling thoughts? Or were they walking home to meet someone that they cared for? Carrying bags of dinner groceries in hand, ready to be splayed onto the countertop and lovingly prepared in between love songs and laughter? I thought of twirling Vivienne around in the kitchen, waiting for our food to finish cooking, her breath lapping my throat like waves as she moved.

"Here you go, sweet and sour tofu, and your tea," Li said, with a soprano lift to her voice as she set the steaming hot plate down in front of me.

"Ah, great, thanks Li, this looks perfect." I nodded towards her in gratitude.

"Enjoy!" She walked away quickly as more people began to file in for dinner. Her daughter was behind the reception desk talking on the phone and writing down takeout orders. I loved family businesses. Why did I deprive her of a family? Why was I so fucking selfish? Was I selfish?

I looked down at my bright orange, thickly sauced sweet and sour tofu, lined with onions, pineapple (Vivienne always ate the pineapple) and slices of green pepper. I unwrapped my chopsticks from their napkin blanket and poured a cup of tea into my small, half oval cup. The faint green grass smell transported me back to hours of conversation and debates with her.

"What are we going to do? Seriously, Vivienne, this isn't sustainable, I can't do this forever, it's totally fucking with me now," I'd say.

"I know, I know. We just need some more time; I need to figure out how I'm going to tell him. I don't want it to blow up into a disaster. Is that what you want?" she would throw back at me, threatening.

"I love you. I want to be with you. That's all I want," I'd say, completely defenseless in her presence.

"I love you, too. You know that, right?" she'd say, smiling angelically, and proceed to feel my legs under the table with her foot. She would always spill sweet and sour or soy sauce on her clothes.

I could feel her absence outlined across the table. Watching me pathetically fumble around the meal, even though she had always been the messy one. I picked slowly at the peppers, eating small bites of produce, slurping boiling hot, weak tea. I was chest deep, bathing in memories, both good and bad, attempting to face the demon and anesthetize myself from the pain and the constant avoidance of pain. So, I sat there with her ghost, for two hours, watching the families and couples filing in and filing out, and ate slowly, wondering where they all were in their own personal relationships.

Eventually, I felt satisfied that I'd faced enough of the upsetting past for one evening and asked for the bill, which came on a small green rectangular piece of paper, a fortune cookie resting on top. I cracked open the cookie and ate a quarter of it, unfolding the long strip of paper with pink writing.

"Sit with silence, and you will hear." I scoffed. As if my life hadn't gone silent for the past year. I felt as if all I heard was fucking silence. Silence and her voice. I needed to hear something else, anything else. I needed her to become silent.

I signed the bill and received my leftovers in traditional white pagoda boxes. I said goodbye to Li and her daughter and walked back in a numb daze to my apartment. I felt somewhat proud of myself; this was the first real place, a place that had been our place, that I had faced since I had lost her. It wasn't as horrific as I thought it would be. It stung, but it didn't kill me, and for that I felt grateful. I was willing to do anything at this point to attempt to move on from her.

I meandered along the sidewalks and curbs to my apartment, my heart thumping against my chest from the sudden injection of salt and sugar after months and months of limited food. I felt bloated and full, even though I hadn't eaten much. I reached my front door and let myself inside, shoving the plastic bag of leftovers into my empty fridge.

I poured myself a glass of tap water and drank it quickly, relishing the liquid to balance out the salt. I found my pack of cigarettes in my bag and lit one in the kitchen, leaning against my counter and blowing smoke into my thoughts. That was some kind of shock therapy, I thought to myself, like when people have odd phobias of peaches or frogs and show hosts bombard the afflicted with hundreds of them to hopefully break their phobia. Being hit squarely in the jaw with those painful and beautiful memories felt cathartic, necessary. I felt like the infected blood had been let out, like I could breathe a little easier, at least in this moment. I was awake and retrospective, starting to search for any holes in my perceived perfect world with her.

I finished my cigarette and decided to give my mind a break and pack for my upcoming trip. I turned on the radio for the first time in weeks to a station that played exclusively wordless jazz, perfect for not wanting to hear any songs with upbeat 'love' lyrics. Plus, it helped to have some background music to take my mind off traveling without her. I dug around in my messy, overstuffed closet for a bag to pack and found my trusty old blue canvas bag, the one we had so often packed together, bringing found treasures and old vintage clothes home from our various travels in the country.

I ignored the urge to be overly sentimental and nostalgic, shaking the bag roughly as if the memories would fly off with my violent movements. I laid it squarely on the bed and took stock of the room and my messy drawers. What does one wear to the desert in April? It's always hot, I told myself, so I packed loose fitting, breathable button up shirts and shorts, plus one pair of jeans. A light jacket for the evenings, and a heavily worn, scuffed pair of white tennis shoes. I certainly wasn't looking to impress anyone, so I overlooked any smart evening attire or date wear, assuming I was going to be alone the whole time anyway. Plus, I was in no fit state to enter into any kind of romantic situation after what had transpired with Jan.

No, what I needed was bare solitude, emptiness, vast expanses of wilderness to think, heal and forget. I finished packing and set my bag down on the floor next to a cardboard box. A box that held her things, our things. I flicked through some of the items, barely touching them, as if they were going to burn me. Clothes, framed pictures of us, postcards we had sent one another, letters I could never bring myself to read again. I kicked the box across the room, not ready to look at any of its innards too closely again.

I crawled into bed half clothed and uncomfortably full, laying without covers as I stared up at the ceiling, as I had for so long now, excited but nervous to go away from here for a while, wondering where I would end up, how it would pan out, how I would feel. Would she come with me? I needed to escape her, but I was terrified of losing her for good.

At a certain time, a varying time every evening, the only thought in my mind was her. Her absence, her voice, our conversations, our sex, our arguments, our frustrations with one another, our differences. Everything played out like an old VHS tape on my ceiling that I was sick of watching. A show my mind forced me to screen over and over in a forensic attempt to extract, file or save memories in their respectful place. But I didn't want to see her anymore, I didn't want to feel her. I couldn't reconcile the woman I loved and the woman who was gone and how I could properly process the absence. What should a human suppress? What does one save, what do they throw away?

After what felt like hours of torturous repetition of her face, I finally fell asleep, and I dreamed of the desert.

10. Vivienne

I woke up sharply to narrow slits of bright California sun across my face. Groggily opening my eyes to my beige, daylit walls. Today was the day I could leave my mind for a while. Today was the day I left this graveyard, a wave of enthusiasm filling my chest. I flung myself out of bed and quickly showered, desperate to escape my stale, haunted apartment for a week. I opened my old fridge to find my leftovers neatly side by side on an otherwise vacant metal shelf, staring up at me hopefully. I grabbed a box and flicked it open, shoving a few mouthfuls of cold, congealed food down my throat before washing them down with warm metallic tap water.

Let's get the hell out of here, I thought, feeling my heartrate pick up pace. I put my shoes on quickly and went to grab my travel bag when I noticed the box—her box— again. In a turn of thought, I reached down and scooped it up in my arms, looking away from its contents and her cursive penmanship on the corner of a postcard. I covered it with her towel to hide the items and headed out of the front door, flying down the stairs toward my ride.

I drove an old 1988 Ford Bronco, the kind that occasionally blew up spontaneously and caused insurance companies millions of dollars in lawsuits. The kind OJ Simpson was famously seen driving down the freeway in a long and heavily televised police pursuit before he was acquitted. I had purchased it from Craigslist for five thousand dollars and it had never failed me. She had been good to me, driving me up and down the length of the west coast, providing shelter from sweltering summer heat and cover in spring or winter storms. I didn't tend to drive much in the city, as parking was such a pain in the ass and everything I needed, from work to friends' apartments, were all mostly within walking distance. It was a little rusty, with dents and bruises dotted around the body frame, but it only made me love it more. Besides, I was also full of dents and bruises. I threw my bag and her box in the back and readied myself to get on the road.

Firing up the engine, I slapped the dusty dashboard in encouragement, proud of the old beast for never failing to start up. I still used old paper AAA maps when I went on road trips; they made me feel closer to my family, to my childhood. The days when my dad would holler back at me and my mom to read him highway numbers or fast approaching forks in the road, following my finger along the red and blue veins of the paper. I preferred this method of travel, regardless of how obsolete it was now. I knew I could rely on modern technology, but where's the adventure in that? I wanted to be totally and completely lost. I didn't know exactly where I was going in life, so I didn't care to know exactly where I was headed on this trip. All I needed was a general direction. In this case, that direction was southeast. I put the old Bronco in gear and turned away from the curb, heading steadily, excitedly, toward the freeway.

Before the highway onramp, I stopped at a gas station to fill up my tank and gather a few trip supplies. At the counter I ordered two packs of their cheapest cigarettes, a bottle of bourbon and a pack of spearmint gum, along with a bag of bright red Swedish fish, my favorite road trip snack as a child. It was also Vivienne's favorite road trip snack. She used to reach across the center console and pretend to swim them into my mouth, laughing as she retracted them quickly. I stopped eating them after she was gone, avoiding even the sight of the unmistakable yellow packaging.

Now, after my Moon Garden shock therapy, I knew this was something else I could potentially overcome. Plus, I really missed eating them. Giving things up you've loved for so long takes severe willpower and effort, and I was sick of her taking them away from me. So, I slapped the heavy bag on the counter victoriously, paid, and headed out of the automatic sliding doors. It was a beautiful day out on the road. Rush hour was long gone, and the highways were wide open to the beast and to my wandering thoughts.

I flicked on the radio and listened pensively to excerpts of written prose on NPR, then to smooth jazz, then classic rock. I glanced dreamily at the tanned brown mountains and swaying yellow wildflowers that lined either side of the freeway as it twisted and ran further east. My hair blew wildly in the dusty hot air, my arm leaning out of the window, burning from exposure. I was feeling my body beginning to exhale, to relax, incubated in the Californian heat.

I looked over at the empty passenger seat, where Vivienne sat beside me so often, where we held hands and rubbed sticky sweat on the worn leather and fought over radio stations and laughed and cried together. Where we discussed so much of our occasionally conflicting views, our childhood memories, our dreams for the future, our past. I hadn't driven in the Bronco much since she had gone. I didn't want to feel her absence, her shadow in the seat, her teasing ghost hands retracting Swedish fish from my hungry mouth.

I thought of her family and our heated discussions about them. How she had endured a strained relationship with her parents. They shared a bitter and loveless marriage and even though that hadn't affected her as much as it maybe should have, she always felt distant and detached from her family. They viewed her as a wild card, a traveler. A flighty girl who skimmed her way through school and lacked direction and legitimate purpose. They were well off, financially speaking, and had raised Vivienne in a religious household, hoping she would grow up and marry a stockbroker or wealthy entrepreneur to take care of her and calm her down. When she eventually introduced me to them, I could tell they weren't impressed.

"Where did you go to school, then, Venn?" her mother asked me, venom in her saliva, judging my every word heavily.

"I went to Santa Monica Community College, before I moved on to Long Beach University," I'd said, looking down at the table, then catching Vivienne's gaze, trying to gain support from her eyes. She always looked nervous around them, as if she was also craving their acceptance and support.

"Do you play golf?" her father asked, dryly.

"I do. I mean, I've played with my father, we used to hit balls after school when I was younger—"

"What's your handicap, son?"

"I don't have one," I said, acting like I knew what a handicap was. I had just enjoyed trying to get the ball in the hole. My dad and I barely even kept score.

"Hmm, I see," he'd said, disappointed, looking over at his wife, who looked at me like a supremely unwanted guest. I thought of her ex, who had obtained a master's degree from UCLA and proudly earned well over six figures. They had most likely welcomed him with open arms and a brand-new golf bag stuffed with golden clubs, thrilled that this prosperous young man had come to save their darling Vivienne from herself.

Now, here I was, hopelessly in love with their daughter and intending on taking care of her for the rest of my life, only to be met with a brick wall and awkwardly sinking like a paper boat. We didn't see her parents much after that first encounter. I knew they didn't like me, didn't approve of our relationship. It wasn't that they deemed me a bad influence on her, it was that I wasn't good enough for her, nor would I ever be, at least in their view. Even though they lacked respect for Vivienne themselves. They didn't know her, her struggles, her secrets, her burning longing for their love and guidance.

Vivienne had stayed, perhaps for too long, in relationships with various men on the basis that her family would finally accept her choices. With me, she knew they didn't accept us, but that someone had finally accepted her. Even if she still struggled with wanting to be seen in a certain light by her parents. In so many ways she was a little girl, begging for their approval, only to be turned away again and again and thrust out into the cold.

She admitted her pain and frustration openly, and we argued about her family often. I would tell her she had to cut them off for a while, take time to heal and focus on herself. That they were selfish, ignorant, that they didn't, nor could they ever, truly understand her. I stayed up with her more nights than I could count, letting her cry into my chest over how her parents would never see her the way she needed to be seen. How they would never take her seriously, would never understand her choices and why she made them.

I tried my hardest not to let a complex build around the situation. I was never usually the type to compare myself to others. I knew, of course, that someone else would always win if I spent my life writhing in comparison. I had wasted too much time focusing on being the right man for Vivienne that I didn't want to waste time focusing on what I wasn't for her. I made enough money. I mean, it wasn't tons, but it was enough for us to be comfortable, to be happy. I knew I wasn't a preppy, golf playing asshole with a nice sports car, but she didn't seem to mind. I didn't have a rich family to fall back on, but she still came home to me, and that was all I needed.

I was delighted to have a partner who didn't let the material pressure of society or her family weigh too heavily on our love. Someone who just loved me for me, despite my moments of insecurity and worry about not providing more for her. She would always assure me that she didn't care. That I was all she needed, and as long as she had me, we would be happy. These considerate words from her perfect, crooked mouth always put my fears to rest.

I wondered, as I drove closer to the desert, if I ever was enough for her. Did she truly see me as an equal or was she simply telling me what I wanted to hear at the time? Was she just a twisted master of manipulation, using me cruelly as her own personal fluffer to plump her self-esteem whenever she needed an injection of pure self-esteem and a hard fuck?

No, no that couldn't be the case. If it was, why would she risk her relationship, leave behind the safety and security of her well-off, well-respected ex? Surely, I meant something to her, too, right? I had accepted her for everything she was and everything she wasn't. She didn't need to pretend around me, didn't need to use me for anything. I didn't have anything to prove, anything to be used for, anyway.

As I drove steadily down the highway, I thought of the scenarios and conversations I had tucked away and avoided visiting for so long, allowing them to play out openly in the forefront of my mind. Laughing at times to myself as I remembered stupid arguments and debates that ended in laughter or the silent treatment or in sticky, aggressive make up sex. She was so incredibly stubborn and incendiary, and we would occasionally dead lock and verbally wrestle to the point of pure frustration and complete exhaustion. Sometimes she grew so angry that she would slap me hard across the cheek and walk quickly away, giving me room to chase her down dramatically and kiss her or apologize profusely until she forgot what we were debating over and eventually melted back into me. Like coddling a child, I would buy her an ice cream or a cookie and all would be well with the world again. Her hot, flushed cheeks would fade back to peachy flesh tones and her smile would reappear, sheepishly, knowing how foolish she had been in her fiery disposition. I would roll my eyes, watching her lap her ice cream sloppily, dripping onto her chest and staining her clothes. Helplessly enslaved by her presence.

The city was beginning to fade into smaller, lesser populated towns and simple gas stations, clothing outlets and dried fruit shops, specializing in local dates and dried apricots. They stretched further and further apart until I forgot what a dense, heavily populated city looked like. Cars thinned out too, a miraculous reprieve, as the road narrowed

from four lanes to two. I took an exit toward the Mojave
Desert and felt a wave of relief, as if I was physically leaving
a broken part of myself back in LA. A part of myself I was
sick and tired of being around. I wanted to remember who
I used to be before Vivienne. The somewhat adventurous,
spontaneous, brave person I was before she showed up and
completely consumed me.

As the morning shifted gently into afternoon and the
layers of warmth changed shape, I took my time to really
absorb the desert surroundings. I drove slowly, letting the
cholla cactus and Joshua trees and vastness of it all sink in,
to mend me. I watched the craggy, rocky old mountains cast
their shadows imposingly down onto the taupe sand while
the little colorful desert birds flew alongside the car, mingling
with dust and wind. I nodded at the field of giant white
wind turbines dancing and twirling on their posts near Palm
Springs. The emptiness of it all brought a blanket of peace
upon me. I felt lighter, warmer, less like a corpse and more
like a human being, doing something for the fun of it and not
just escaping reality for mental survival. It was a feeling so
alien to me now. Was it even possible to enjoy myself without
her?

After nearly three hours on the road, I decided to look
for a place to call home for a week. I avoided booking online
bed and breakfast places and tourist hot spots to make it
more of an interesting mission, to allow myself more time to
think and more peace from the crowds of partiers and, God
forbid, honeymooners.

After driving on a two-lane highway for half an hour or so, I was spit out into a small, sparse desert community. A cute little town seemingly frozen in time.

Every sign was as bleached and weathered as a whale bone. Liquor shops, strip malls, rusty antique stores and small grocery or service shops lined the sides of the highway, hoping to entice passing trade. At the very end of the road, before the open desert and highway began again, I spotted my new digs: the Cactus Corral Motel.

An old yellow framed light up sign advertised a pool and jacuzzi, color TV, AC and HBO. It looked perfect. A true oasis in the desert, so I pulled the beast in and turned off the engine to let it cool down for the evening, proud that she had delivered me safely to the desert without blowing me up, even if I had morosely considered the reprieve that might have allowed me.

The parking lot hosted only two other beat-up work trucks, filled with gardening and roofing supplies, most likely a stopover between construction jobs. It wasn't a desirable motel by any means. Perhaps it was fifty years ago, but not any longer. There were not any bachelor parties or fun girls' weekends held here. It was on the edge of the infinite abyss, the kind of place you only stopped when you were desperate to sleep after a long drive or needed to pick up a gram of coke from the local desert dealer before a night out, driving aimlessly in the dark.

The thin metal rails along the balconies had faded and chipped into a coral pink from a once-dark red. The old pool, a kidney shaped bright bean, sat empty, lonely, while the hexagonal hot tub bubbled its streaming jets for no one. Striped navy plastic umbrellas swayed in the desert wind and old brochures lined the sides of the well-worn reception desk. I flicked through them as I stood and stretched my cramped legs. They advertised various levels of adventurous outings and clean family fun: skydiving, tortoise spotting, rock climbing, water parks, sky trams.

I rang the knackered brass bell for service and a short, stout man appeared from a hidden side office; looking as old and as weathered as the motel itself. He looked leathery, tired. As if he'd seen a million men exactly like me in his lifetime and had borne witness to all of the shady and creepy situations that play out in the dark corners of the desert. I wondered how many dead bodies had slept silently in the trunks of this parking lot, pre-burial, never to be located again.

I also wondered if he knew how to recognize a murderer now. Were they shifty, nervous? Too keen for a room, breaking out in an unnatural sweat beneath the icy air conditioning unit? Did he know who was having an illicit affair? Did he ever use his own rooms to have an affair? Maybe he was celibate, or perhaps a total pervert, inserting pen cameras into the walls to spy on unassuming new couples making love. Maybe he threw wild, drug-fueled parties and huge orgies here when it was deep into its 1970's heyday, before age and the sun dried everything up and people moved on and became more responsible and boring. Maybe he had lost someone he loved. Or maybe he was just a normal person, trying to get through each day alive, like me.

"Do you need a room, son?" he asked, monotone.

"Yes, I do, for six nights, please."

"Six nights? You goin' to an alien convention, or somethin'? No one ever stays that long," he asked, laughing roughly. His voice had a scratchy kind of twang that echoed off the walls of the office.

"No, I'm just taking some time off from work. In fact, I don't really know what I'm going to do. Do you have any suggestions?" Maybe he would surprise me.

"Bar down the road does Western Wednesdays, they usually have a local band, or a singer. You can eat there, too, if you want. It's pretty good, been around forever," he said dryly, as if he'd said this same spiel to lonesome travelers for decades.

"Okay, cool, yeah, that sounds great. Thanks for the tip."

"That'll be four hundred and fifty dollars, plus tax and cleaning fee. You smoke?" He didn't seem to care about my answer, and I noticed a soft pack cigarette box on his desk, so I answered honestly.

"I do at the moment, yes, but I can smoke outside, it's no problem, I..."

He waved his hand around before saying, "I'll put ya in a smoking room, then. Ashtrays are provided, you'll be charged extra for any stains or burns though, so I'd be careful." He shoved his thick glasses against his face while he added the bill up on an old calculator with his chunky, hairy fingers.

I noticed a wedding band on his finger; a simple faded, gold band.

"So…are you married?" I said, breaking the rhythm of the calculator pressing, causing him to look up at me with a slightly exasperated annoyance.

"I was, yeah. Why? Are you?" he asked, attempting to make conversation back. We were both terrible at this. I can't be in a room with someone and say nothing.

"No. I mean, I came close to being married once, but I lost her. It's kind of why I'm really here, to do some…some soul searching, I guess." I looked down at my shoes, kicking the cold tiles like a sulking child forced to be on holiday with their parents. Just talking about her always sent me into a strange, despondent daze.

"You don't need to find your soul, man, you need to get yourself a bible. Get to know Jesus, he's the only one who can save your soul. Hell, he saved mine. Here's your room key. I'm here 'til midnight if you need anything else. Otherwise, you'll have to come around in the morning. Enjoy your stay and the search for your soul. I'm Randy, by the way."

"Right. Thank you, Randy, and uh, thanks for the advice." I nodded politely and walked out of the freezing cold lobby into the radiating hot sun.

I didn't need Jesus right now; I needed a stiff drink. I didn't have the capacity or strength to go looking for a savior or committing myself to any new religions. I always found it curious how people deemed it appropriate to tell you what religion you needed to ascribe to within minutes of meeting them. It suddenly struck me that I was in a different part of America now, a more honest, more conservative part. Still, I appreciated any conversation that got my mind away from her, even for a few minutes.

I parked the old Bronco in front of my room and grabbed my bag and bottle of booze, leaving her box of belongings in the back before locking the doors. I couldn't risk someone breaking in and stealing her things, after all. I walked up to the second floor of the shabby motel and robotically checked into my smoking room. I wasn't prepared for the change in scent and stepped back after being immediately hit with a wave of baked-in stench. Stale sheets, an old, wet ashtray aroma, fast food remnants, desert sex and sweat. A slight undercurrent of synthetic floral room spray making a pathetic attempt at masking the permeated smell. I wondered what kind of salacious scenes these walls had witnessed through the years. It reeked of something awful, but it was cheap, and it was a room I could smoke in if I wanted to. It was all I needed for my week of hedonistic escapism.

I sat delicately on the floral printed, scratchy and unravelling bedspread and looked at the paintings that adorned the walls of my simple room. Desert paintings, one of a man riding a horse through what looked to be Arizona, not California, but hey it was still the desert, I suppose. Another was desert flora and fauna, a list of local plant and animal species that could be found in the area, which I studied attentively for a few minutes. I sat at the small wooden table provided and looked across at the empty metal chair and clear, empty ashtray. The loud air conditioning unit turned on and blew cold air so hard and fast it blew my hair back.

I stared at the wall for a while, uncertain as to what to do next. I had no official plan, no itinerary, no one to hang out with, no one I wanted to call and talk to. I lit a cigarette and thought for a while, sitting with the bad and beautiful thoughts again, allowing myself to try and process them in the dark room of my mind.

11. Vivienne

Our first trip was to the Northern Coast of California near the border of Oregon. The first real trip we took together, openly, as a non-secretive, actual couple. We went in her 2001 black Honda Accord and packed everything we thought we would possibly need, from camping equipment and firewood to binoculars, even a disposable camera to capture this new and exhilarating love we had finally managed to grasp and hold on to. We were so elated to finally be free of our constricting empty relationships. Free to love each other out in the world, to not be sneaking around, hiding our messages, our pain, our lust.

We meandered north through the state for over two weeks, stopping at rural campsites and sleeping openly under pine trees, looking for constellations, eating dirt-filled sloppy campfire meals and stinking of firewood smoke. We bathed in the icy rivers, splashing each other's cold, naked bodies and played horribly timed jokes on each other, pretending to be a bear or the elusive sasquatch. Eventually collapsing together in pain from the laughter or anger that ensued as a result.

When we wanted to treat ourselves and take a hot shower, we would stop in motels like the one I was in currently. Cheap motels off the side of some lesser traveled highway, thematically tuned to its surroundings, whether it be the woods or the mountains or the coast. The Breeze Inn, the Lumberjack Motel, The Summit. We would check in quickly, hardly able to resist touching each other for the few minutes it took to sign the paperwork and swipe our credit cards, immediately rushing out of the lobby to our rooms and fucking against the thin walls of the space.

Eventually we'd peel ourselves off of one another, hours later, to seek out much needed nutritional sustenance, a shower, or to watch strange local television shows or stern religious sermons. The strict, heaven or hell kind Vivienne grew up listening to with her grandparents. We would invent weird, sometimes gross cocktails out of what was left in our grocery shopping larder, adding orange slices to cheap light beer or drinking vodka mixed with instant coffee and sweetener. Dancing to the local fuzzy radio station, before falling back into our hazy, infatuated sickness and biting, squeezing, coming all over each other's worn skin and smearing those cheap sheets with various bodily liquids. We stained the coast, literally, with our love and our fueled desire for one other. It was the happiest I had ever been or felt I could ever be in my life.

Now I was here, in this little room, all by myself. No

weird cocktail recipes, no radio dancing, no stained sheets or crooked teeth marks on my skin. Just me, looking at local desert flora and fauna in this freezing cold, stinking old room. A dead orange cigarette butt lay in a thick glass ashtray like a squashed caterpillar.

It was nearing 6 pm. The sun was beginning to sink down sluggishly, as if heat stricken, leaving a blazing red hue burning across the sky and the mountains. I felt it was too early for Western Wednesdays, but maybe I could go and sit in the cafe for a while, watch the people coming in and out, pick ambivalently at my food. I enjoyed getting out of my own head and wondering what kind of pain was going on in other people's lives, it was a welcome distraction. I considered for a brief moment what the fuck I was actually doing here. Would I reach any type of healthy conclusion, or just sink deeper into sadness? It could go either way, I thought, feeling as empty and ambiguous as the lonesome desert landscape itself.

I showered beneath the rusty old shower head and cowered under its pitiful pressure as it dribbled out onto my skin like spit. I had only been here for a day and I already stank of dust and sweat. I was starting to feel like an old cowboy, weathered and worn, like Randy.

I rubbed the small white motel soap bar over my body and rinsed the dust out of my hair, eventually turning off the shower and drying my skin off with a scratchy towel. The room was freezing, artificially cold, like a fake film set of Alaska, so I reached up and abruptly shut off the AC. I'd felt frozen for so long, I needed some comforting warmth in my bones again.

I decided on wearing my only pair of jeans, a cotton button up 'evening' shirt and my worn-out tennis shoes. I didn't pack any nice clothes, anyway. I assumed Western Wednesdays and the Cholla Roadside Cafe and Bar wouldn't be offended if I showed up dressed casually. I poured myself a shot of bourbon in a plastic ribbed cup and drank it slowly. They always have these ribbed plastic cups in motels. Why do I have to see her everywhere I go? Can't I just have one fucking day where I don't encounter anything that reminds me of her?

I finished my drink, letting the harsh, smoky aftertaste coat my throat, and got up to leave. Here goes nothing, I thought, my first night in the desert, alone. What's the worst that could happen?

I left my car keys on the room table, putting only the hotel key in my pocket alongside my wallet, and headed down the stone balcony stairs that led to the road facing the highway. The desert looked drastically different at night. Everything took on a softer, more heavenly, albeit bleaker tone. A man pushing a beat-up metal shopping cart behind the motel stopped to have a look in the dumpsters, collecting cans for recycling. Birds gathered around a leaky garden hose tap, grateful that another sizzling day had ended, and they could finally drink in the liquid of life. Now they just needed to survive the night, the predators. I stood still, realizing we were all trying to survive something. Homelessness, the harsh faces of nature, death, loss, heartache, addiction, disease. Anyone who isn't trying to survive something should consider themselves extremely fortunate.

I wondered if I was dragging out this pain on purpose, afraid to finally let go of it, of her. Perhaps I should have been over it all months ago, fully moved on by now, living happily, truly healed, dating someone new. I shook my head. I had to remind myself that healing isn't linear, it isn't straightforward, there is no guide, no manual, no right way to do it. I guess it was going to take as long as it was going to take. I had a newfound sympathy for humans walking around with an empty chest and a full mind. Pretending they were okay until they arrived at home and removed the mask.

I lit a fresh cigarette and walked a half a mile or so down the road to the Cholla Cafe. It was another old school roadside cafe with a big red and white sign that lit up the dark, tempting late night drivers to pull off the road and have a hot meal. There was a small wooden sign outside that read 'Western Wednesdays, Live Music and Dancing! 5$' in black and white lettering. There were already cars parked in the dirt lot in the back and front, so I felt a bit of hope that I wasn't going to be the only sad, lonely loser here. Misery loves company, after all. I did enjoy western music, too. I grew up listening to Patsy Cline, Dolly Parton, Johnny Cash and Marty Robbins, so I was up for hearing whatever they were going to put on. I was up for anything that removed me from myself.

As I walked through the front doors, I saw the cafe to

my left, the bar to my right. Guarded by a tall, ripped and tanned security man covered with dark blue tattoos and a black paisley head bandanna. Behind him, another door led into the venue space. I turned left into the moderately filled café—occupied mostly by families and older couples—and asked the hostess for a table for one. The older woman, straight out of Thelma and Louise with her striped waitress garb and cute white curly hair, topped with a small paper hat sat me down at the counter on a stool and handed me a menu with a big green cholla cactus drawn onto it. It felt sticky with years of road trippers' hungry hands.

"You want somethin' to drink, hon?" she asked me, sweetly.

"Uh, just water, and maybe a beer, please?" She kind of reminded me of my mother. Just a little older, and a little more orange.

"What kinda beer, hon?" She looked bored and busy.

"Surprise me." I tried and failed to wink, hoping to make her smile. She didn't notice.

"You got it." She disappeared into the kitchen.

I never really drank beer anymore, not since my twenties anyway. I didn't want to get drunk too quickly, or even at all if I didn't plan on staying here long. I knew if I wasn't careful, I could easily fall into another dark spell of consuming way too many sedatives and cigarettes to medicate my pain. Maybe I should go back to the hotel after dinner, watch a film, engage in something, do some kind of writing. Maybe I could be productive for once, positive, sober. For the first time in over a year.

"Here ya go, hon." Pam, so said her name tag, set down my drinks, a nice cold Mexican beer and a thick plastic cup of ice water. "You ready to order?"

"Um, yeah, sure, what are your specials?" I asked, for asking's sake. I didn't really care what they were or what I ended up eating.

"Chili tonight, burger's always good, too."

"Can I just have the quesadilla with salsa, please?"

"You got it." She grabbed my menu from my hand and flitted away again, her hair moving like a soft cloud along the ceramic, cracked tiles. It didn't seem like I was getting far with attempting conversation around here.

As I waited for my dinner and drank my cold beer, I looked around at the couples and families eating and talking, pondering their life stories curiously. Where they were heading, where they were from, what their secrets were. I used to love going to roadside diners with her. She would always order something plain, like a grilled cheese sandwich with French fries or a piece of carrot cake for dinner. I swear she did this to be more endearing to me. As if I could see her any other way. She demanded to sit next to me in a booth, instead of across from me, so we could hold hands under the table. I was always conscious of how sick we must have made people, cozied up together in a booth, holding hands and eating, watching her spill ketchup on her clothes and slurping chocolate milkshakes loudly, seductively. We even met in the bathroom and fucked slowly in a roadside town of which I can't recall the name. I looked at the ketchup stained on her lacy blouse collar as I bit her neck.

We fought in diners, too. When I asked her to be more focused, to choose a career path or a passion and stick to it. To do something she liked instead of working for people she hated. Men who would hit on her and stare at her, always trying their luck, to no avail. I would call her childish and immature and baseless when she didn't know how to debate or defend her arguments and walk away brashly, which only incensed her more. But even after all the arguments, the voice raising, the anger, the slapping, the tears, we always ended up together. In diners, in hotel rooms, in our apartment, in our life. My body felt drained of life again, I focused on her dirty feet leaving the room as I zoned out into the booth in front of me. Stunned in past pain.

"Your ques-o-dilla, hon. You want hot sauce or anything?" Pam said, ripping Vivienne's face and feet from me. My hand was curled tightly around my ice water. I hadn't noticed, so I unclenched the cup.

"Yes, yes please, thanks." I looked up and shook my head.

"Here you go, enjoy." She grabbed a full bottle from across the counter and set it down beside the plate.

I took a few bites of the quesadilla, chewing it slowly while I observed the other diners talking in their booths. I sipped my ice water, which felt cold and refreshing after my warm day of driving, coupled with the fact that I had been severely dehydrated from my diet of cigarettes and coffee and booze. Everyone in the cafe seemed to have heat exhaustion except the people working there, who were buzzing around like road runners, picking up and dropping off food to tables of transients.

I could hear music and movement happening in the venue space adjacent, rising above the noise and clamor of the kitchen and diners. Sound check, with various levels of volume, voices and instruments bursting forth and testing notes. I continued to peel away small bits of my quesadilla off, dipping it into my salsa and chewing it blankly, watching, listening, feeling totally empty and alone in a room full of people.

The music was starting now, and people were paying their checks and getting up to go next door and check it out.

"Can I interest you in any dessert?" Pam asked me, looking down at my partially eaten meal.

"No, I'm okay for now, maybe later in the week. Can I just grab the check please?"

"Sure thing, hon."

She was back within a minute with my bill and a red and white mint wrapped in a clear plastic wrapper. I paid the bill, leaving Pam a generous tip. I chewed on my mint and headed over to the venue side to see if I could find something suitable to occupy my clouded mind for the night.

The space was a decent size for a roadside club, with a small, half circle stage in the center and enough space to dance or to stand, whichever suited you. A four-piece band played the guitar, drums, stand-up bass and mandolin, with a female lead singer playing country songs, some covers and some of their own music.

She was tall, with thick soled boots and tanned olive skin, long, straight dark hair down to her waist and a round apple shaped face. She looked like she was born in the desert, the way some people looked like they were born in the snow. She began to sing a new song and her voice lingered and cooed in a kind way, similar to Joan Baez or Joni Mitchell. She closed her eyes when she sang, even if she appeared to be very comfortable in this space. She had a sweet voice; accompanied by the music of her band, it sounded good, and I was impressed by them.

Vivienne loved music. Old music, new music, world music, anything that sounded good, anything with soul. She introduced me to obscure and interesting underground bands, groups of talented musicians who seemed to stay hidden from the limelight. She dragged me to shows against my will, thinking they would be tragic and sound terrible, only to leave me eating my words and dancing, well, fumbling with her until the early hours of the morning. She tried to learn every instrument, from the guitar to the piano and harp, giving up after a week of it not clicking. She sang everywhere, in the shower, on a walk, while she cooked. Her voice was broken and out of tune, but silky and angelic to me.

I watched this mysterious, moonlight western singer croon and sway and dance to the songs as more people filled the room. Older couples were dancing to old tunes and singing along, others were moving and swaying alone, some simply leaned against the wall and watched, fascinated or drunk.

I walked to the darkened bar and ordered a drink, the singer's voice continuing to play in the background. I ordered another bourbon on ice and drank it slowly, turning to face the singer as she introduced the next track. She had a real maturity about her, an older soul kind of essence. She seemed bold and confident, like she knew herself well, at least from what I gleaned from her voice and her mannerisms. I watched the older couples embrace and dance in each other's loose, tan arms. Swaying in small steps across the floor, smiling. Would I ever grow old with someone, or would I end up the old creep who leans against walls and looks at young singers hungrily? I hoped not the latter.

After an hour or so of watching the band and the people who attended the show, I decided to go outside for some air and a much-needed cigarette, an oxymoron that didn't escape me. I heard the singer say they were going to take a quick break and have a drink before playing some more 'old timey tunes' and the crowd broke up to do the same. I stepped out of the front door past the tattooed security guard and stood against the wall to smoke by a rusty trash can.

"Can I bum one of those?" a loud voice asked me. I hadn't seen anyone else out here, so it scared me a little. For a second, I thought I was hearing voices.

The singer was tall, maybe 5'8 or 5'9, with a full, stretched-out figure and very tanned, golden-brown arms. Her big brown eyes and long dark hair reminded me of

Cher. I laughed a bit to myself, remembering that Sonny
Bono was the Mayor of Palm Springs before his premature
death. Here I was in the desert, a schmuck and a Cher.

"Well? Can I?" she prodded again.

"Hey, yeah, sure, sorry." I fumbled in my jeans pocket
for my pack of cigarettes and handed her the box nervously.
Visions of Jan hitting my face shot through my brain. Don't
engage. This is not good for you, walk away, go back into the
bar.

"Got a lighter?" she asked after putting the cigarette to
her lips.

"Oh, sure, here." I flicked the metal wheel on my lighter
and touched the flame to the tip of the cigarette.

"So, I've never seen you here before. You're not from
around here I'm guessin'?" she said, exhaling smoke into the
lamplight.

"Ha, how did you guess?"

"I know everyone who lives here, I've been playing here
for two years," she said, almost sad, like just saying it aloud
was a dead end for her career.

"Oh, is that right?" I smiled, attempting to be polite.

"It's a small place, mostly everyone is from out of
town, especially guys who dress like you." She looked me up
and down and pursed her lips in a judgmental grin. Here
I thought I was dressed shabbily, over casual. I guess in the
desert I was dressed too well.

She was wearing a pair of white jeans and a patchwork quilted crocheted top, which contrasted starkly against

her bronze skin. She looked like something out of 1960s Tennessee. I watched her smoke her cigarette, lost in her own thoughts, the kind of thoughts bored, small-town girls thought when they were stuck somewhere playing the same gig over and over.

"Do you ever sing in LA?" I finally asked her.

"Not yet, we're still kind of figuring out our style, I guess. I'm still in school here, too."

"Oh, what are you going to school for?" I asked, genuinely curious.

"Psychology. I figure it's the easiest way to get out of this shithole. Plus, I think all of that stuff is really cool." She looked forward hazily, blowing out white smoke into the black desert air.

I watched her for a while, unsure as to what I should do. I didn't want to make her uncomfortable or find myself in another despicable, embarrassing situation as I had with Jan. I decided to keep things light.

"So, what's your name?" This was light, right?

"Sage. You?"

"I'm Venn, with a V. Sage, huh? That's pretty apt for being from the desert, don't you think? Were your parents hippies or something?"

She laughed through her teeth, blowing the last of her cigarette smoke toward the ground.

"My real name is Sara, Sage is just my stage name. My parents broke up a long time ago. My mom left when I was like, six, ran off with some guy and moved to Oklahoma. I haven't seen her since."

"Jesus, shit, I'm sorry…" I didn't know what to say. A relative stranger just shared a horrible truth with me, and I was caught short for words.

"It's cool, she left her guitar, and I got her voice. The rest doesn't really matter. I'm over it. It's all good, me and my dad are really close anyway."

She looked forward blankly, and we both knew she was lying to herself. I recognized the pain of a daughter who needed her mother. I decided not to pry any further.

"So, do you want to go back in?" I asked lightly.

"Yeah, in a second. Why are you here? In the desert, I mean. Are you, like, a mountain climber or something?"

"A mountain climber? Ha! No, nothing like that. I'm here just trying to, I don't know, get some new air."

"Come to the wrong place to get some air, man," she said sarcastically.

"I didn't mean literally. I needed to get away from LA for a little while."

"Do you have a girlfriend, or a wife?" she asked brazenly. It sounded like she was checking off a questionnaire she used for different humans after bumming their cheap cigarettes between weekday shows. Only the person she was asking changed.

"No, not anymore," I croaked out.

"Hm. I see. Well, come back in, we can finish this conversation later, huh?" She smiled a bit as if trying to lift me out of my headspace.

"Cool, yeah I'll see you back in there." I waved a limp goodbye.

I watched her disappear back into the venue and heard her voice speaking over the microphone again on the other side of the wall, reintroducing herself and the band before playing another western song. I thought, for a moment, that I should walk back to my motel. Maybe I could sit in the jacuzzi for a while and relax, do some real thinking, stare at the desert night. I almost turned to the road and walked back, but as I approached the front door of the venue, I stepped inside and back up to the bar, taking my seat to watch long, tall Sara sing her western desert songs.

12. Vivienne

As I watched and listened, my face placidly looking forward, I wondered how I would ever realistically date another human again. After Vivienne, I didn't know how to talk directly, flirt properly, or read romantic signals aimed toward me any longer. Every wire was crossed and fucked up and fried. Maybe I would become one of those burned-out people who was killed off and hardened by their true love experience and lived the rest of their days out in some remote cabin in the woods, without friends or romantic companionship ever again. I could always learn some kind of valued trade, a carpenter or logger. Something that kept me away from the general public for the remainder of my life. Maybe I should get a dog, some old gentle gal who I could bore with my stories and theories. I sat pondering the possibilities of my open future, raising my eyebrow to myself after each new idea presented itself, while the twang of the mandolin played gently beyond me.

I didn't want that, though. Ultimately, I still believed in

love. I knew I wouldn't ever find the exact kind of love I had shared with Vivienne, but I could, potentially, find something similar, something unique still, something real. I wondered how people were drawn so deeply into certain characteristics of humans; the same characteristics that could repel someone else. How did physical chemistry work? Was it a beautiful coincidence of serendipity or just a matter of chance and timing? Was I supposed to learn some cosmic lesson from losing Vivienne, or did I have residual bad karma and deserved to be brutally assaulted by the universe for my past mistakes?

I pondered these existential thoughts while Sage, or Sara, or whoever she was, moved her way through the western hits of the 70s and 80s, singing sweetly in tune with her band and swaying slightly, controlling her audience. It was almost midnight now, so I ordered another drink on ice and sipped it slowly, folding my square paper napkin into small origami shapes, debating what to do next. I wasn't feeling particularly tired, at least not physically. My mind was mentally beat and frazzled, but I knew I wasn't ready to sleep yet. So, I stayed put, sipping, folding, sipping, folding, wrestling demons in my mind.

Over time, the band wound down and stopped playing, ending their final song with a round of applause from the dwindling audience and thanking them earnestly for their attendance before sending around a tip jar. I watched as Sage drank a light beer and talked to her fellow bandmates, laughing occasionally and helping them pack up their instruments. Was I waiting for her? Am I being weird? Maybe I should get out of here, I thought, second guessing my decision to stay.

As I was fumbling around hypotheticals in my mind, Sage came over to me and grabbed the box of cigarettes out of my shirt pocket, which surprised me. I wasn't used to women touching me anymore, and she did it so comfortably, like we were old friends. She put a cigarette to her glistening lips and said six words.

"You wanna get out of here?" A mischievous smile broke across her face.

"Yeah, sure, where do you want to go? I'm in the Cactus Corral Motel down the road." I pointed my thumb in the direction. "It's not much or anything…"

"We can go to my place," she said confidently. "My car is outside, wait here for a sec, 'kay?" She held my shoulder.

Sage walked up to her bandmates and bid them good-bye, whispering something I couldn't quite hear. After she said it, they all looked up at me and laughed together, so I could only assume they were making fun of the dumb Hollywood loner who thought he had a chance with her.

She walked back over to me, set her empty beer bottle down and looked at me expectedly. "You ready?" She rattled her keys.

"Yeah, sure, let's go."

I paid the bar tab and followed her out to her dented gold Toyota sedan. She moved papers and empty cups from the passenger's seat and directed me to sit down, so I followed her orders. I didn't know where we were going, or what she was planning to do, so I sat quietly, awaiting her guidance.

"I just need to make a quick stop at my friend's house, is that cool with you?"

I looked at the clock lit up over her car radio; 12:45 am. What could she need to get from her friend's house this late? But I didn't question it aloud.

"Yeah, sure, whatever you've got to do," I said. It's not like I had anywhere else to be.

She pulled out of the roadhouse and drove onto the black, desolate highway. Only a handful of vehicles could be seen in the distance, small red and white pairs of lights floating across a black sea.

After about ten minutes of winding in and out of smaller roads, she pulled up to a manufactured trailer set in between families of cacti and rocks and told me to wait in the car.

"I'll be right back, 'kay?" she said assuredly, as if she did this all the time.

"No problem, I'll be here," I said, trying not to appear freaked out. It was a sketchy scene. Rabid looking dogs with metal chains around their necks were barking at me from behind a chain link fence. I rolled up the window and listened to the radio in a poor attempt to drown out their cries, pondering my suddenly odd situation. Why did she ask me, of all people, to come here with her? Was I easy prey, a limping gazelle with a flashing sign over my head? Maybe people actually were attracted to brooding, quiet, depressed people. Maybe unavailability is indeed alluring, as pop culture and film want us to believe. I certainly wasn't fully available to anyone any longer.

Fifteen minutes later, Sage scared the shit out of me by banging on the window and shouting "BOO!" I recoiled and caught myself, instantly realizing what had happened, which made me smile sourly. What was I doing in this strange driveway, in the middle of the desert, with this mysterious woman? Maybe she was going to kill me and rob me, drop me off in the middle of nowhere and let the buzzards pick my bones clean. She got in the car and turned on the engine, illuminating the sand and sending dust into the rearview mirror.

"Did you get what you needed?" I probed.

"Yep. Still want to come over?" She looked at me squarely.

"Yeah, sure, let's go." At this point I felt like I had nothing to lose. We both seemed a bit lost, a bit vacant, a bit bored. Misery loves company.

She drove further down the desert road, turning right onto another sandy dirt road, and continued a while longer. It was pitch black, and I had completely lost track of where we'd come from and where we were heading. Everything just looked dark, only illuminated for brief moments by the car's dim headlights. You could tell she was a local, she knew exactly where she was going. To me, however, every cactus, tree, bush, mound of sand looked virtually identical to the next.

She eventually turned left and pulled the car up to a small, square wooden house set against the lonely hills of the desert. A house that at one point had probably resembled a buttercream yellow color. Now it was chipping and revealing patches of bare wood against its beaten frame. A large American flag waved proudly from a flagpole to the right, shivering in the silver moonlight. Yet another muscular dog moved around inside of the house, peeking its blocky head through the curtains and barking out of the windows at us, flapping its large jowls. I wasn't sure I was ready to get my face mauled off tonight, especially by some wild desert beast. I suddenly second guessed coming out here with her. Before I could say anything, she turned off the engine and nudged me to get out.

"Let's go!" she said, excitedly.

I got out and shut the door silently, looking up at the dimly lit house, the barking dog, the shabby exterior. Then I glanced up at the stars, billions of them so brightly illuminated and clear, a celestial extravaganza of light. I couldn't get over the view as I stood there, stupefied, below the expanse of it all. For a moment I forgot myself, a feeling I so rarely felt these days. Maybe desert life wasn't so harsh after all.

Sage grabbed me under my arm, pulling me from my elevated reverie, and led me up to the front door—which had thick metal bars over it—and unlocked the door to let us inside, using keys with an iron bottle opener keychain attached. The muscular dog quickly ran over and jumped up onto her legs, scraping her jeans and licking her face. I stood back warily, not wanting to piss off the scary looking animal.

"This is Joey, he's really sweet, he just looks mean!

Aren't you, baby?" She rubbed his head with her palm and the dog ran back into the living room, jumped onto the beat-up leather couch and laid his head down on the cushions. "You want a drink or something? I have tequila, or soda, or tap water." She went to the vintage, avocado colored kitchen and took out two glasses.

"How long have you lived out here?" I asked, attempting to get to know her.

"A few years. It's okay, I guess. If the AC works."

"Do you like living in the desert? I mean, you must like the view at night, at least, right?"

"Yeah, it's pretty. I don't know, I've never known anything else. It's boring as fuck around here, though. Not much to do besides sit around and hide from the heat and drink or smoke for fun. That's how I got into playing music, I didn't want to end up in jail from boredom."

She handed me my cup with a small amount of clear tequila in it. I drank it slowly and we sat quietly for a while, musing, as I took in the surroundings and scents of the house. Fluffy, quilted pillows, shaggy carpet, wooden walls, an old tv on knotty, stained pinewood furniture. It reminded me of my grandmother's house. It smelled like cigarettes and dog hair and old potpourri. It occurred to me that I didn't know what she did for work. Did she make any money from her music?

"Want to take some Molly?" Sage finally said, breaking my observations of the house.

"Some Molly? Like, as in ecstasy?" I thought she was

joking. I didn't think people still took E.

"Yeah, that's what I picked up from my friend's house. It's supposed to be super pure, they got it from Vegas. Have you ever done it before?" she asked.

Suddenly I felt hot and nervous. I hadn't done drugs in years. I dabbled in my teens and early twenties, taking small amounts of cocaine or party pills at night clubs and shows, occasionally smoking weed or taking hallucinogens in the woods with my friends, but that was ages ago. I felt like an old man being asked to partake in something I had totally forgotten how to do. This was exactly what middle aged people meant when they said they were 'too old for that.'

"I don't know, I haven't done that in a long time, I don't know how I'd act," I said truthfully.

"Then don't think about it. There's no pressure, you can just take a little bit. It'll be fun!" She shook the small plastic baggie of white powder in front of my face, and I laughed nervously, realizing how strange this situation was. This morning I was driving in my car alone in Hollywood. Now, I was in the middle of the desert with a mystery woman who wanted me to take drugs so she could possibly harvest my organs and leave me for dead in this dilapidated prop house. Then I had a morbid thought: maybe dying in the desert wouldn't be so bad, after all. I wasn't living a life full of meaning, anyway. At least, not anymore. I was half dead already, so I made a choice.

"Alright, sure, let's do it," I said, shrugging.

Sage got up and grabbed a CD case and her town li-

brary card, with a small picture of her head on it, and started
to pour the contents out of the bag onto the CD case. It was
the iconic TLC album, FanMail. I watched intently, fascinated as she created little rows of white lines and pretended
as if I remembered how drug etiquette was supposed to play
out; giving the illusion of someone who'd indulged many
times before. Her slender fingers lifted and separated piles of
powder as she hummed, and I tried to psyche myself up for
whatever was coming next.

She rolled a dollar bill into a tight tube and bent down
to take the first row of powder up into her nostril, leaning
her head back and sniffing in roughly to get the last remnants
from her nose as she wiped it with the back of her hand. She
turned and reached across the CD, handing me the rolled-up
dollar bill. I tried to act like I'd done this recently, wondering
if she could see through my fumbling bravado. She didn't
seem to notice or care. I leaned down and mimicked her
actions, sucking the same amount into my left nostril and
leaning back to let it flow down. Turns out taking recreation-
al drugs is like riding a bike.

Sage got up and turned on the faux-silver painted stereo
in the corner, putting on some kind of disco-electronic dance
music from a compilation CD, and began to move and dance
to the beat. She came over and grabbed me by the shoulders.

"Dance with me!" she begged, trying to feebly pull my
weight up from the ground.

I got up and fumbled stupidly around the shag carpet in
my dirty tennis shoes, which kept getting caught and sticking

to the long rug, causing me to trip over myself. I wasn't feeling much happening from the drugs yet. I was feeling a little drunk, though, so I held onto that feeling and allowed myself to loosen up a bit around her. She was dancing by herself to the music and seemed to be in her own world, totally oblivious to the fact that I was beside her.

I watched her curiously, and suddenly I felt overcome with warmth. My mind and vision seemed to blur and slow. Sage looked like a tall, tanned fairy, twirling and moving magically in front of me while the colors in the house began to pop and stand out. I was feeling more animated now, and I let the feeling of warmth move through my veins as it slowed my constantly analytical mind down. Laughing at how I had somehow arrived here. I felt totally relaxed in this moment, with this stranger, within my body. Vivienne flashed in my mind, but I violently pushed her away, and in a flash her face was gone. Maybe I should take mind-altering drugs more often, in addition to my other crippling vices.

I started to dance quicker alongside Sage, grabbing her arms and holding her body while she twirled and giggled and danced next to me. She handed me the CD case, with TLC's faces now shining and blurry before me, and pushed the rolled-up dollar bill into my hand. I snorted another white line and handed it back over to her, so she could do the same. We passed the drugs back and forth before she turned the volume knob up on the stereo and continued to encourage me to dance with her. The dog slept soundly on the sofa as if he'd witnessed this scene a hundred times before and grew bored of it, kicking his legs deep in sleep, probably chasing roadrunners.

I no longer felt any reservations about my peculiar situation. I was exhilarated, confident and airy—my body was as swift as a river. I started laughing and dancing harder, feeling my body with my fingers. I bent down to look at Sage in her eyes, which were as wide as saucers set inside her round, golden face. Then, like an electric shock I wasn't expecting, she leaned in and kissed me, grabbing my face and hair roughly, pulling my body against hers and kissing my mouth deeply, her tongue in my throat. I kissed her back, my body feeling like melted butter against hers.

She reached her hand under my top and rested it against my chest before she began to slowly unbutton my shirt. I was covered in a thick layer of sweat from dancing, but she didn't seem to notice. I helped her take the shirt off and she took her own crocheted patchwork top off, tossing it to the floor. We danced on the shag carpet to old disco tracks, topless, for another few tracks and kissed in between, laughing loudly and marveling at each other's bodies.

I was so light, ebullient and perfectly cloudy. Thoroughly detached from my body, my mind, my shattered past. I wanted to stay in this warm, comforting, safe little pocket of escapism forever. Maybe I could move to the desert, maybe I should call my family and friends and tell them how much I loved them. I had been such an insular, aloof asshole for so long. I hadn't been able to express how much they had all truly meant to me. I reached for my phone and could tell immediately that it was dead. Fuck, I needed to remember to actually charge these things.

Sage grabbed my pack of cigarettes and lit two for the both of us, smoking and dancing topless in her little dated, desert abode. She was truly beautiful, moving like a rattlesnake across the linoleum tiles and swinging her small breasts around freely, blowing smoke throughout the room, laughing like a wood nymph. I don't think she'd ever realize how grateful I was for her, in this moment, relieving me from nearly a year and a half of constant pain and mental torture. This was a true mental vacation from the bullshit and agony I had found myself trapped within, day after day.

We fell to the ground, exhausted and sweaty from dancing, our hearts pounding in our ears from the mixture of drugs, booze, nicotine and excitement. Sage continued to kiss my neck and shoulders, as I played with her hair. It felt like dark, silky water between my fingers, and I became fixated on the feeling of it. I failed to notice that she had taken my jeans off and thrown them across the room, near where the dog was now snoring in his sleep.

She grabbed my face and kissed me deeply, rubbing her tanned body against mine and sucking firmly onto my mouth, biting my lips. I kissed her back, holding her hair in my hand, feeling her warm rib cage beneath my palms, skin that felt as if it held the heat of the desert within it, as she rested her weight on top of me. I knew I was only feeling synthetically good, but I didn't care. This wasn't going to last indefinitely, but I wanted it to. I was so high and floating that I didn't want to come down and face my depressing, flat, empty reality.

As we continued to kiss and touch each other in our drunken drug haze, a sharp light suddenly flashed across her face, accompanied by a low rumbling that somehow caught my stoned attention. First as an interesting orb that I wanted to touch, appearing soft and slow moving. Then the dog started to bark again, which shocked me out of my ethereal state and frankly scared the shit out of me. A loud, piercing, guttural bark that itched my brain and made my ears hurt. Sage jumped away of me quickly, looking terrified.

"Fuck, he wasn't supposed to come home tonight!" she yelled, her eyes huge and black. She looked back at me in a panic. I could feel her heart racing from across the room.

"What? Who wasn't supposed to come home to-night...?" I mumbled in a contorted tone. I was feeling exceptionally high now, my warm body rolling in waves of distorted delight.

"My dad! Hurry, get your shit and go!" She grabbed my shirt and threw it at me in a wadded-up ball. It hit my chest and felt like a ball of warm, soft cotton. Her arms covered her naked chest as she looked at the front door.

"Your...dad?" was all I could manage to croak out in my ecstatic, slow state.

She fumbled to put on her crochet top, backward, and started to fix her hair, running through it with her long fingers, straightening up and pretending she wasn't also high as a kite.

"Get out! Go, leave!" she yelled at me again, shooing me away with her tan hands.

My sluggish drug brain couldn't fully comprehend the magnitude of the situation. Everything had changed so quickly. One minute we were on the floor kissing and now I was standing half naked in her living room being told to leave the property. I didn't know what to buy into, so I stood there, idling like a high idiot, touching my sweaty face.

Sage looked into my largely dilated eyes, worried, wondering why I wasn't heeding her directions. Then her gaze turned immediately back to the front door as the lock was being turned by an outside key. Suddenly, a large, imposing man entered the room, a familiar looking man. Even in my elevated state I knew exactly who he was in an instant. Tall, bronzed, bandanna, covered in dark tattoos. It was the fucking security bouncer from the Cholla Club, the Western Wednesday's guy. This was her father? I cocked my head to study him. It was most definitely the same guy. The same *huge* guy.

"Hi, Daddy, I thought you weren't going to be back tonight..." Sage said in a sweet, high voice that hummed in my ears. I stood there like a dried-out scarecrow, reveling in ecstasy with my head cocked to the side like a dope, still not believing this was happening to me.

"Who the fuck is this guy?" was all he said, pointing his huge finger at me angrily. This wasn't good. I knew this wasn't good. His deep voice cut through my fuzzy state a bit, and I looked at Sage, pleading telepathically for help.

"This is Venn, don't you remember seeing him? From the show tonight?" She smiled nervously, glancing over at me.

He walked briskly over to me and stared into my eyes like a sharp sword through my skull. "How old are you, boy?" he growled. His hard, weathered face demanded an answer.

"Thirty-five," I croaked out. I couldn't focus my eyes. This was a horrible position to be high in, and I knew it.

"And do you know how old she is?" he roared at me, his face reddening in anger.

I felt sick. I abruptly realized I didn't know how old she was. She was so mature, she was drinking, she was playing music in an adult club. It hadn't occurred to me; I was so inside of my own head I forgot to ask how fucking old she was. Stupid, stupid, stupid. Before I could answer he spoke to me.

"She's seventeen, pal! Ever heard of statutory rape?! I ought to kill your punk ass for even touching her!" He pushed my chest violently against the fake wood-paneled wall.

"I– I didn't know, sir, I, uh," I rambled. Fuck, I was really high and now I was about to die in the desert. It never failed to amaze me just how quickly situations can turn sour.

I looked at Sage for some kind of moral support, but she just shrugged innocently and said, "Actually, I'm eighteen in a few months." She bit her lip.

"Why didn't you tell me?!" I screamed at her, feeling stupid and like a total creep.

"Get the fuck out of here before I blow your brains out, guy!" Her angry father pulled a small, shiny silver pistol out of his denim trousers and held it against my bare chest.

This was really happening, I told myself, letting a rational voice speak to me, cutting through the high. I held up my hands and swiftly moved past both of them towards the door.

"I'm sorry. I'm really sorry, I didn't realize…" My words were shameful and slurry.

"Bye, Venn! See you around sometime?" Sage yelled as her father slammed the door shut against my back, causing me to jump forward. I could hear them arguing in the living room behind me, her father scolding her in a muffled tone as I stood bare chested on the porch of the house, atop the black ocean of sand and beneath a million stars.

13. Vivienne

The day Vivienne decided to finally end her relationship with her ex, she instructed me to wait for her call. She said she would meet me in the park between our two apartments after she had broken the news to him, and we would discuss our options moving forward. I spent the entire day pacing my apartment nervously, feeling sick and heavy. My girlfriend had gone to visit her parents in Virginia, so I had the place to myself, but it didn't make it any easier on me. I glanced around at my partner's possessions, the things we had bought together, notes she had written to me in an attempt to be cute or romantic, and scolded myself. I shouldn't have led her on for so long and continued to be so selfish. I should have ended things with her the day I met Vivienne.

After waiting for what seemed like an eternity, Vivienne finally called. She had been crying, I could tell immediately, and it occurred to me that I had never witnessed her cry. The thought of her beautiful face crying in pain made me tense up.

"I did it, it's done, he knows," was all she said, in a flat, slightly sad tone which made me feel a little bitter.

"Are you okay? What can I do?" She was only down the street from me, but it felt like she was across the world.

"No. Now, you need to do the same. I just feel horrible, you know? I feel like a total heartless bitch. He didn't suspect anything. I can't stop crying." She began to wail breathlessly on the other end of the line.

At first, I felt a slight sting of jealousy, hearing her cry over another lover. I felt like she should have been resolute in her decision, remembering why she was leaving him. It was for me, for us, for our relationship. Soon though, those immature, selfish thoughts gave way to logic, and I remembered what a caring, considerate woman Vivienne was. She had just done something hurtful, ending a long-term relationship with someone who was once her best friend, someone she shared a home and significant time with. Ending a chapter of her life that although she no longer felt she needed to be a part of, still played a role in her development as a human. I should respect and encourage her mourning process. After all, soon that would be me, and I would need her to do the same. The thought made me feel sick. Could I break up with my partner as easily? I wasn't as brave or as concise as Vivienne. I was weak.

"The manager said he has a studio available, if I want it," she said glumly, through tears.

"Okay, do you need help moving? I can come over, whatever you need me to do."

"Can you meet me in the building? He's left, I don't know where he went, he just drove off. I can meet you on the other side of the apartments after I see the manager, maybe around two?"

"I'll meet you there, Vivienne. I love you, everything will work out, I promise, okay?"

"I love you, too. See you at two." She hung up.

I stared down at the phone in my hand. I couldn't quite believe it. After a year of what ifs, of sneaking around, of almost indulging in our most primal instincts and abstaining, one of us was now cut free. Separated from the chain that held us back and open to loving freely in the daylight. I paced around my apartment until 1:50pm, then ran the two miles to Vivienne's apartment building, feeling light as a sponge and as heavy as iron simultaneously.

When I arrived, she was already in her new, completely empty studio, aside from two suitcases, looking around with puffy, drained eyes at the downsizing of space and view. The new fishbowl apartment was one square room, with a small side kitchen, a fire escape window balcony and a view looking onto the busy hospital across the street. She sat in a slumped ball on the floor, looking up at me with painfully red eyes and runny makeup.

I sat beside her and scooped her firmly into my arms, holding her like a limp teddy bear while she cried heavily into my shirt, smearing snot and salt all over my clothing.

"I just feel so horrible, like a really shitty person," she cried.

"You're not a bad person…You just followed your heart; you did this for us." I realized I was terrible at consolations. I never made my girlfriend cry, at least not that I knew of, and I had never cried in front of her. I was rusty at comforting someone.

We lay on her empty studio floor, entwined silently until the evening. Vivienne cried against me on and off until she ran out of tears. I held her close, comforted her, trying to say and do the right things to show her she had made the correct decision in choosing me. I pondered how I was going to tell my girlfriend that it was also over between us, and that I couldn't stay with her for another minute, perpetuating the lie.

Just as I was inventing scenarios and conversations of breakups in my head, my girlfriend called me. Vivienne lay there like a ragdoll, curled up on the floor, exhausted, while I went outside to answer my current partner's call. She was as cheerful and blissfully unaware as ever, telling me about her family outings, the southern weather and how she was spending her days, adding to my agony how she missed me and couldn't wait to come home the next day to see me.

Fuck. I felt overwhelmingly guilty and awful. Here, I had the love of my life in a ball on the floor beside me in tears and on the phone, I had my current partner excited to come home to be with me indefinitely, maybe forever in her mind. Everything about this situation was impossibly difficult, no one could win.

I said my goodbyes quickly and hung up on my partner,

feeling waves of heat and shame. I strode back to the carpet and lay on the floor with Vivienne, wrapping my arms
around her unmoving body. We spent the night there, curled
together on that empty floor, engaging in nothing more than
holding one another. She was too fragile, too upset for any
sexual tension or romantic endeavors. I held her through the
night, until I had to leave for work the next morning. Then
I covered her with my jacket and assured her she would be
okay, that I would call her once I had ended things with my
girlfriend, and we would be together finally, once and for all.
She kissed me goodbye, and I held her cheek, before forcing
myself to leave her in her new world, alone.

Work went by quickly, far too quickly for my liking,
and I didn't want to face my girlfriend when I got home.
She would no doubt be waiting for me, an excited, ignorant
expression on her face. Only for me to crush her instantly,
ending what she deemed to be a perfect relationship.

At 5 pm, I nervously walked the short distance back to
my apartment, taking my time and considering my words
carefully, replaying what I was going to say over and over, attempting not to falter in my hypothetical delivery or responses to her anger. I needed to do this, I needed to be brave, to
be brutally honest. I couldn't succumb to weakness and pity
for her. I didn't love her, she deserved to be with someone
who could truly love her the way I never could.

As soon as she heard me come through the door, she
jumped up from the sofa and ran to greet me, smiling before
giving me a painfully close hug, expressing how much she

had missed me. I choked on my practiced words and attempts to act coldly. Do it now, you must do it now, I thought. Tell her it's over, tell her it's done, stop prolonging the pain, for both of you.

But I just stood there quietly. My mouth went dry and my throat weak. I couldn't formulate separating, hurtful words. All I could manage to eventually say was, "I missed you, too."

Fuck. No, no, no. Don't tell her that, don't lead her on. I stared beyond her face into the wall, imagining Vivienne crying on her empty apartment floor, waiting for my call.

My girlfriend held me closer, her head resting against my chest, stopping to look up at me. She broke the quiet pause between us. "I was thinking…maybe we could go away somewhere together? How about a little beach vacation, or a long weekend in the woods?"

Oh god, I had really fucked myself here. Now, not only had I not broken things off with her, but I had also somehow further dug myself in a hole by making her think we needed to 'get away' on a romantic secluded holiday together. This was very bad. My eyes widened and my body tensed up. End it, tell her now, my brain screamed. But my words had a mind of their own. All I could say as I stood there rigidly, holding onto her with my loose, flabby arms, was, "Yeah, sure, that would be nice."

I told my girlfriend I needed to make a work call outside while she hummed and made us dinner. I felt completely sick and disgusted with myself. I wasn't able to do it. The one thing I needed to do in order to be free, to be with Vivienne, and I was too much of a coward to pull it off. I was now further leading my girlfriend on and still lying to her, emotionally and physically cheating on her, and pretending everything was okay between us when it was the antithesis of okay. I walked across the street and called Vivienne from the empty playground in the park. Her line rang once.

"Hello?" she said nervously, slightly out of breath. I wondered if she had moved from her studio floor all day.

"Hey, are you okay? How are you feeling today?" I tried to kill time before she found out what a weak piece of shit I was.

"What happened, how did she take it?" She cut straight to the point. I flinched and bit my lip, shaking my legs nervously, leaning against a rusty jungle gym.

"I…I didn't do it. She's just too nice, I couldn't do it, I couldn't hurt her. I'm sorry. I don't know what to do," I croaked out pathetically. I wanted to hit myself.

There was a pause before she spoke, clearly letting the weight of my words sink in. "What?! You didn't end it? What the fuck, Venn! How could you?" she screamed, vitriol building in her voice.

"I just couldn't do it; I didn't want to hurt her. I think, maybe, I just need some time…to figure it all out." What was I saying? I couldn't believe the words falling out of my mouth.

"Okay. Fine. Take your time. Go back to your loveless relationship and sleep in your loveless bed and waste your life. I ended my relationship for you, I went through the pain and hurt of breaking another person's heart and moved out of my home to be with you. Now here you are, too much of an asshole and a coward to do the same. Never fucking call me again." She hung up abruptly, leaving me in shock with my jaw dropped open.

I stood there, in that empty playground, totally blindsided. I didn't know what I had expected Vivienne to say or do. Had I genuinely expected her to wait for me while I continued to pretend in a lifeless relationship? Of course she wasn't going to wait around for me to get my shit together. In the span of an hour, I had lost the woman I loved, deciding in turn to be with a woman I don't think I had ever loved.

As I walked back to my apartment, where my girlfriend was happily cooking us a meal in content unawareness, I couldn't have felt any worse. I kicked the dirt and held my head down in shame. I couldn't explain my actions to myself. Why hadn't I just ripped the band-aid off and ended the dead relationship? I was willing to avoid pain at all costs to not hurt an innocent party, but by not hurting my girlfriend, I was now hurting myself, and even worse, hurting Vivienne.

As I slowly entered the apartment and took off my shoes, a wave of sadness engulfed me, and I felt as if I had suddenly been encased in concrete. I looked around at all our shared things and felt nauseous, a writhing knot forming in my stomach. I had just made a huge mistake and I knew it. My girlfriend came over and hugged me again, holding my cold, unmoving body while I stared at the ceiling and cursed myself.

"Everything okay?" She smiled at me.

"Fine, just work stuff," I said coldly.

"Well, dinner is ready!" she said cheerfully, plating up colorful dishes of hot food.

I looked over at her lovingly prepared meal. Surely, she couldn't actually be this happy, this naïve? Was this half-hearted partnership enough for her? Was she pretending or fooling herself into believing this was a mutually happy, healthy relationship? Or was she simply doing everything she could to keep me around, suppressing her gut intuition about how distant I had become over the last year, how complacent, and how she'd pretended not to notice?

"So, what beach should we go to?" she chimed, looking into my eyes with a hint of desperation mixed with hope.

"I'll see what's available tomorrow." I picked over my food with my fork, Vivienne's face burned into the forefront of my mind. What was she doing now? Was she crying over me the way she had cried over her ex?

My girlfriend looked at me, then at her plate and back at me, waiting for some kind of sign, a layer of excitement or love from me that couldn't be conjured up. At that moment, I felt completely trapped in a hell of my own making.

That night, we lay in bed together. My girlfriend attempted to make love to me, frowning and offended when I couldn't grow erect for her. I lied, saying that I had jacked off that morning, which to my surprise she bought, not bothering to ask for anything else. She moved over and cuddled my chest, running her hands in my hair.

"I love you so much," she whispered, before drifting off to sleep, failing to notice I hadn't returned the sentiment. I stared up at the ceiling for hours, wide awake while my girl-friend snored lightly against my skin, wondering how different this night could have been.

14. Vivienne

I spent that summer on autopilot, scared to upset the gentle, fragile yoke that was my pitiful undoing. I couldn't call Vivienne anymore, she had emphatically prohibited me from doing so, especially since I still hadn't ended things with my current partner. There was no point in calling her unless I had news that she wanted to hear. Who knows, maybe she had already moved onto someone else. The thought itself was a bullet to the chest. Picturing her touching another human, kissing anyone else, filled me with a jealous fire.

Instead, I buried my thoughts in work, in self-loathing, in books, in anything that kept my mind away from the idiotic misstep of not ending my relationship, continuing this miserable charade, pretending I loved someone I didn't. My girlfriend played house that summer while I merely existed, barely remembering the passing of days. Everything I saw and heard and felt reminded me of Vivienne. Eventually I knew I would have to sleep with my girlfriend, so as to not totally give away the notion that my love was long gone. I did so painfully and quickly, feeling all the while that I was, in fact, cheating on Vivienne. She didn't seem to notice any difference in my behavior.

I thought of Vivienne every day. I wondered if she had returned to her rich boyfriend, begging him to take her back, sucking up to him with her big puppy eyes and charming him into believing she had just had a brief crisis of thought instead of an affair. Or if she hadn't gone back to him, what she was doing instead. Had she decorated her little studio? Was she sleeping well in her new bed without me? Did she think about me, miss me? Did she loathe me for the weak scum that I was?

I picked up the phone to call her multiple times a day, always putting it back down and shaking off the idea that Vivienne would ever truly forgive me. I was a piece of shit, a spineless coward. I had hurt her and humiliated her, and she would never love me for that. So, for three long and arduous months, I stood stagnant. Still, she was all that consumed my thoughts, while the puppet of me attempted to resemble a live-action boyfriend to my unaware, gleeful girlfriend.

We went on the beach holiday, pretending everything was fine and singing to radio songs like happy campers on the road. I stared out of the window sadly. Why wasn't I here with her? Why wasn't she on this trip beside me? Everything beautiful and painful and sad reminded me of her. Every song, I sang to her. Being heartbroken over someone while in a relationship with someone else was a tough act to juggle. We spent the weekend on a beach in foggy Oregon, playing at being a real couple, strolling through the Pacific Aquarium, staring at various electric colored fish and trapped mammals. Me, eating lunch unenthusiastically while she spoke to the mask of me, the actor, the fraud. Her, reading her glossy fashion magazines and watching her boring, shallow reality TV shows in the hotel while I sat in the corner pretending to read a book, pining over Vivienne and dissecting my stupid decision to stay away from her.

After what seemed like eons, we finally packed up and drove back to LA, with me sitting silently for most of the drive down. I couldn't tell if my girlfriend knew I was mentally distant, or if she just didn't care. Maybe she was one of those people who preferred to be in a loveless relationship than to be alone.

Once we finally arrived home, it hit me like a brick wall. I had reached my limit. I couldn't go on like this. *We* couldn't go on like this. I couldn't spend another day pretending to love someone when my heart was with someone else, and finally, for the first time in years, I truly realized how cruel it was for me to prolong someone else's happiness for my own selfish needs. I knew it was time to end it, once and for all.

I approached my partner, who was gingerly pulling sandy clothes out of her suitcase and placing them in the laundry basket. Touching her shoulder, I turned her toward me. She looked at me in a loving yet quizzical way.

"Hi, honey, are you feeling okay? You've been quiet all day." She looked hopeful, like my response would have nothing to do with her, or with us.

"We need to talk," I said flatly, standing firm in my decision.

"Okay…" She set the clothing down on the bed and sat down, bracing herself. We both knew what 'we need to talk' meant.

"I don't know the right way to say this…" I began wondering if I should do this after all, but I knew what I needed to do. "I just think…I think you deserve someone better, something better than me. I feel like we've been growing apart for a while, and it's nothing that you've done, you've been great to me, I just don't have anything to give back, I can't give you what you want, and I'm sorry." Make it about me, I thought selfishly, how I was the problem. Even though it was true.

She looked confused, then angry. Her face went from hopeful to upset in an instant. "What?!" she yelled, her cheeks turning a radish red.

"I just think we would be better off apart, I…"

"No. I heard you the first time, I am asking why you're saying this, why now, Venn?"

"I just think we've been growing apart for a while, and I stayed because we're such close friends, so we could—"

"Friends? Close friends?!"

"We both know it's not working. I care about you…but I can't do this anymore, I don't know what to say…I'm sorry, Grace."

"I moved across the country for you, I quit my job for you, stayed with you and stayed positive despite you being a selfish, introverted, self-serving asshole! You think I've been happy here? You never even talked about marrying me, or having kids, Venn. All you've done is waste my time." She wasn't wrong. I stared at the floor and took her scolding. Now I was two for two. I had fucked up royally and hurt two people I cared about. I deserved whatever was going to happen to me. I deserved to rot in hell for this.

"I knew something was off, I just didn't want to admit it to myself," she finally said, after reflecting for a while, quietly sitting on the edge of the bed.

"Grace, I'm so sorry, I'm really fucking sorry." I meant it. I should have never been with her to begin with, I could never give her what she needed.

"I don't want to hear it. I feel like I've wasted years of my life. I truly thought you might get your shit together and propose to me this year, now you're dumping me. I look like an idiot," she said curtly, adding quickly, "Are you fucking someone else?" She turned to look me dead in the eyes, tears of anger building in her wide, blue eyes.

"No, I'm not." It was the truth, technically.

She accepted this hollow answer and began to put her dirty beach clothes back into her suitcase, the suitcase she had just packed a week before, excited about a romantic vacation with her loving partner, the one she thought might propose to her. I sat on the bed watching her pack, numb. This was what I had wanted, what I had needed to do three months ago and failed to do. It was difficult, but not as difficult as staying together had been. Although I felt selfish and wretched, I also felt a sense of relief, that we could both move on and be truly happy with other people. Now, I just need to find a way to reconcile with Vivienne.

I knew this wouldn't be easy. For all I knew Vivienne had cut me out of her mind and eliminated me as a potential lover and partner, and I deserved it. I hurt her, I hurt myself, I'd let her down, why would I deserve her forgiveness?

We hadn't spoken for over three months. She might not even live in the city anymore. The thought of her no longer being down the street from me made me choke on my saliva. I left my now ex-girlfriend sitting silently, packing up clothing in our bedroom, and I walked outside, to the same park where I had blown everything up and ruined my chance at being with Vivienne. I dialed her number slowly, and for the first time in over three months, I allowed it to ring.

It rang seven times. She's never going to answer, I thought. She hates me, I knew it. I placed my finger over the button to hang up.

"Hello," she said, from the phone resting in my hand. I fell onto the woodchips, her voice seeped like honey. Sad, crystallized, fucked-over honey.

"Vivienne, I did it, I ended it, I broke up with her."

"You broke up with her? Actually broke up with her? I thought you 'couldn't do it'?" she said, mocking me.

"I know what I said, I told you I just needed time, but I did it, it's over now. She knows."

Vivienne stayed quiet for a long time. I could hear her breathing, could almost hear her trying to process what I had just told her, debating whether or not she should stay on the phone with me.

"Why now?" she finally said, harshly.

"I just needed time; it didn't feel right before. I know I fucked up, I'm sorry. What can I do, Vivienne?"

"What do you want, Venn? What do you actually want?" She sounded bruised.

"I want you; I have always wanted you, I just didn't want to hurt anyone."

"You hurt me," she retorted.

"I know. I know I did, and I'm sorry. Please, I have to see you," I begged.

"Come over, same place." She said after a long pause and hung up.

I felt a surge of excitement. Despite the awful mess I had made with Vivienne and the bomb I had just dropped on Grace; I had finally accomplished what I'd needed to do all along. If I could beg Vivienne to forgive me and gain her acceptance again, perhaps once the dark clouds had cleared and we had healed, we would all have a chance to be happy, to be together.

I walked back to my apartment and told Grace I was going for a walk. She didn't respond, pacing back and forth, aggressively shoving items and clothing into bags and suitcases, crying softly. I wanted to comfort her, but I was terrified of not being able to hold my ground, of falling back into my old pattern of pretending it was okay, so I left her alone.

I ran as fast as I could to Vivienne's apartment building, dodging dog walkers and pedestrians and almost getting hit by two cars and a bus, all angrily honking and shouting obscenities at me. I couldn't see any of my surroundings, just the familiar blocks as they passed and marked my path to Vivienne. When I finally reached her rusty fire escape stairs at the back of the building, I ran up the six flights quickly, skipping and tripping over the metal steps until I reached her window.

She was sitting quietly at her wooden desk, facing the wall, seemingly lost in thought over what had just transpired, a phone clutched in her hand. She looked confused, sad, numb, all at once. I tapped on the window, which shook her out of her stupor, and she let me in. I contorted and climbed my tall frame into the small window and stood before her, ashamed. I didn't know what to do; I wanted to kiss her, to hold her and beg for her forgiveness, but she didn't move, her body language uninviting.

She looked thin, too thin, as if she had stopped eating completely over the past three months. Her once full, healthy face looked pale and sallow, small bags under her forest eyes. She looked as if she had cried herself to sleep for months or hadn't had any sleep at all. She was dressed in a simple cotton shirt and jeans, standing stiff and cold, looking into my eyes for a full explanation.

"Well, let's hear it," she finally said.

"I'm sorry. I ended it, it's over," I said again, hoping that hearing me say it in person would make her believe it was real.

"And, what? Am I supposed to just be okay now? You really fucked me over, V. We had a pact, and you didn't keep your end of the deal."

"Vivienne, I know, please, I couldn't do it that day. You should have seen her face; I just couldn't do it. I know I fucked up, I'm sorry," I pleaded. She stood still.

"Do you know how bad these last few months have been for me? I drank every day, I couldn't sleep, I couldn't eat. I fucking hate you right now." I thought she was going to hit me.

"I know, and I accept that. You can hate me forever, but I love you, Vivienne, I love you and I want to be with you, forever."

She loosened her body a bit, as if I had said a secret password to unlock her coldness, and she started to cry, which hit me like a punch to the gut. I could see the physical and mental stress I had caused her by simply failing to keep a promise, and it became blatantly evident that I was the one who needed to be punished. I was willing to do whatever it took, however long it took, to work my way back into her good graces.

"What now?" she said, in between gasps and tears. I couldn't stand back anymore, so I moved forward and held her, which only made her cry harder. After a few minutes of standing against me limply, her arms moved up and clasped around my back, squeezing harder while she cried.

"Now we can be together," I said, kissing the top of her head.

"But how can I trust you? You might just go back to her. How do I know this is real?" Her eyes were swollen and red, her thin face looked blue and strained.

I grabbed her face in my hands, looking her firmly in the eyes, and said, "I'm not going anywhere, you have to believe me."

We sat on the cold kitchen tiles and held each other in silence. For the first time in nearly four years, we were holding each other in total innocence, without the cloud of adultery or secrecy shrouding us. We were allowed to just be in love, to be hurt, to be vulnerable. No alibis, no curfews, no hiding our calls, no more sneaking around or hurting other people. We were just there, together, in pain and in love, watching the light turn dark as we cried together, entwined on her floor.

15. Vivienne

I stood on the soft sand of the cold desert in my boxer shorts and tennis shoes, still astonishingly high and not noticing the crisp desert wind hitting my body and giving me waves of goosebumps. If anything, it was a beautiful sensation against my skin. I could still hear Sage arguing with her father, as I watched the American flag flapping loudly in the wind and nearly full moonlight, debating my next move.

How the fuck was I going to find my motel? I was in the middle of nowhere, with no car, no pants, no phone, no direction, incredibly high on ecstasy and drunk on alcohol. I questioned going back to the house, asking if I could have a ride, before recalling the feeling of Sage's dad's steely pistol against my chest. I realized that perhaps I didn't want to die tonight, so with no other suitable options before me, I decided to walk into the unknown.

I tried to calculate time in my head, to no conclusion. It was about 1:30, 2 am maybe when her dad violently kicked me out of the house. How long had I stood there in the cold?

A half an hour perhaps, so it must be around 3 am. We drove for fifteen, maybe twenty minutes, considering all of the twists and turns in the road, but which direction did we come from?

I followed the sand and dirt road until I reached another identical sand and dirt road, then another, passing more little square homes with more American and military flags and old cars or motorcycles outside. More barking dogs frightened me out of my sedated state, before moving swiftly along in the dark. Another road. More cacti, more bushes, more sand, more rocks. My old tennis shoes dug in and tripped over various unknown items, lit by the glistening moonlight. I wondered if I was traveling deeper into the desert, if I was going to end up on one of those tacky cold case mystery shows. I could see the shitty headline now: 'Naked man found dead in desert hills of California.'

More little dark square houses, more sand, more rocks. I was starting to feel quite cold now, so I put my shirt on and buttoned it up. I picked up my pace to generate some heat, trying to stay on dirt roads, avoiding any dark rock or bush that looked like it could potentially kill me. The last thing I wanted to do was step on a rattlesnake or scorpion and die a slow and terrible death out here.

As I walked, I thought about everything that had happened over the last few months. This was the first time, the first place, where I could sit with my thoughts openly and analyze them without any distractions. I couldn't do anything but walk forward and think, so I thought. I thought about my family, my parents. I wondered what my brother was doing on the east coast. We barely talked to each other now, he was so busy he couldn't even come to the funeral, which had only caused further contention in our already strained relationship.

I thought about Texan Jan, and laughed to myself, seeing my breath fog before my face. I replayed our primitive bedroom fiasco in my head and instead of punishing myself for being so vulnerable, I decided to be gentle on my drunken, heartbroken actions. I had asked her to hit me in the face. I needed to acknowledge the pain I had been feeling for so long, the deep, wallowing, agonizing pain that culminated in asking an unwilling stranger to physically beat it out of me. I wondered where she was now. Was she dancing in some club with another, more together partner? Was she sleeping soundly in her warm bed, preparing for an audition in the morning?

I thought about Sage. Wild, mature, dancing, way too young for me Sage. Was I developing a new pattern with women? Without even realizing it, she had kindly removed me from myself. Even though she was underage, and I should have been more responsible in my approach to the situation, she had given me a gift. She had allowed me to escape, to feel something, even synthetically, to feel alive again, for a brief moment. I thought of her behemoth, scary father pushing his gun against me and played out scenarios in which that could have gone horrifically, terrifyingly different. For once in a long time, I was grateful I didn't end up dead. I realized, as I walked and tripped and chewed my cheeks, intoxicated, that maybe I had wanted to live, that I wanted to heal, I wanted to try again.

Then, after happily avoiding her all evening, I thought about Vivienne. I stopped and looked back up at the sky, the moon, the dark shadows of the mountains, and I thought of her. Was I always the problem? Should I have tried harder? Would that have kept her here with me? Did the gods take her away from me because I was actually just a fucked up, confused human, unworthy of her love, her kindness, her forgiveness? I thought of the times we quarreled, the harsh, cutting words we said to one another in anger, the times she ran away and came back to me, before we apologized and made up. I thought of my cold, tense demeanor towards her, how I blamed her for her actions, made her feel ashamed of her family, her decisions, her past. How I tried to change her. How I watched her spirit die before me as her eyes turned to stone, as if it was her fault. Maybe I was actually the disease that took her away this whole time, and I just never wanted to admit it.

I sat down on a smooth rock, hitting my bones against the hard surface, and started to cry, quickly building into a sob, then a full-on screaming wail. I cried hard into my dusty hands and dug my feet into the sand below me, listening to my sobs echoing off the blue mountains in the distance. Flashes of beautiful and terrible memories hit my mind like sharp pellets, each one making me cry harder than the next. From the night we held each other on her empty apartment floor to the day I lost her forever. I had loved her more deeply than I had loved anything else, more than I had ever loved myself.

"Vivienne, I'm sorry, I'm so fucking sorry," I said out loud, to the bushes and rattlesnakes and cacti. Wiping snot and tears from my face, I felt drained, and relieved. I hadn't allowed myself to let go for a long time, hadn't allowed myself to remember it all so clearly. How it had really happened, how it truly was.

I sat there, on that rock in the desert, and cried until I had nothing left to cry. I held my ribs again, to prevent myself from falling apart completely and descending into the depths of despair. I pondered my weaknesses, my raw emotional state, my physical and mental wellbeing. Would I ever be able to offer another human more than a partial piece of me again? Could I ever truly heal, or is this damage irreparable? Would it heal into a hole, or a scar, or worse, would it never heal at all?

I felt the sand between my hands and listened to the wind blowing through the mountains and the tall thin bundles of Mormon grass. I thought about my next moves, what I should do when I returned home to LA. Was this all my life was now? Should I continue to go to work daily, suppressing my woes and drowning my thoughts in booze and cigarettes, starving and punishing my body? Should I move away, go off the grid, live somewhere I could no longer remember her face?

I must have been sitting there, deep in contemplation

and tears, for a while. The sky was changing, the mountains growing lighter, with glimpses of the ridges coming into view. The sun was coming out of its slumber. This was both positive and negative. I could now see where I was walking, but how long would I be able to walk under the desert's oppressive heat?

I forced my sluggish, dehydrated body to move forward, to get up. It was so heavy with sadness and weak from the evening, the drugs, and months and months of dull heaviness. I walked down the dirt road toward a house, easier to spot now that the sun was making its appearance. I noticed a long green garden hose jutting from the side of the house, so I pounced on my opportunity to rehydrate and quench my thirst.

Falling to my knees in front of the nozzle, I turned the tap clumsily and guzzled old, rusty water. I shut the tap off and put the hose back the way I'd found it, before another pissed off desert dweller came out and blew my head off for drinking their water. I knew how important liquid was in the desert, and how important individual privacy and property rights were to others. I didn't take that for granted.

For another hour, walking into nowhere, I watched a magnificent, magical desert sunrise float above the mountains like a giant lemon, slowly working its way into the sky like a bright hot air balloon, causing me to stop in my journey multiple times to admire its glorious view. The sun and moon will always show up for me, I thought. They are something I can depend on.

Eventually, to my utter relief and shock, I stumbled onto a road. A real, graveled black top highway. "Thank fucking God," I said out loud, smiling to myself, excited to not be dead, to have made it through the night alive. This was what I had wanted all along, sheer survival. I just didn't think it would actually happen.

Only now I didn't know which direction to walk in, or how far I'd come, or where I was. I figured if I could successfully flag down a passing car, they could give me a ride to the nearest town, and I could find a phone to use. After all, my phone, wallet, and room key were in my jeans pocket at Sage's house.

I stood on the road, scratching my head, which felt wonderful. I was still semi-high from my drug indulgence, but I was slowly sobering up. My skin and bones were warming under the sun, to my relief. A car passed, so I waved my arms frantically, attempting to stop them. Workers in a paneled work truck. They barely took any notice of me, passing as if I was a lump of roadkill on the side of the highway.

I soon remembered, as I looked into cars and trucks with their drivers eyeing me perplexed, that I didn't have any pants on, and I was waving my arms like an escaped psychotic maniac. I could only imagine what passengers in cars thought of the human before them.

Still, I persisted, waving down every car that passed, hoping to invoke some kind of pity, encouraging them to stop and give me a lift to safety before I met my untimely death on the hot road.

After ten or fifteen vehicles passed with no luck, a beat-up white Dodge truck slowed down and skidded onto the shoulder beside me. A rough looking older man with a worn veteran's hat and a shaggy white beard sat straight-faced in the driver's seat. There was a coffee cradled in the beat-up cup holder, dog tags hanging from the rear-view window. I ran over to his window, relieved and supremely grateful.

"Where you going?" was all he said, nonplussed by the fact that I was in my underwear and covered in sand and dirt.

"I don't really know which direction it is, the Cactus Corral Motel, near the state highway? I would really appreciate it if…" I trailed off. Maybe this guy was going to kill me. I stepped back from the window, wondering if I should wait for the next car or take my chances.

"That's just up the road, a few miles at most. Get in," he said dryly, looking forward at the road.

I flipped the door handle and got in quickly, without weighing my options. I sat on the already sun warmed, worn leather seats, feeling like if there was a god or gods looking out for me, they weren't ready to end me just yet. Unless this was some kind of sick trap and this guy killed hitchhikers as a hobby.

We sat in silence as he put the truck into drive and rolled away from the sandy shoulder. Both of us looked at the illuminated vastness. I was exhausted from dancing and crying and walking.

"So, what happened to you?" he finally said, half smiling as if he hoped it was bad. He recognized a city dweller alright.

"It's a long story," was all I could manage to say, my mouth dry as I eyed his coffee cup.

"Well, whatever happened to you, consider yourself lucky, kid. A lot of crazy shit happens in the desert." He laughed, slurping his coffee loudly.

Within a few minutes, I began to recognize the little town where my motel was. Seeing the familiar font of the Cactus Corral made me calm down and flood with feelings of safety and warmth. I had made it, somehow. He pulled into the parking lot, and I turned to let myself out, turning back to the good Samaritan who had rescued me.

"Hey, thanks a lot, I really appreciate it. Um…?" I held my hand out, realizing I didn't know his name.

"Sal," he said, shaking my hand, before adding, "Be careful out there, kid." He laughed again.

"I'll try, thanks again, Sal, you really helped me out." I shut the door and watched him drive away, standing alone in my dirty boxers and button up shirt.

I saw Randy pottering around inside the motel office and realized I needed to get another room key, as I didn't have my pants anymore. I let myself into the already freezing reception room; Randy certainly adored that air conditioning.

"What the hell happened to you?" he said, looking me up and down in one quick swoop. He blushed, seeming embarrassed to see me in my boxers.

"It's a long story," I said again, deflated. My dusty hair was blowing beneath a cold vent. "I need another room key. I lost mine last night."

"No problem, son, let me get one for you. I won't ask any questions." He reached behind the counter and produced another key with my room number attached to it on a plastic green circle. He handed it to me in a singular motion.

"Thanks, Randy, have a good morning," I said, exiting the cold building and relishing the warmth on my skin outside again. I walked up the battered stone steps to my room, glancing over at the empty pool and hot tub. The work trucks were gone; the only vehicle sitting in the parking lot now was my Bronco.

I let myself into my room and collapsed on the still-made bed. Not bothering to wash my face or change my clothes, weak and nauseous and a little bit high still, but mostly tired from staying awake all evening. The pulsing adrenaline of the night started to wear into pure sleepiness. I looked at the alarm clock as I closed my eyes, feeling my weighted lids shut easily. The clock read 7:12 am in bright red numbers.

16. Vivienne

After I had won myself back into the favor of Vivienne's hesitant heart, the night I climbed through her window and begged for her to be with me, for good, we slept together for the first time, physically. After a year of not having sex, we fully indulged in every desire we had held back on in guilt. We fucked on her floor, in her bathtub, in her little iron-framed bed, and on the kitchen table, covering each other in bites and marks and bruises. She took out her anger on me, which I accepted happily, before we collapsed, covered in saliva and come, into a deep sleep. I took the next two days off work, scared to leave her side out of fear she might change her mind.

Once we were allowed to be with one another, we didn't quite know how to be together. Our phones no longer rang with our former partners' names, stunning us with fear. We no longer adhered to a strict curfew; we didn't have to hide any longer. Grace moved into another apartment on the other side of town, then back to Virginia, but not before leaving me a long, angry voice message on my answering machine about what a piece of shit I was. I accepted it, I was a piece of shit for doing what I had done to her, I knew that, but perhaps now she could really find someone who would fully love and appreciate her. I never figured out if she'd found out about me and Vivienne, but I didn't want to think about it. All I wanted to think about was my new life, my future, my everything, with Vivienne.

After a month, she moved in with me to my apartment, the apartment I'd shared with Grace for years. At first, we argued over this fragile detail. She staunchly hated finding things Grace had left behind or forgotten. She hated the bed we slept on together, the things we had purchased for the home. I tried to remedy this by taking her shopping for a new mattress, new dishes, and new decor to make my home hers, ours. This seemed to ease the awkwardness.

Over the next year, everything was perfect. Well, close to perfect. Slowly, we introduced each other to our friends, the ones who didn't know anything about our illicit affair, pretending we had met at a premier after our former relationships had naturally soured. We wanted to avoid any judgment or gossip that could possibly taint our blissful honeymoon period. We held social dinners and game nights at our apartment, inviting our friends and colleagues over. We naively pretended as if we had been together all along and had never faced the uphill battle of not being allowed to fully be with one another. We rarely discussed the pain and obstacles we faced to reach this point.

It was, without a doubt, the happiest period of my life. Days melted together like sugar and work flowed by in an instant. I couldn't wait to come back home to see her. I thought about her skin, her lips, her laugh and couldn't help but smile and glide through my small existence. I took days off work to stay at home with her, in our unpolluted private world. We would drive to the nearby mountains or canyons, talking loosely about everything from politics to pollinators.

We couldn't keep our hands away from one another; if we weren't holding hands we were kissing, or fucking, or feeling one another, almost in disbelief that this was real. She would climb onto me and stare into my eyes, capturing and sealing my being into her memory like amber.

We developed a pattern of hobbies, cooking foods from around the world, or attempting to, trying to mimic each recipe as the creator had intended it, occasionally substituting ingredients that sometimes worked in our favor, sometimes didn't. We discovered new little restaurants and dined at well-known, well-liked restaurants, finally feeling safe to show affection and go on dates in public, seeing new films in old theaters, always holding discussions or debates afterwards, like we were real critics of the silver screen.

All that time with her felt slow and sweet, like my life had meaning, had flavor, depth. I felt like I was getting to know myself, the real me, through her. She didn't seem to mind my many flaws—how I could be emotionally closed off or aloof or shy around her friends, my strong, stubborn opinions, or the different backgrounds of our families. We held a fake wedding in our apartment that summer, where Vivienne dressed in a two-dollar thrift store white dress, and we danced and consummated our 'marriage' before watching the sunrise on the roof of the apartment building and falling asleep glued to each other's bodies.

When the Pacific Ocean tide was low, we would drive to the beach in the evening, searching for hidden natural treasures with our flashlights. Starfish, sea anemones, hermit crabs, the rare Pacific octopus or small jellyfish washed ashore, which Vivienne would always try to throw back into the sea, staring sadly at the inanimate body floating lifelessly back to shore, sometimes crying over it. Once, we even witnessed the elusive California grunion run, a mysterious event where millions of the tiny, silvery fish flood the beach, flapping and slapping their thin bodies against the shore. We stood in amazement, calling each other over to reveal what we had found, falling into the cold sand beneath us and making love, surrounded by fluttering mating fish and bright moonlight. My heart swelled and ached with love for her. Through every discovery, every discussion, every disagreement, every silent treatment, I was wholly addicted to everything that she was.

We traveled all around the west coast, visiting every state park in the northern states, taking trains, boats, cars, bicycles to explore the different landscapes together. Making her scream in orgasm in a field, against a tree, in the snow, as she did the same to me. We would cut stares into each other like glass, like wild animals. I never could fully believe that she was actually in love with me as much as I was in love with her. I would catch myself staring at her, wondering if I had just imagined this beautiful creature in my mind, made her up from fragments and matter, only to reach over and touch her, to realize she was indeed very real, and she was there with me.

That first year together, as they usually are, was the best year of my life. Everything felt new, magical, perfect, even when it wasn't. Those little annoyances and personal dislikes don't make an obvious appearance, their every movement coated in a glossy sweetness that enshrouds you both in a hazy, drunk infatuation. I didn't notice anything that bothered me about her, except that I wanted to spend all of my time with her. I didn't see anything sinister brewing beneath the surface, any serious problems taking root, festering. She never led me to believe anything was ever wrong between us, either. We spent each day together as if it was our last, making it count.

This is exactly why they say love is blind.

It wasn't until the second year I started to notice the slipping in our routine. The little cracks, the holes. My work was catching up to me, and my boss began to hold meetings warning me to get my shit together and produce better work or she'd be forced to lay me off, telling me I could no longer take time off flippantly, scolding me for my weak performance.

My family was frustrated that I had stopped calling, stopped visiting. My friends noticed I stopped asking to hang out, especially Will, who expressed his concerns openly, questioning if our relationship was healthy considering we never got together anymore. I felt bad, of course. After all, I hadn't cut anyone off on purpose, I was just too involved in my obsession with Vivienne to pay attention to anything else. I didn't know how to please everyone, how to reconcile and save my relationships before they were burned away forever. Vivienne was the only person I wanted to see, to talk to, to be around. I didn't know how to balance everything in a healthy, mature way, the way I had managed to before I met her.

Vivienne struggled as well. Without telling me, she dropped out of school and applied for more low paying jobs in grocery and retail. She couldn't seem to manage her time outside of me, either. She brought it up over dinner one evening, fearing my reaction.

"I can't do it anymore, Venn, I just kept falling behind. I needed to get a job," she said glumly.

"But what about school? Your future, your career? I thought that was what you wanted?" I said, probably too aggressively.

"I thought you didn't care what I did, as long as I was happy? Do you not feel that way anymore?" she asked, immediately defensive.

"Does working for minimum wage make you happy, really happy?" I sounded like a fucking snob.

"It makes me happier than selling my soul for a paycheck, Venn," she responded, gritting her teeth before adding, "Maybe I don't want to be rich. Look at my parents, they're rich and they aren't fucking happy!"

"It's not about the money, V, I just want you to live up to your potential. Doing this, quitting school, eliminating opportunities…" I was starting to sound like her father, and I knew it. She scowled at me in hatred.

"Do you think I don't have any usable skills? Opportunities? I can fulfill my potential by beating my own path. School isn't for everyone, you knew I was like this, Venn!" she screamed, before getting up, going to the bedroom and slamming the door behind her, barricading herself inside while I watched our dinner turn cold, my head in my hands.

She was right, I did know she was like this. This was exactly why I had fallen in love with her to begin with. She didn't care about climbing the social ladder, obtaining wealth or accolades, following in her parents' hollow footsteps. She wanted to be a free-spirited bohemian, an artist, or a writer. She didn't want to feel trapped in a dead end, soulless office job chasing the dollar.

But that attitude unfortunately didn't pay our bills. I had spent so much time and money funding her artistic endeavors that I was spending more of my own paycheck, my own savings, even though my own career was on the line, sowing those silent seeds of mutual resentment that bury and root when that first blissful year has worn off and the fruit begins to rot.

Still, despite our flaws and arguments, we were still in love with one another. We made up after every petty argument, every outrageous emotional episode, every sour disagreement. I didn't want to argue about money with her, didn't even want money to exist and infect our world. I truly adored her, and wanted to support anything she wanted to do, even if it hurt our finances and forced me to work overtime. She was flighty, sure, she changed her mind more often than not, and dropped out of courses halfway through, but she was still inspirational to me.

As someone who had followed the school route exactly as the world expected of me, I admired her freewheeling, carefree style. I genuinely respected her bravery and ability to take risks, so I let her figure herself out in our relationship, whatever it was she thought she needed. I wanted to be her pillar of strength, her protector, her friend, especially when she stopped talking to her family, who cut her off verbally for a year, citing her inability to take life seriously as afflicting them with unneeded stress. It caused ever more emotional and physical strain on her, on us. Strain I attempted to make up for, perhaps in futility, with petty money, inventive outings and unconditional love.

17. Vivienne

I woke up in my hot, stuffy motel room at 3:03 pm, dehydrated as a prune. My head was groggy, and my stomach
twisted with desperate thirst and hunger. I pushed my sweaty
body from the polyester fabric of the bed and stumbled,
ungracefully, to the bathroom. I stood with my hand weakly
against the wall to steady myself above the toilet, peeing a
hot, dark shade of nutrient-deficient orange.

My body was caked with dried sweat, sand and dirt, my
hair matted and gritty with particles and grease. Blonde cactus needles poked out from my naked legs. I turned the tub
faucet on and let the bathtub fill, before filling a plastic cup
with water from the sink and guzzling nearly half a gallon,
until I felt almost satisfied. My head was throbbing intensely
from the combination of the hangover and comedown from
the drugs I'd ingested with Sage.

Fuck, Sage. Yet another strange night amidst the darkness I had found myself trudging within now. First, I made
someone punch me in the face and now, on my supposed

solo vacation, I was caught with my pants down next to a teenager, high on ecstasy before nearly having my head blown off, before walking through the desert half naked and crying in the middle of the night. I was really succeeding at life. I used to be a normal, responsible, typical person. I used to care, assess my actions with some forethought and consider the risks involved. I seemed to have thrown all logic out of the window and replaced it with reckless abandonment and inconsideration.

I lowered myself slowly into the hot water, feeling my body loosen as I submerged myself entirely. My muscles started to relax, my breathing calmed, and my limbs went limp. I had forgotten how superbly relaxing a bath could be. I'd avoided them for over a year and a half, as they always reminded me of Vivienne, of us entwined, talking, bubbles flying around the room, washing each other's hair, kissing, our naked bodies covered in soap. The time I sat in the tub with her in her little studio and told her how much money I earned, praying she would accept this amount even if it was a far cry from what her previous partner could offer, professionally laying out a five-year plan for a home, savings, even money to help her succeed in her own endeavors.

In this little motel tub, I let those fond memories flicker in and out, without allowing them the power to cripple my thoughts. I wanted to enjoy relaxing in hot water, simply, while my hangover subsided, and let it be just that for as long as I could. Before the darkness of her memory took hold of me again and I was written off for yet another day.

I lay in the tub for over an hour, sitting with my fuzzy thoughts. No music, no television, no traffic noise, no AC unit. Just silence and still water. I felt an invisible web of numbness falling around my body. Partially from feeling so awful physically, but part of me knew I was beginning to mentally reject feeling like shit, always wallowing, constantly mired in pain and regret and self-doubt. As I scrubbed my body clean of desert dirt and drug sweat, I felt a little bright surge, a foreign feeling of hope flowing through me. A notion that perhaps I truly wouldn't feel this low forever, that suffering isn't indeed as definite as it seems and somewhere inside of me there was fresh blood and skin waiting to be revealed beneath the vast layers of scabs and bruises.

I decided to pull myself up, literally. I lifted my body out of the tub and dried off using old towels with little green cacti embroidered on them, a small CC below the cactus. I wondered who had used these towels before me, if they were upset, in love, depressed or just stopping over for the night. Motels are the keepers of many secrets.

I figured I should probably eat something soon—I hadn't eaten since last night after all—but where? I didn't want to go back to the Cholla Cafe out of fear of running into Sage or her massive, gun-toting dad, so I settled on driving until I found something suitable. I wasn't feeling overly picky, but I needed something to offset the headache, to settle my nerves and ease my tense stomach.

I dressed in old cotton shorts and another long sleeved, white button up shirt, as I had left my jeans at Sage's house.

Shit. My wallet, my phone. I only had about fifty dollars in cash in the glove compartment of the Bronco. It was going to have to be a cheap week. I didn't even know where she lived, so I couldn't drive over and get them back. I groaned to myself, another obstacle, another stupid, directly negative consequence I needed to live with.

I stood on the balcony and lit a cigarette, which instantly caused my head to swell and flood with dizziness, a terrible idea. I put the cigarette out and drank more water. Just as I was pondering how to call and cancel all of my bank cards, where to get a new phone and the tedious, mundane task of obtaining a new driver's license, someone called over to me.

"Hey, kid!" It scared me at first. I never expected people to call out to me anymore. When you're always in your head, people yelling at you really shocks you awake. It was Randy, looking as sturdy and tanned as ever, running over to me with a white plastic Dollar Tree bag. I walked down the flight of stairs to meet him in the parking lot.

"Hey, are you okay?" I didn't know what else to say.

"Tony Padilla's kid dropped this off for you, around two this afternoon." He handed me the bag, searching my face for answers, attempting to piece together what had happened to me the night before. So Tony was his name. Pistol waving, red faced, huge Tony.

"Oh, uh, thank you, what is it?" I was lightheaded, squinting in the afternoon sun. I took the bag and opened it carelessly in front of him. A fountain of relief poured noticeably from my eyes as I dug into a plastic bag containing my wallet, dead phone, and jeans. I couldn't believe my luck; maybe I did have some good karma stored somewhere. A small note floated on the top, reading simply:

Hey Venn

Sorry about last night, I hope you'll forgive me.

Maybe I'll see you around when I'm a famous singer in Hollywood :)

~Sage

I laughed, feeling like I was reading a note from my little sister, which made me feel guilty and sick. I mentally blocked the vision of her and I kissing half naked on drugs in her living room and just sat with the appreciation of her returning my belongings. It really was a small town; she must have remembered me mentioning I was here. I tucked my wallet into my back pocket and threw my bag with my phone and trousers in the footwell of the Bronco.

I happily waved good evening to Randy as he returned to the motel office, then fired up the engine. I needed to drive, to think, to explore the area more. I hadn't really seen much of my surroundings coming in, and after last night I figured I should introduce myself a little. I wanted to make a good impression before barreling in like outside riff raff and getting myself into any more trouble.

I drove west, past the Cholla Cafe and Bar, shivering a little as I drove past, weird memories of drugs and skin and dogs floating to the forefront of my mind, then past the gas station and little antique shops and rusty old liquor shops with people hanging around out front, smoking. I listened to the radio, a local desert station which seemed to focus on mid-century artists, the station was a little fuzzy coming through my speakers, which only added to the ambience of driving through the desert during sunset.

After about ten miles of straight highway and small inclines and declines, I noticed another cafe, a little diner to the right of me, so I pulled in. An old sign flashed 'Hi-Desert Diner - Open 24 Hours' proudly in yellow and black font. It looked moderately busy. Again, with families, road trippers and truckers looking for some reprieve from the long, lonely expanse of road. I parked the Bronco and headed inside, hungry for food and distraction, still feeling a little sick from lack of food, water and the dry heat.

"Table for one?" the waitress asked me, looking me up and down, smiling through her auburn-colored lipstick.

I nodded and followed her to a window booth. She handed me a menu flatly and left, returning with a large glass of iced water. I drank it quickly, feeling the cold liquid work its way through my starving body.

"Do you want to order, or do you need a few minutes?" she said.

"I'll just have a grilled cheese, with fries, please," I asked politely.

"Sure thing. Anything to drink?" She scribbled my order onto a small paper pad.

"Water is good, thank you." She took my menu and walked away.

I don't know why I was ordering Vivienne's normal diner fare. I was beginning to recognize a pattern of desensiti-
zation tactics, without realizing it, and was allowing myself to
face small things I'd ruthlessly avoided and denied, to avoid
the pain of missing her.

I thought of the last grilled cheese she had ordered
with me. We were in the mountains, a small lumberjack style
place serving blue plate specials and no-frills, all-American
diner food. She avoided looking me in the eyes, after another
discussion about jobs that had fallen through, and her general airiness and lack of direction. She sat across from me, not
next to me, quietly chewing her bright orange rubbery grilled
cheese and solemnly dipping her shoelace fries into ketchup,
chewing slowly, looking into space. I stared at her, searching
for my bright, excited lover, seeing instead a sad, lonesome
child in her place.

Today, I sat and ate my food slowly, quietly. I felt instantly better on a biological level, my body happily accepting any
form of nutrition, and my rich headache started to slow to
a gentle, even pulsing. I looked around at the people dining,
some laughing and some eating alone, always wondering
where they were going, if they were happy, if they were
trapped.

I ate a handful of oily fries before I felt uncomfortably
full and decided to get the rest to go. After declining dessert
and paying the bill, I headed back out to the Bronco, not
exactly sure what to do next. I noticed a small bar across the
highway. What the hell, I thought, conveniently forgetting my

past mistakes in favor of a quick buzz. I've got nothing else to do, no healthier alternatives that appeal to me. So, I placed my congealed leftovers on the passenger seat and crossed the empty black road to the other side, telling myself in absolute, certain terms, do not go home with anyone tonight.

Upon entering the minimally lit, simple bar, I surveyed the scene. A few people were playing pool in the back, knocking the balls over the soft green surface. A few turned to look at me, giving me that familiar 'you're not from around here' stare, before returning to their drinks or conversations. Fleetwood Mac played in the background, humming through the worn speakers.

I sat on the stool in front of the bar and ordered a cheap whiskey on ice. I wondered how long I was going to self-medicate, drinking my discomfort away, avoiding the raw feeling of anguish. Was I becoming a full-blown alcoholic, or was this widely accepted as common practice when you're mourning and heartbroken? Surely all those sad songs, poems, lyrics and paintings about loss and heartache commingled with a mind-altering substance or two.

I was thinking about this, the loss of a partner, the pain of separation and grief, deep in my mind, zoning out, still holding my drink.

"You okay there, honey? You look a little sad," a sweet, elderly voice said to my side. I looked over to see a short woman, nearly my mother's age, with blonde and gray hair holding a light beer. She had kind, soft blue eyes, looking at me worriedly, as if I was one of her children.

"Hi," I said, still surprised she had spoken to me, I must have really looked like shit. I rubbed my eyes, as if it would shift the growing bags beneath them. "Yeah, I'm okay, I've just got a lot on my mind, I guess."

"Looks like it, you're really starin' into space over there. What's weighin' on you, sweetie? Girl trouble?" She smiled a little bit.

"Hah, yeah, something like that," I said, looking down despondently.

"Well, let me tell you something, people come and go. The person you've gotta love first is yourself. I know that's not easy to hear, but listen to an old, wise broad, love your-self first, honey, the rest will come later." She patted my back, before returning to her beer and taking a small drink.

"What about you, what makes you happy?" I asked her, unsure as to where this raw curiosity came from. It was nice to feel someone else's pain, someone else's darkness.

"Same as you. I lost my husband a little while ago, Mateo. We'd been together, gosh, almost forty-five years. He died of a stroke, right in front of me. Now all I have is my son, and my cats." My eyes widened. I was looking at a ver-sion of myself, only inside a different, older body. She must have recognized mourning as soon as I walked in. "I'm Ivy, nice to meet ya." She stretched out her hand, a small gold wedding ring with a little diamond still on her finger, a little tight.

"Venn, nice to meet you, Ivy." I smiled back. I felt like she was my guardian angel, sent to tell me something important.

"What brings you to the desert?" she probed.

"Nothing, I just wanted to be in the middle of nowhere, you know, to get my mind off of things."

"Good place to do it." She laughed, taking another swig of her beer.

"How do you do it? I mean, how long has it taken you to move on?" I asked, hanging on for her answer, hoping she didn't tell me something I wasn't ready to hear.

"I don't think you ever really move on from love. I think it kinda changes form or moves on to something else. If someone comes along and changes you, you're unlikely to forget them, no matter how long they stayed around for. Do you believe in reincarnation? Past lives and all of that?" She raised her eyebrows, knowing she was now in unfamiliar territory.

"I don't know, maybe. I definitely feel like it's possible. I think, sometimes, feelings can't be denied," I said honestly.

"Well, I believe in 'em. When I met Mateo it was like we'd known each other forever, even before this life. We never felt uncomfortable around each other." She looked down in silence.

"What's the secret?" I asked, trying to occupy her.

"To what?"

"To a happy marriage, a happy relationship." I wanted to heed her advice, I wanted to know.

"There is no secret. You gotta respect each other, you gotta compromise. You have to learn to laugh, be patient, not turn your back on them when they're in trouble. No one is perfect, honey. Youth wears off, sex wears off, and all you've got left is each other. You've got to love them for who they are, not who they ain't." When she looked into my eyes, she really did remind me of my mother.

"You're right, Ivy. That's some of the best advice I've ever heard. God, you're like a monk, a monk who drinks light beer and lives in the desert." We both laughed.

We sat talking, wise Ivy and I, until well past 1 am. We talked about everything, from where she grew up (Redding) to how she met Mateo (working for a railroad line) and their subsequent love and marriage, resulting in a son, David, who worked for the same railroad line his father had worked for and was now happily married with two young daughters. Ivy continued to live in the house she and Mateo had purchased in the desert after they retired, and even though she lived there alone, she felt content, felt she was at home. We talked about my family and my job, then we spoke about Vivienne. We made each other laugh and for the first time in a long time I felt like I had met someone who truly understood me.

I decided, for the first time in months, not to get totally drunk. I knew I had to drive home, and I didn't want to wind up in a small-town jail after this enlightening conversation. I bid sweet Ivy adieu and thanked her for her pleasant company, promising I'd come to visit her again someday, before asking her to look me up if she was ever in LA. She patted me on the back and wished me well in my journey to the unknown. I paid for her drinks and headed back to the motel, into the desert night, processing and replaying our conversation.

As I drove, I thought about what made a relationship successful. Truly successful, not delusionally successful. Were people brought together by circumstance or chance? Did true love ever transcend social status, background, financial situations, vast differences? Or did we just kid ourselves, so frightened by loneliness that we settle for anyone who keeps us from sitting with the pain of being on our own? I enjoyed being alone, having time to breathe and to think, left to my own devices. At least I had, before Vivienne. Now, for the first time in years, as I drove that desolate road back to my rented motel room, I realized that I felt lonely. Not just lonely in her absence, but lonely in my being. I needed someone to talk to, to confide in, I needed to be held. Only the thought of a stranger holding me, anyone that wasn't her, made me feel sick.

Maybe I should see a doctor, get some sleep or even depression medication. Maybe I should see a therapist. Then perhaps I would have a sounding board and some rational, objective solutions to choose from before making any life altering decisions. But those options all seemed so hollow to me, nothing sounded like it would work, would remedy the emptiness I felt without her, and I knew it.

I pulled slowly into the Cactus Corral and noticed another car in the parking lot, a small white hatchback type. Who else had arrived while I was out? As I walked back to my room with my cold leftovers, I heard people laughing. A playful, high-pitched laugh coming from the pool. A young couple, half naked and bronzed, laughed and taunted each other within the bright lights of the inner kidney bean, teasing and splashing water onto one another's skin in a careless manner. My body and heart ached listening to them. I wanted to hate them, but I could only exhale, remembering how I felt when Vivienne and I were in their position. I mentally wished them the best, fretting about the downfall and stark reality that emerges from these once-carefree moments of infatuation.

I shook my head and let myself into the room, tossing my food into the mini fridge and stripping off my underwear, before climbing into bed. I thought about Ivy, I thought about Will and Agnes, I thought about her cold body in the mountains, rotting. I turned on old black and white films and drifted off to sleep sometime around 3 am, still holding my ribs in place.

18. Vivienne

Vivienne May Van Valkenburg was born on a sweltering summer day in June, in upstate New York. Her mother attended Oneonta University before accepting a job to teach in the Theology department in Columbia while she completed her PhD. Her father studied business at Columbia University, and they met serendipitously when they bumped into each other in the street, him nearly knocking her mother onto the sidewalk in her heels. Her father repeatedly apologized and insisted he make it up to her by buying her a coffee in a nearby cafe. Her mother would say later that he had planned to bump into her when he noticed her down the street approaching him, so he could ask her out on a date, but he would deny it, claiming it was 'fate.' Her mother and father were initially liberal, artistic and politically active, before making serious money, before sheltering themselves within the confines of their conservatively myopic peers, before they lost their love for each other.

A year after their fateful meeting they were married and

her mother was pregnant with Vivienne's sister, Leigh, before having Vivienne seventeen months later. Her mother was back to work six weeks after she was born, leaving the two sisters in childcare and with their grandmother.

They lived in the outer suburbs of New York until she was five, relocating to Berkeley, California for her mother's career. Her father continued to trade in stocks remotely and travel often across the globe for his work, never attending his daughters' school plays or sports games. Vivienne and her sister attended a private Catholic school until she was fifteen, with Vivienne getting kicked out twice. Once for bringing a pack of cigarettes to school and making her friends all smoke one, and the other for bringing a Playboy magazine she had stolen from her father's closet, much to the dismay and embarrassment of her parents, who couldn't be bothered to scold their daughter for her thoughtless, attention-seeking antics.

Vivienne was left alone often, both of her parents working late or holed up in their offices. She allowed herself to explore the surrounding neighborhoods, to get lost, to daydream and spy on her neighbors with binoculars. She questioned everything, from creationism to the legal system—again, to the dismay of her parents and educators, who pushed her to tow a more traditionally conservative line.

She did the opposite. She fought with her former teachers about God and the teachings of religion, the cracks and contradictions written in the bible, but she continued to pray and believe in some sort of God. She studied art and science

and blew off mathematics and attending local church services. She first tried smoking weed at thirteen and experimented
with almost every other drug by the time she turned eighteen. She made out with her girlfriends and dressed minimally, expressively proud of her body. She experienced many
suitors and had even more crushes, constantly charming and
flirting her way through life. She loved the attention but also
desperately needed alone time, or she began to itch and lash
out at those closest to her.

She graduated high school, to the surprise of everyone around her, before taking a year off to travel around
the states in her little used car, to 'find herself,' she had told
her father. She worked every minimum wage job under the
sun, from waitressing to customer call centers to clothing
retail, doing small stints in local community colleges before
eventually dropping out, citing emphatically that traditional
education wasn't for everyone. Avoiding the long lectures,
arguments and disappointment showered upon her monthly
by her family.

She relocated to Hollywood to get away from the
academic world and her family, to feel what it was like to
be totally on her own, working two and three jobs at once,
dating various shades of losers, drug-addled guys who took
all of her earnings and rinsed her kind naivety. Finally, she
met her successful, spineless ex and moved in with him. The
ex her family had loved, the one they thought would save her
from her troubled past.

By the time we met at that horrible film premier, I could

sense she was still in the process of healing, still angry. We were both similar in our desire to be surrounded by equal parts company and solitary confinement, as well as feeding off our discomfort and mutual pain. I didn't have anywhere near as much anger or pain as Vivienne had, she always had more restlessness, more longing, but we recognized a certain kind emptiness in each other, and knew we could potentially help to heal each other, even if it was in some kind of fucked up, diagonal way.

It was in the second year after moving in together I noticed how hurt Vivienne really was. When the initial lust and constant pawing of one another wore down, when real life crept in and money, jobs, and paying the bills took precedence over hot sex and carefree road trips. I would catch her crying alone in the tub, relentlessly, scratching her arms until they bled and saying she wanted to leave this earth, that it was too full of pain, too full of suffering. Everything weighed on her mind. Every painful thing from the welfare of animals to global water drought, poverty and lack of sexual education and accessible healthcare.

She would lock herself in our bedroom and cry, or stare out of the window, vacantly, refusing to eat or drink until she nearly fainted and I had to almost force her to consume something. This regular occurrence made it extremely difficult for me to know the best approach to help her. So, I tried many; I coddled, I left her alone, I cried with her, I assured her she was safe and that I wouldn't leave her, I offered to pay for a volunteer program abroad. Occasionally this method worked, but other times it didn't, and I was left with my head in my hands, unsure how to solve her enduring sadness.

She took her anger for her parents out on me, blaming me for living a normal, supported life with my family, who had loved me without pushing me. A family whom I ate dinner with and conversed with often, devoid of drama or any major issues. She was fiercely jealous of functional family relationships and begged me to play that role in her life.

And I tried. I tried to be her mother, her father, her sister, her friend, her mentor, her tutor, her lover all at once. It was completely fucking exhausting. I was constantly shifting roles to be what she needed at that moment, in addition to earning most of our finances and keeping everything flowing seamlessly. Some days she would sleep until 3 pm, others she would spring out of bed and work a full shift, coming home to paint and cook and dance with me.

I couldn't tell if my life was easier or less complicated before her, but I knew I never wanted to be without her again. It's not that I felt sorry for her or needed to save her; she would have slapped me for even having the thought. I knew Vivienne was strong, she was just wounded, and she loved me, as a crutch or as a partner or both, and I couldn't leave her on her own. For as long as she'd have me, I would love her.

No one wants to admit it when they're deeply in love and their relationship begins to dissolve. No one wants to admit that their partner is falling apart, or that they aren't doing enough to protect them, to make them happy. I lived delusionally within the valley of utter denial for another year, watching in pain as Vivienne locked herself mentally and physically further and further away from me. The impromptu dancing in the kitchen died, the cooking broke down to eating lousy takeout or cooking for ourselves at different times, the sex dwindled to nothing. Vivienne even pushed me off violently when I attempted to kiss her.

Her sadness swelled and crested, and there was nothing I could do to remedy it. If I even brought up medication or therapy, she would argue with me, citing sheer ignorance on my part, saying I never really cared or understood her to begin with. Much to my upset and frustration. I was trapped in a chokehold of our own creation. I couldn't leave her, she was the most exhilarating and complex person I had ever met, and I knew finding anyone even close to her would be nearly impossible.

I also knew I couldn't go on like this for much longer, fearing her mood toward me day in and day out, wondering what I would come home to, if she would even be there, if she would be gone, if she would be dead.

19. Vivienne

I woke up at 11 am. The familiar desert sun peered through the dark curtains of the motel, greeting me cheerfully as the harsh sun often does, oblivious to its own power. I could hear the young couple from the pool getting into their vehicle, probably dressed in sun hats and tropical fabrics, heading off to brunch before exploring the many desert activities together.

I stretched and felt my body, running my hands over my stomach and bony rib cage. My head wasn't throbbing, I didn't feel too hungover, considering. For the first time in what felt like forever I didn't wake up feeling like total shit. Was this progress? Is the fog lifting? I shook off the thought and washed my face, before putting on a shirt and my trusty old jeans and combing my hair with a little cold tap water. Looking into the mirror, I still looked ragged, but I was starting to see fragments of myself again, even if they were blurry and abstract. I could see familiar attributes that recognized me back. I didn't want to look too long.

I smoked a cigarette outside, watching the various cars pass the motel and admiring the expanse of the desert and mountains in the daylight, feeling the heat creep up my clothing and wrap around my skin like a blanket. I stubbed out my cigarette and threw the butt away before firing up the Bronco and heading east.

I stopped in another small, all-day breakfast diner, sitting alone against the window as I'd grown so accustomed to, ordering two scrambled eggs and a coffee. I even read the newspaper, a new yet familiar concept to me. I hadn't noticed or cared about what was happening in the world for almost two years. All I was concerned about was my own selfish needs, and the absence of Vivienne. I had forgotten how relaxing it was to sit and read something, the news, the beautiful and horrible and interesting facts displayed before me, causing me to smile and squint and frown and absorb what I was reading.

I finished three cups of black coffee and, miraculously, finished most of my scrambled eggs as well, before tipping my waiter and climbing back into the Bronco, driving due east, onto the next unknown adventure of the day.

I had seen a sign for a modern art museum on my route in from LA, so I decided to find it on the map and drive over to have a look. I hadn't been to a museum since I'd lost Vivienne, so I figured this would be another painful test of the system. I genuinely missed looking at art, even accompanied with those painful reminders, and I wanted to see what the desert museum had to offer.

I pulled into the modest parking lot, admiring the curved, mid-century architecture of the building as I walked to the office and purchased a ticket for one from a kind man who looked as tired and old as the desert itself. I meandered through the Alice Neel and Agnes Pelton exhibitions, oil portraits of humans, beautifully harsh landscapes, and incredibly personal portrayals, immortalized in paint and mixed media.

I was caught off guard by the sudden realization that I was truly enjoying dissecting and analyzing this art alone. I didn't need to discuss or argue about its context or allegorical meaning with anyone. I was enjoying being completely by myself, taking my time without rushing on to the next exhibit, lingering from piece to piece, examining and contemplating the individuality and tone of the art, absorbing their own special, subjective meaning to me and letting it stain my psyche.

When I left, I felt lighter, full. Not just of yellow eggs, but of raw, artistic beauty. I had stepped outside of myself and allowed myself to be bound by something other than my own thoughts and mistakes. I was feeling extremely grateful for public museums and natural spaces, for art in general, remembering that all humans were just here trying to understand their purpose in the limited time we were allotted.

I passed a United States Postal Service and decided to purchase some paper and a pen. I sat outside of the office on a worn, wooden bench and wrote letters. I wrote to everyone I could think of. I wrote to my brother in New York, telling him I was sorry for what an asshole I had been these last few years, how I missed him and our former closeness, and that I wanted to eventually visit him on the east coast. I wrote to my parents, telling my father I would come and visit, I promised, telling him how much I missed him, how much I missed my mother and the memories and ease of my childhood.

I wrote to Will and Agnes, thanking them for their constant support and dedication to our friendship, even though I had been a flimsy, arrogant and pathetic friend for over a year and a half. I wrote that I admired their love, their mutual understanding of one another, and how I would always value them as individuals. I told them I would see them when I was back in town, and to try my hardest not to be such a sad mop around them. I finished each of my letters with 'Sincerely, Venn.'

Lastly, I wrote to Vivienne. Five blue lined pages of words I could never say to her, words I'd forgotten in anger, words I never thought she would hear even if I had said them aloud. I wrote how incredibly sorry I was, how much I'd truly loved her and still did. How committed to her I was and feared I always would be, even now that she was gone. I included that perhaps, even surprising me, we were in many ways unhealthy for one another, causing each other unnecessary pain within the veil of true love. I felt my arms go cold and eyes well up as I penned these words to her, feeling every emotion hit me at once. Finally, I finished my thoughts, before signing:

With love forever,
Venn.

I put my letters into their envelopes and addressed them to their various destinations, carefully filling out the names in all caps. I licked and sealed the envelopes, placing a neat American flag stamp in the right-hand corner of each one before dropping them into the metal mailbox to be delivered. All except Vivienne's, of course. I folded her letter and placed it into my jeans pocket. Perhaps I just needed to write everything down, to let my thoughts pour out, to let myself say what I was thinking out loud. I had kept my feelings so tight and close to my chest, not letting anyone into our sacred little world. Today, I let the pen and paper in, and it felt healthy, like I could maybe let a little more of her go.

I continued driving with no plan and nowhere in particular to go, which felt nice, passing oddities, art and old burned-out car wrecks half buried and swallowed, sinking into the sand. I passed a small rock and crystal shop, which I stopped into. I had always found geology fascinating. The way sediment and earth and pressure, along with minerals and biological chemistry, created these beautiful, often rare and totally unique formations. A small-statured woman with long dreadlocks and geometric tattoos was working in the shop, listening to meditative music. She glided over in her thin sandals to speak to me as I was admiring the vast array of stones and crystals, knowing nothing about their properties and healing powers.

"Looking for anything specific?" she asked in an upbeat voice.

"I don't think so. I was just curious about all of the

rocks," I said, dully.

"These are crystals, they are very powerful," she corrected me, looking slightly offended that I'd referred to them as mere rocks.

"Oh, I see. So, which one heals broken hearts?" I asked, half-jokingly, not expecting her to answer.

"You will definitely want the rose quartz. This harnesses a powerful healing energy. It has a direct line to the heart chakra, perfect for healing the wounded heart," she said emphatically. I noticed she was covered in jewelry containing different metal-wrapped crystals.

I looked at the dusty pink chunk of raw mineral, cocking my head to the side curiously, perhaps skeptically. I wondered if a small crystal could actually heal a broken soul or resuscitate a dead heart. The price tag said five dollars each, so I picked one up and purchased it from the kind crystal woman.

"I hope this helps you, be well," she said in a soothing, peaceful voice as I turned to leave, her bright teeth against her tan skin glistening toward me.

"I hope it does too, thanks," I said, not totally convinced, but hopeful. At this point I was willing to try anything before I drank and smoked myself to death.

The day rolled into evening, softening into darkness again. In the desert, every sunset is a masterpiece. The vermilions fade to crimson and bright screaming oranges, settling down to indigos and cotton candy blues, before a blanket of dark slate sucks up the sky and the stars begin to peek out from their hiding spots. I decided to head back to the motel, stopping at a small grocery store to buy a sandwich, a bottle of whiskey and some cigarettes on the way.

I smoked with my arm out of the window, letting my fingers flow up and down through the warm desert wind as children do when they're bored on family road trips. It was such an incredibly barren place, yet I felt more alive than I had in years. This vast wasteland was weaving in and opening something unfamiliar inside of me, some kind of cathartic catalyst. I wasn't trapped in such a small cage anymore, no longer constricted by considerable mental affliction and daily reminders of her. Maybe you need to feel vast emptiness in order to truly understand the concept of fullness.

I arrived back at the Cactus Corral feeling introspective and good. I'd had a purgative and pensive day, and I felt tired, in a good way for once, without the fog of substances. The couple's car was still gone—they were probably off enjoying a fabulous candlelit meal—and I seemed to be the only person there. Even Randy wasn't around. I decided to go swimming. I hadn't packed anything to swim in, so I went down in my boxers, using the little cactus towel from my bathroom. I brought my cigarettes and some water and set them down with my towel, leaving my motel room door open so I could hear the faint radio music drifting down to the pool area.

I dove arms first into the neon pool and let my body float in the womb-like abyss of the body-temperature water. I turned and twisted like a baby in the stomach of its mother and closed my eyes, thinking of absolutely nothing. Not Vivienne, not my normal distractions, my heaviness. I floated and felt nothing, and it was exactly what I needed.

After an hour of floating in the pool alone, I moved on to the hot tub, letting the entirety of my body relax against the pounding jets. I lit a cigarette and stared at the sky. The view still astounded me, and I understood now why people live in the desert despite its faults and harsh climate. I watched for falling stars or satellites or UFOs and let my body absorb this feeling. I thought about my mother and brother and what my colleagues at work were doing while I was here under these stars.

I couldn't tell if I was losing my mind or finding it again. I was beginning to notice that I was mentally talking to myself, the way two friends would, occasionally making myself laugh or smile. I didn't know if that was normal, but I didn't really care. I didn't feel the need to call anyone and talk on the phone. I was enjoying my own company again, and I was okay with the fact that the way I sat with myself was unconventional.

Around 11 pm I went back to my room, prune-skinned, pale and quiet, reflecting over the subtleties of my day. I dried my thinning body off and crawled into bed like a hairy spider. I felt whimsical and, surprisingly, turned on, so I jacked off crudely to the thought of making love in the dark desert night to an unknown shape, imagining only moonlit glistening skin and illuminated rock. I didn't see her face, didn't feel her skin or smell her hair. I thought of no one in particular, releasing my fluids over my stomach and chest with a heavy gasp. I fell asleep covered in come with the desert radio on. I didn't hold my ribs together, crippled in pain. I didn't cry, and for once in a long time, I didn't dream of her beside me.

The next few days in the desert mirrored the days before. I woke up after a decent night's sleep, grateful the day had finally arrived, and I had made it through another long night. I washed my grimy face, stood bare chested in the sunlight, smoked a filthy cigarette, and contemplated my hollow existence on the motel balcony. Occasionally, I watched Randy walk from his office to the back of the motel and out of view. I considered my heavy heart, my pounding head, my scrambled egg future. I thought of her and of us, how we used to be and how we were toward the end, how I'd never thought I would be suddenly navigating a world where she no longer existed.

I'd drive the highways for miles, occasionally stopping in at various shops or local spots to let the engine cool down, drowsily exploring small handmade crafts, desert art antiques run by kind, leathery owners, or indigenous cactus gardens. I spent hours mulling along the stretches of road, taking my time, taking it all in, stopping to catch my breath and admire the beauty of the desert, thinking of everything and nothing.

I consumed small, greasy portions of food in local diners and spoke to the people working there, although they were occasionally too busy or short staffed to maintain a fluid conversation with me. In quieter times, they would talk to me out of sheer necessity to pass the hours before they were finally free to go home. Wherever that home was in the void of hills. Sometimes conversations developed into fascinating theories about the world, about the desert, about Hollywood, the good old simple days. Others were quick interactions they'd had a million times with a million other people. I'd chew my food slowly and look out of the window toward the sunny, tarred highway, never changing, wondering where everyone was heading, how unique it was to be in the same place at the same time, doing the same exact thing.

I explored the outer perimeters of the desert on foot, where the houses thin out and the veins of sandy roads lead to nowhere but more desert. I climbed soft ochre hills, hiked to the top of small, craggy mountains, strolled casually through spiky fields of cholla cactus and ancient Joshua trees. I considered the purpose of everything, their counterparts and functions, stopping to smell the various sagebrush and Mormon grass, picking up interesting, billion-year-old rocks and studying them before losing interest and laying them back down in their depressions, letting them bake in the sun.

I criticized myself and my former actions as I walked, kicking the sand and scoffing while recollecting certain memories. I shunned myself for my mistakes, my shortcomings, my flaws, but I tried to be easier on myself, easier than I had maybe been in the past, attempting to forgive myself. I told myself that I did the best I could with the situation. I tried to forgive Vivienne, too, for hurting me. For the endless nights I spent awake, worried about her safety, her mental wellbeing, for constantly giving her more attention than I could give myself, for her cruelly lashing out at me. For the callous words she spat towards me in her animosity. Words I may have believed at the time, but now I could see they weren't entirely true. Just an aftereffect of an emotionally charged conversation and an attempt to be hurtful toward me in the moment.

I thought about the good times, the most painful for me to think about. The seemingly infinite ocean of fluttering smiles, laughs, kisses, adventures and memories we shared when we were happiest together. When we fully trusted one another and felt it was us against the entire world, before the infection of doubt and reality spoiled and ruined our silk cocoon.

I thought of me, down on my knees against a rocky tidepool in late March, begging her to marry me against the windy night and slipping a small Edwardian ring on her finger, before falling into the sand. She had said yes, of course. She screamed in her exuberance and held me, and we felt that we would be together, fighting against all of the judgment and trials, all of the bullshit, until the end of our days.

These are the memories I avoid recounting in my scattered, broken mind. The ones that make me feel queasy and weak. These skin-bare memories, so raw and cutting that I nearly fall to my knees on the blanched earth and attempt to catch my breath, to force myself to take another step forward in my cramping and pain and the memories that make me cry.

How could something so pure, so enriching become so noxious? How did she suddenly mold and rot towards me, towards herself? What precisely was happening in her mind that differed from my own, and why couldn't she communicate her feelings with me? What was the exact day, the exact moment, the emancipation of self to eliminate her once attached body from mine? When was her mind made up, thoroughly, so absolute in her decision to follow through with what she did?

20. Vivienne

On my last evening in the desert, I decided to take myself out for dinner. A kind of ever-familiar solo date, where I would sit across from my former self and chat quietly within my thoughts. Only this time, I decided to treat myself to a full meal and possibly even a dessert, to bid a proper good-bye to my dry, cathartic, arid home for the week. A home I'd fallen somewhat in love with, despite its harsh exterior and a few questionable decisions on my part.

In fact, the harsh exterior was exactly why I had fallen in love with the desert. There was no false hope, no maybes, no obvious oasis. The desert was as honest a companion as I could possibly hope to find, the kind that told you without sugarcoating or skirting around the issue, that you are fucked up and need to look deeper into yourself to figure it out. The desert was my mirror, my cold slap in the face, my harsh reality, the seed of all things beautiful, of life and death. That same cruel, seemingly dead environment had begun to heal me in unexpected ways, even brought forth something new in me, some kind of recognition. A small, tentative tendril of hope, renewed faith in myself. A morsel of belief that life was indeed possible without her.

I decided to walk down to the Cholla Cafe. Of all the little desert diners and cafe eateries on offer I'd seen this week, this was the diner where my trip had begun, so I deemed it only fitting that I also ended my trip here. Despite the disaster with Sage and her father almost killing me, which now made me hang my head in embarrassment when I recalled it. Despite all of that, it was a wonderful little cafe. Full of charm, teeming with reality, no bullshit, no Disneyland theme, just real people living real lives, eating somewhat real food.

I dressed methodically while the old motel television played infomercials for hair loss dyes and 'revolutionary' knife sets in the background. The kind that reminds you of staying up too late in your childhood, flipping through the channels aimlessly, settling on a loop of infomercials just to be able to watch television, just to have some company in your insomnia. I thought of how many inventors sat in their offices, brainstorming these hopeful, million-dollar ideas, and how many succeeded.

I slid my jeans on and tied my trusty tennis shoes, the shoes that had led me out of the desert, literally. The shoes that walked me through museums and cactus gardens and crystal palaces. They were beat up, full of holes, and covered in dirt; they were my physical body depicted in footwear. I got up to look at myself in the mirror again, something I was beginning to grow more comfortable doing, even though I still looked like hell. I glanced at myself, studying my sunken, tired green eyes, my thin body, my oily quaff of hair. I searched hopefully for recognition from the parallel face, looking for myself again. I did look a bit more tanned, which I appreciated, even preferred, over the pale, floury tone my skin had taken on in the past few months due to the endless days of refusing to leave my apartment.

I saw pain, but within that sad, lonesome face I saw a tether of resilience. At least that's what I hoped it was. I felt and looked fucking tired, zeroing in on the huge bags under my eyes. I was tired. I was tired of feeling this way, tired of losing infinite hours to her and her memories and grieving for her, tired of not sleeping properly. I stared at my ragged face and body and felt like I wanted my life back, my intentions, my ambitions, my mind. I was tired of feeling indentured to a woman who was gone from my life forever.

I stopped looking at my gray face in the mirror before I became too analytical, too upset or worried, deciding instead to take some of my autonomy back and have a decent last night in the desert. This was my trip after all, why does she have to dictate everything I do, every emotion I feel, I wondered, angry at her ghost for trying to control me. I snatched my key and wallet swiftly from the table, opened the door and headed down the stairs, past Randy's office and the bright pool, down the quiet, desolate highway and toward the Cholla Cafe.

As I approached the brightly lit cafe, I noticed a familiar

car, a gold sedan parked out front of the Cholla Bar side. Beside the sedan, an older model Harley Davidson bike parked diagonally in the next space. It was a Tuesday evening; Western Wednesdays was tomorrow night. I shook my head as I entered the cafe, trying to use my hair to hide my face and keep a low profile, as if it would work. I could hear people laughing and talking in the bar, along with people practicing their musical instruments. Just find a booth and eat your meal, I thought, stay far away from the Cholla Bar.

I walked quickly to the furthest booth in the corner that I could find empty and sat down facing the road outside, slightly covering my face with the menu and feeling a bit sick that I had kissed and danced with a teenager. I remembered how great I felt, how happy I was, how liberating it all was, and how wrong it all turned out to be. Why can't I just find someone normal, someone good for me, someone who understands me, I—

"Any drinks, hun?" It was Pam again. Good, kind, constant Pam.

"Hi, how are you?" I said cheerfully, trying to get the image of Sage dancing topless out of my head, trying to look like an innocent diner customer and not a creep.

"I'm fine, business as usual. Drinks?" she said, undeterred by my pathetic charms.

"I'll take a 7Up, thanks," I mumbled. She thought I was a creep. The whole town probably knew by now.

She returned promptly with a soda and a striped plastic straw, setting them on the table beside my wrist. "Have you decided?" she asked, boredly raising her eyebrows, pen and pad ready to scribble my order down.

"I'll have the, uh, the buttermilk pancakes, please." I felt like I was about five years old, ordering breakfast on a Sunday with my folks.

"Half stack or full?"

"Half, please"

"Eggs?"

"Scrambled. Thanks." I handed her my menu and she flitted away again, hair bouncing lightly as she disappeared into the flurry of the kitchen.

I pursed my lips and crossed my legs beneath the metal table, glancing outside at the highway, watching the lonely cars driving quickly past the cafe and out of this small town, without taking any notice of its simple appeal. I wondered if I should load up the Bronco and drive until I couldn't recognize my surroundings anymore. To a place where I could begin entirely new, from scratch, without any recollection of this life, my old life, my life with Vivienne. Perhaps I could become a small vegetable farmer or one of those guys who carves bears using chainsaws and sits on their porch all day pondering the beauty and philosophies of life, instead of obsessing about the dead and buried past. Maybe I could force myself to be someone completely different. Maybe I could be alone for the rest of my life.

As I was musing about my potential new career and where I would inevitably live, a stack of fluffy, hot pancakes appeared before me, smelling of rich butter and vanilla.

"Anything else?" Pam asked, impatiently.

I smiled. "That's it, thank you."

She walked away without a word.

I looked at the stack of cakes in front of me, trying to remember how to be truly hungry, how to really enjoy food. I mechanically rubbed butter on top before ladling maple syrup from a dispenser, letting the liquid dissolve into the pancake sponge while I psyched myself up to eat a full meal.

I cut a small bite from the edge and let the salty sweetness coat my mouth. It hurt to chew. I hadn't chewed food properly in a while, more inhaled or swallowed carelessly for the past two years, so I chewed, and I tasted. I surprised myself by ordering pancakes, my childhood favorite, but as I glanced around at the highway, I felt a hint of emotion strike me, a tiny wave of happiness, a smile. I was eating, I could enjoy food, maybe truly enjoy food in my lifetime again. I continued stabbing pieces of soft cake and letting it sit in my mouth while I savored the texture and flavors, before moving onto my scrambled eggs, which again, to my surprise and relief, I finished nearly all of my plate.

I felt proud of myself, proud of this small but important accomplishment. As I sucked the rest of my soda through the straw and pushed my empty plate to the edge of the table, I welled up with a sense of relief, bloated with satiation, reminding myself that even the smallest fragments of growth relayed a larger truth. I could heal, I would heal. If I could eat again maybe I could date again, work again, sleep again, even love again.

"All done. Wow, you were hungry this time, eh?" Pam asked dryly, but in a kind voice. I let my paranoia about Sage fade.

"Yeah, yeah, I guess I was. It was really great, I'll miss this place," I said, feeling overwhelmed with the thought of returning to LA.

"I wouldn't miss it too much, there's nothin' but a whole lotta sand and dirt." Pam laughed, as if she was trying to comfort herself, as if she had tried to leave and always ended up back here, in this town, in this diner.

"Could I have a piece of cake? Maybe a chocolate cake if you have one, to go?" I asked, surprising myself again.

"Sure thing, I'll get it wrapped up for you." She walked toward the refrigerated section that housed a massive array of baked delights, gingerly cutting a slice of cake and placing it into a small white container.

I had always carried a massive sweet tooth in my life before, especially on vacation. I could easily pack away cake, donuts, cookies and chocolate bars in one sitting, if you let me. I hadn't been able to enjoy baked goods since I lost Vivienne, but something was returning. I knew that now. More importantly, I felt that now, so I ordered the damn chocolate cake. For me, and only me.

"Well, have a safe trip home, kiddo. Maybe we'll see you again out this way sometime." Pam smiled, reminding me of my mother as she placed the check on the table, along with my wrapped-up piece of cake.

"I'll come back, I promise." I smiled up at her and she

tapped the table with her brightly painted nails before walking away to attend to a small family. I guess that's how they
say goodbye in the desert.

I left her a twenty-dollar tip and placed it under the
sugar jar. I waved goodbye on my way out, feeling full and
introspective, yet emotionally lighter, as if parts of myself
were warming and beginning to grow back, like seedlings in
the spring or a severed starfish arm.

As I headed out, I saw Sage smoking with her bandmate
outside. Fuck. Of course she was outside the exact moment
I'm leaving. Why does this always happen to me? I grabbed
a local paper from the metal stand and put my head down as
I took a sharp right and walked swiftly north back to my motel. I thought I was out of the woods, that she hadn't noticed
my escape, when suddenly a sound rippled in my ears.

"Bye, Venn!" I heard her scream from behind me, followed by a loud giggle.

I ignored it, picking up pace to a near jog until I reached
the motel's parking lot. With just my car and Randy's car in
the parking bays, I felt like I was really returning home. But
I wasn't ready to call it a night just yet. I decided to put my
cake in the mini fridge in my room to be consumed later,
while I listened to the radio or watched tacky infomercials. I
headed back down the stairs and towards the highway again,
this time heading the other direction toward the small bar
across the street. I could hear Sage and her friend laughing
down the road. God, it really was a small town.

I let myself into the small bar and sat down on a stool

beside an older man, surveying the familiar bar scene. It was only 8 pm, but the bar was already pretty crowded. I guess there isn't much else to do in the desert than drink and socialize on a Tuesday evening.

I ordered a whiskey and water and sat watching people play darts and sing karaoke. They all possessed a familiar look, an air of golden, hardy resilience and strength, dotted with just a bit of loneliness or pain. They reminded me of John Wayne, the way he hid his feelings in favor of playing a tough role.

I thought about how I must have looked to them, in my dirty jeans and ratty tennis shoes and sallow skin. They knew an outsider instantly, but they were probably once outsiders too, or are outsiders just by living here. So, in a way we were all outsiders, all running from something, healing for something. I didn't want to go home at all. I wanted to live on the outside.

"What are you drinkin'?" a deep voice to my right asked me, lifting me out of my fantasies of becoming a dried leather bag of skin living out my days in the desert.

"It's whiskey, I don't know what kind, he didn't tell me," I admitted. They don't appreciate showoffs here, anyway.

"Ha, that'll be the cheapest rocket fuel they got, then. You look like you don't come to dives much." He looked at my clothes, then at my hair, smiling crookedly through dry, chapped lips.

"I actually prefer them, much more honest." It was true.

"Well, a bar's a bar, I guess. As long as they have cold

beer and stay open late, I don't really care what it is." He laughed as he drank his Corona with a lime in it.

"I'm Venn, nice to meet you." I held my hand out to him.

"Charlie, nice to meet you, Ben." I didn't correct him.

Charlie looked about sixty-five, maybe younger. I couldn't truly tell age with desert folk; everyone was so rugged and tanned. He had dark hair with gray wavy streaks gliding through it beneath a trucker hat. He was wearing a short sleeved, cotton plaid shirt and a pair of light blue, worn in Levi jeans.

"How long have you lived out here, Charlie?" My conversational skills were improving. I was interested in talking to this man instead of just pretending, playing along. Another small seed of hope.

"Only about four years. I moved out here from Wyoming. I had a little ranch there, cattle mostly. What about you, how long you been out here?"

"I just came to visit, to get away from things for a while, work, my relationship..."

"Oh, your old lady, huh? I bet she's missing you now!" He laughed, spitting beer particles on the bar.

"No, she's gone. She's been gone for a while, I just needed to get away from it all."

"Oh, shit, I'm sorry, man, I didn't mean to laugh." He looked at the floor, embarrassed.

"It's okay, don't worry about it. I mean, I'm still trying to figure out how to, you know, move on from it all. I keep trying to speed up the process, but it doesn't seem to be working." I took a sip of my whiskey, looking forward glumly.

"Can't speed up grief, man. It takes as long as it's going to take." He looked down at his bottle, morose, and suddenly the mood felt very bleak between us. Charlie became quiet, almost as if he was holding back tears of his own haunting memories. I didn't know if I should break the silence, so I sat still, looking down at the floor, unsure what to say.

"I lost my son a few years ago. Suicide. Shot himself in the field behind our house," Charlie said haggardly, choking on his words. "He was gay, but he never told us, he wrote it in his suicide note. Felt like he couldn't be himself in this world, not where we were anyway. After he was gone, my wife and I split up, just couldn't take it anymore. We sold the house, and I moved out here. Don't know where she went, we don't talk much anymore. Still miss him every day, still punish myself for not knowing, not asking more, for, you know, being a bad father. He was all I had. I'd do anything to bring him back." He drank his beer, pushing his lips together, looking at the floor.

I realized we were two humans sitting together, medicating in our pain, over two very different relationships over two different periods in time, but emulating the same formula. Grieving the loss of people we loved, people we would always love, and people we would never get back. I was beginning to detect a familiar pattern in the desert, a pattern of pain, of loss, of remorse. I knew Charlie's pain was far different than my own, and I felt naked in my selfishness. We sat quietly together, drinking the last of our drinks in silence, reflecting on both of our lost relationships vacantly, the way your eyes lose color when you discuss effectively permanent loss and fall back into your thoughts and memories.

"Well, shit, how about another round?" Charlie finally said, slapping the bar in an attempt to rattle himself from his loss.

"Sure, let's do it." I smiled at him, encouragingly.

I was more than happy to sit here and drown with a fellow sufferer. After all, finding people who share a similar affliction at the same time is rare, and I wanted to hold on to this fleeting companion for as long as I could.

So, we got two, then three more rounds, and we talked. He asked about Vivienne and my family, and I told him. I asked about his son, and he told me. We celebrated the mutual understanding of one another's unique sadness and talked about how losing friends and loved ones in your grief is just further collateral damage, par for the course, an expected fallout of losing part of yourself.

Charlie told me about his new life in the desert, rigging and setting up solar panels and connecting satellite dishes for local cable networks. He told me he didn't miss raising cows, too many problems with livestock, but he missed the ranch, the seasons, the snow on the mountains and the forest. When I asked why he didn't go back he said he couldn't face it, not yet at least. The desert was to him what it was to me, a reminder of death and decay and survival in its most bare and brutal form. Forcing people to bleach their sorrows in the constant sunshine and heat.

After another round of drinks and discussing everything from the Vietnam war to living off the grid, pesticides in farming and various conspiracy theories, I asked Charlie if he would ever actively look for love again, wondering if his response would mirror my own.

"I already lost the love of my life," he said, frowning.

So, I'm fucked, I thought.

"But that being said, I wouldn't mind having someone around to keep warm at night, to laugh with. There's always a possibility." He smiled at me, in a fatherly way.

"Do you think it's possible, finding love again, or is it just companionship?" I asked nervously.

"Of course, anything is possible, man. Love is always possible if you're open to it. If you can get past your bullshit and open up to someone. Anything is possible." He laughed heartily, which made me laugh, and we knocked our glasses together, for the possibility of love again, before swallowing another harsh shot of cheap whiskey, feeling it burn all the way down.

I paid my bar tab and bid Charlie goodbye with a big hug, thanking him for making my last night in the desert a special one, and for his words of wisdom and honesty. I wished him luck on his path, wherever that led him, and told him I hoped the loss of his son became a little bit easier to bear. He shook my hand and told me to have a safe trip back.

As I left, I thought about coincidences and chance, two ideas I never put much stock into before now. What were the chances I would sit next to a man going through a similar experience to what I was feeling at the same time? I shook my head and laughed drunkenly at the coincidence, before crossing the empty black road to the Cactus Corral Motel and sitting down on the curb beside the Bronco, thinking about everything. The week, the drugs, the food, the driving, the desert. I felt happily drunk and bitterly confused, slightly sick, both mentally and physically, at the thought of returning home.

I pushed myself up and sloppily unlocked the back door of the Bronco, causing the overhead light to turn on, making me squint and cover my eyes. It was late, close to 2 am, and the roads were tranquil, quiet. The small shops and cafes were dark. Only the bar had more than two cars parked in its driveway. I looked back to the seat of the Bronco at the box, her box, the box with our most favorite souvenirs and special pictures in it, and I sighed. I reached in and pulled the box toward me, catching a glimpse of the dark tops of our heads together on one of our trips somewhere. I didn't look, it was too painful. I held the box in one hand and closed the door with my left elbow, walking down the road, past the motel, into the deep abyss of the desert.

I walked for what felt like a mile or two along the highway with no cars or streetlamps to guide me, walking drunkenly on the side of the road, dusted with desert sand and silence, holding a box. Finally, I turned off to a dirt side road and followed it by moonlight until I reached a clearing. The mountains lit up along the ridges looked like white whales' teeth, covered in spots of dark algae. I dropped to my knees and began to dig a hole with my hands, scooping out still-warm sand and tossing it to the side.

I looked at the box in the moonlight. The menacing, horrendously painful square of memories that held the history of my heart for the last few years, the contents of which could kill me if I let them. I poured the contents of the box into the hole and ripped the cardboard into little pieces, covering the mound with tiny black squares before removing my lighter from my pocket and flicking the flame on the edge of the card.

As it started to burn, it illuminated parts of the box I didn't want to see. Her face, her handwriting, her gifts to me. Before long, I had a small bonfire of wood and paper and photographs, curling and squirming beneath the moonlight and heating my forehead. I stared into the flames remorsefully. I was on my knees, drunk, full of sadness, but I couldn't cry. I didn't want to cry over her anymore. I wanted to exorcise Vivienne from my life, to be rid of her constant and agonizingly tight grip on me. I didn't want to forget her, but I wanted to move on from her. I watched the pile burn until it was almost reduced to ash, then I reached into my pocket and retrieved the letter I had written to her earlier in the week, pausing before tossing it into the fire.

"Goodbye, Vivienne," I said quietly as I watched the flames engulf the five-page letter I'd penned, pouring my soul onto paper with all its hurt and confusion and emptiness. Finally, I tossed the rose quartz on top of the ashes and buried it all beneath the ground, kicking mounds of sand and rock back into the pile, covering it up, until there was nothing left but smooth sand and pale moonlight.

I felt a sense of draining, a release of some kind of emotion, even if I couldn't quite identify it yet. Something felt calmer, looser, a bit more relaxed. I exhaled, feeling the discomfort of wanting her and succumbing to letting her go.

I walked back to the motel along the highway, occasionally looking up at the stars and smiling. I thought of Charlie, Ivy, of Sage, of all the people I'd met and connected with here, those who reminded me that human connection is still accessible if you allow yourself to let others in.

I walked past the sleeping Bronco, jumping up the stairs back to my room, the familiar and comforting stench of stale cigarette smoke and synthetic flowers hitting my olfactory senses upon opening the door. I was going to really miss this place. I sat on the edge of the bed and lit a cigarette, dragging the ashtray over from the side table onto my lap. I smoked slowly in silence, listening to the soft buzzing of the AC units and electricity around me. As I smoked, feeling uncomfortably serene, I remembered with drunken delight that I had a piece of chocolate cake in the fridge, a revelation that made me laugh like a madman.

Cigarette still dangling between my lips, I opened the little mini fridge to discover my chilled chocolate treasure, ready and waiting for me. A small white Styrofoam box with a napkin and plastic fork atop it. I opened the clamshell lid to reveal my saccharine lover for the evening, my decadent chocolate cake, and took a bite. It was incredibly sweet, fudgy, with sugar crystals crunching between my molars and sending an electric jolt through my veins.

I felt a sense of happiness, of pure joy. The thought alone caused me to panic. Was I supposed to be happy, joyful? I sat on the floor and ate my cake and smiled to myself, about absolutely nothing in particular, before falling into my decorated bed, covered in chocolate cake crumbs and dust. I watched the moonlight sneak through the window curtains as I drifted off to the sound of the ice machine rumbling next door.

21. Vivienne

I woke up at 10:14 am, stale, hard chocolate cake crumbs and icing nubs flattened on my forehead and chest, my arm dead and numb from hanging diagonally off the side of the bed throughout the night. Today was the day I had to drive back to LA. I felt a sense of loss, a deep sadness about leaving this place. I had made some genuine breakthroughs in my travels here, in such a short period of time.

Then I remembered the box. I had burned it all, her letters, the evidence of our mutual and unabashed affection for one another. I sat up in bed and felt an instant pang in my forehead, causing me to lay down again. I burned all of our things, I thought again, a drunken, split-second decision that separated her even further from me. I couldn't dwell on it for long; checkout was at 11 am and I needed to get moving.

I forced myself out of the bed, passing the empty Styrofoam cake box on the floor—streaked with fudge lines and crumbs—and took a quick shower. I washed my whole body, gliding the soap along my chest and legs before drying off and drinking four glasses of tap water. You're always parched in the desert; the water felt like it dried up the second it hit my throat.

I thought about my trip, how I felt a little bit more whole, more like myself again. I smiled, a real smile, and looked around at my little room while I packed the remainder of my things in my blue canvas bag. I lit a cigarette—for the road, I said to myself—and waved goodbye to my little desert home, throwing my bag over my shoulders and shutting the door behind me. I was greeted gleefully, as I was every morning, by a powerful and painfully bright blanket of sunshine. A kind of sunshine somehow so different from what I was used to in Los Angeles, a much more concentrated version.

I walked over to Randy's office and found him inside, glasses on, reading the Hi-Desert Proclaimer, the local newspaper. He barely looked up when he saw me. It was the look I'd become accustomed to seeing in the desert, the look of knowing people won't be here long, a look of non-attachment.

"So, today's the day, huh? How was your week of soul searching?" he asked, semi-jokingly, his eyes peeking over the top of his thick glasses. I looked at the headline glaring at me: 'UFOs Spotted Over Palm Desert, Are Aliens Real?'

"You know what, it was perfect. I don't really want to leave," I said.

"That's the desert for you, kid. She's a real harsh lover, the kind you don't forget easily." He laughed, but I knew he'd said that a hundred times to a hundred different people.

I handed my key to him, and he placed it back on its hook behind the desk.

"I'll be seeing you." He held his hand out.

"Thanks, Randy, for everything. Hopefully I'll be back sooner than later."

I shook his hand and headed toward the door, pulling it open before he shouted, "Have a safe drive, kid, and, hey, don't forget to pray! Jesus is always listening!"

I waved politely and headed toward the Bronco, which was now baking in the late morning sunlight.

As I tossed my bag onto the back seat, I noticed the absence of the box and remembered our letters and photographs turning to ash in the middle of the desert, buried, like her, in a hole in my chest. It was bittersweet to see her things gone, a separation of necessity, for my own sanity and survival. I hopped into the driver's seat and started the engine, taking one last look around the little motel oasis before driving off down the highway.

I passed everything that had become familiar to me over the past week. The Cholla Cafe, serving its hot breakfasts for hungry families and workers. Next door, the Cholla Bar would be setting up for Western Wednesdays this evening with Sage singing her vintage tunes and her father guarding the door. I wondered if she would meet someone and take them home tonight. Maybe she would meet someone her own age and not some suffering sap who was too stupid to ask her how old she was. I laughed again, replaying the evening in my head as I drove on.

At the edge of town, I stopped at the little gas station that appeared to provide the whole county with fuel and supplies and filled up the tank for the journey home. I took out my flimsy paper road maps and decided to take a scenic route, through the mountains over Idyllwild and down to the Los Angeles valley, before returning to my old life, my old apartment, my old job. Hopefully this time I won't be the old, depressed me. I wanted to hold on to what I had felt here, what I had learned, what I had let go of.

So, I drove. I drove long, windy desert roads, marveling as I had the first time over the infinite valleys and jagged mountains, the giant wind turbines, the outstretched, spiky Joshua trees, the pale-yellow sand and dust devils kicking up in the distance. The sun warmed the left side of my face as I listened to old country songs on the radio and let my mind wander.

As the mountain roads climbed from rocky desert into thicker patches of tall trees and eventually dense forest, I felt my body relax. I inhaled the deep, earthy smell of pine and bark, commingled with soil and mountain flowers, and I couldn't stop smiling, occasionally pulling over to explore small trails and paths leading into the woods. I wasn't ready to let go of this new sensation, this refreshed lease of life. I sat on a felled log and ate a sandwich from the service station, followed by some very warm Swedish fish, and let the forest engulf me in its towering wisdom, before climbing back in and continuing my drive, passing small mountain cafes, little log cabins and thrift shops, wooden bears carved by chainsaws posed in different, welcoming positions.

The road wound slowly back down the mountain, through thinning trees and tall grasses, and before I knew it I was spat onto a big highway and well on my way into LA, rejoining the congested traffic and familiar gray freeways that spaghetti sharply along the state. It was strange to see so many cars clumped together after seeing so few for a week, feeling so far removed from this overpopulated world. Everything looked grubby, busy, and apathetic. Drivers sat bored and bloated in their vehicles listening to the traffic updates and car accidents or roadside work that had caused frustrating backups on their commute home.

I sat with them, staring out of the window placidly into the stale, polluted air, attempting to guess what the people around me were thinking or feeling, if anything. My new high of freedom and release was wearing off and I was beginning to feel the heaviness of reality fall swiftly against my shoulders as I inched closer to my freeway exit and turned off toward my stagnant apartment. The apartment waiting for my return, full of dirty dishes, messy memories and dried blood.

I groaned as I made the last turn onto my street and pulled the Bronco into the parking space. I took a deep breath and exhaled as I stared at my building. I wanted to drive away, leave it all behind, fuck my job, my apartment, my savings. I wanted to go back to the desert.

But I didn't. I mumbled to myself anxiously as I collected my belongings and headed up the stairs, nervous as to what ecosystems and fungi had taken over the walls during the week I'd been absent.

I unlocked the door and let myself in. The place stunk of cigarettes and dirty laundry and old food. Not the nostalgic, cheap stench of my motel room but the musty funk of someone who hasn't been living for the last year and a half. It smelled like death.

I tossed my bag on the floor and decided not to let my newfound serenity escape this easily. I had a choice to make. I could go out, get drunk, smoke until my throat burned and leave this all to further decay, or I could take positive action and change it. So, I rolled up my sleeves and walked to the kitchen sink, recoiling at the sight and smell of stagnant water and mold covering the dishes. I turned the radio on, which was playing old jazz, and began to wash them, one by one. Then I dried them with a fresh towel, until they were all clean and put away in the cabinet. I wiped down the counters, which were coated in crumbs and old sauce remnants, then cleaned out the fridge, which was empty but laced with colorful blobs of unknown liquids and rotten milk.

Next, I went to my bedroom and gathered my laundry, the sheets, still covered in my own now-brown blood, sticking out of the top like a muffin. I thought of my pain again, how terrible it was to ask Jan to punch me, how I'd needed it. Then I wiped the thought away and shoved the sheets into the washing machine along with the other clothes I'd neglected to wash for weeks.

I gathered the various impromptu ashtrays, beer bottles, cans, and actual ashtrays filled with piles of smelly cigarette butts and threw them away in the already overstuffed trash can. Tying up the bursting bag, I carried it downstairs to add to my other neighbors' household garbage.

I returned to a disheveled, unmade bed, with a bare mattress covered by a thin duvet. I rifled around in my closet, avoiding her old clothes, for a pair of matching pillowcases and a clean fitted sheet, before making the bed properly for the first time in a year. I swept the hardwood floor next, creating little mounds of dust and crumbs and hair and mysterious other particles, making sure to carefully sweep around the remainder of her boxes, the ones I hadn't burned in the desert.

I hadn't realized through the cloudy months of sadness and grief how disgusting my environment had truly become. A once clean, orderly, well-tuned machine was reduced to a decaying squat. I emptied the last dustpan of grit into my waste bin and looked around, feeling proud of what I had accomplished in such a short time. I tugged open each of the window blinds, and the windows as well, letting the last of the evening light filter through and dance on the plain walls. Then I lit some old incense I found in a drawer, to mask the smell of depression and cigarettes. Now my apartment smelled like a 1920s boudoir.

I decided to go down to the corner grocery store and buy some food for my empty fridge. As I perused the aisles, I felt more excited by the labels, the colors and offers before me. I thought of simple meals I could make, easy recipes I could handle cooking for one. I bought coffee, a four-pack of beer, milk, butter, rice, lentils, tortillas, two types of pasta, three cans of beans and a block of parmesan cheese, along with a head of broccoli, four tomatoes, a bunch of bananas, a pineapple, six oranges, three lemons, two limes, a carton of eggs and a box of cornbread mix. This would do for the week.

At the checkout line, I threw a bag of peanut butter M&M's on the conveyor belt, the way I used to when I was with her. I observed my colorful array of food, not the simple pot of noodles or microwaved mush I had been used to over the past year. Food that looked flavorsome and full of nutrients. Once I'd paid, I gathered my bags and thanked the cashier before heading back to my apartment.

That night I didn't drink. Well, I didn't get drunk, which felt like a small success for me. I drank two beers with a lime wedged into the bottle and listened to the soft radio, after eating a delicious but simple dinner of rice and beans with corn tortillas, topped with plenty of habanero hot sauce.

I lay in my clean bed and thought about the open desert. I felt depleted and lonesome for her—the desert, that is. The feeling of emptiness and vastness somehow contradictorily made my heart feel fuller than it had in years. Maybe she was a harsh lover, and I was just her servant. I wanted her back.

I thought of Vivienne and Jan, Sage, and the other people I'd met and seen and pondered what my type was.

I didn't know if I had one anymore. I wondered if I should try dating again, but the thought made my mind and chest recoil as if I had been stung in the heart by an angry wasp. I turned onto my side and wondered about how long I could feel physically this way, how some days it waxed and waned so easily. Others, it plastered and drowned me to the point of catatonic suffocation.

I stared at the outline of her boxes in the corner and tossed and turned until I found my way back to the comforting silence of sleep.

22. Vivienne

I returned to work, a little lighter and more motivated. Not a minute too soon, either, as my boss was sure to inform me. People had noticed my lack of effort and sliding enthusiasm toward projects, which she admitted was costing them valuable time and money, not to mention further projects. I apologized and promised that I was in a better place now, that I could focus, do the work required of me, get back to the way I used to be. She seemed reassured. I thanked her for allowing me the time off, stating it was invaluable to my work and mental well-being moving forward. I knew I was cutting it close, so I tried to put on my best act.

Will called me that Friday evening, excited and anxious to hear about my big trip to the desert. He was as giddy as a schoolboy to listen to every one of my dusty adventures and the recounting of stupid and unique situations. He invited me to a show at a nearby music venue that night, a band I'd never heard of but sounded interesting, which I agreed to. After all, I desperately needed to get out of my house more, make more of an effort to see the people I cared about, even if I had to force myself.

I dressed in casual but nice clothes, black jeans with black boots and a clean white shirt, paired with a simple, lightweight jacket. I grabbed a fresh pack of cigarettes and a new lighter from the liquor store and headed down the street to meet Will outside the venue around 9 pm, without Agnes, who was at home grading her students' projects. He gave me a big hug and looked me up and down, in his ever cheerful, positive manner.

"Well holy shit! If it isn't the rugged old explorer back from his travels out west, the writing romantic, the hobo rambler!" he yelled jubilantly as I blushed.

"Yeah, yeah. So, you got your letter, I take it?"

"I almost cried, man. Agnes did cry. What did you do out there, peyote?" he joked.

"I wish. Not peyote. I thought a lot, I did a lot of driving, I met a few people. It was cool, I think it was good for me, in some way," I said, smiling a little.

"Well damn, man, that's great. Hey, this is really great. How are you feeling about things? You look a lot better, anyways. Did you meet anyone interesting out there?" He raised his eyebrows hopefully.

"Uh, kind of. I met a girl who played music, but it was totally fucked up. She didn't...She wasn't..."

"She wasn't what, a human? Did you get abducted out there? I know weird shit happens in the desert." He laughed as we walked toward the front door. I was glad to drop the subject.

We paid the cover and went in. It was relatively crowded for a smaller Hollywood venue, with a lot of typically well dressed, beautiful and artistic types mingling around, talking with cold drinks in their hands.

Will bought me a drink and we sat at a table, talking about everything I could recollect from my trip. I told him about Randy, and Sage, which caused him to erupt in laughter and scold me, before saying 'Mothers, lock up your daughters, a perverted prowler is on the loose!' causing me to shrink in my chair and melt into a puddle of shame and embarrassment.

I told him about snorting drugs, getting kicked out of her home with a gun to my chest and how I walked through the desert until I caught a ride back. All to the frozen, wide-eyed amusement of Will, who told me it served me right. I went on to say how she had returned my things and I was back on the straight and narrow from then. I told him about the museum and the cafes, the quartz crystal, but I didn't tell him about burning the box, I kept that for myself.

The band started to warm up, causing people to gather in front of the stage and limit their conversation. Will dragged me out of my chair, memories of sand and guns still in my head, and stood next to me in the back of the crowd as we watched the band begin to play. They were good, a mixture of folk and blues with instruments like a steel guitar and harmonica. They opened with a light folk song and people were dancing and hollering along. I stood there, feeling a warm composure flowing through my body, watching intently and feeling grateful that I was out of my house and back in the world.

As I watched the band wind down the first song to a roaring round of applause and cheers, I felt happier. I looked over at Will and he smiled at me, looking at me in a familiar, not worried way, unlike the way he'd been looking at me over the last two years.

"Do you want another drink?" he asked.

"Yeah, I do. Just a beer, thanks, man," I said, patting him on the back before he disappeared into the crowd.

The band was introducing themselves to the crowd and talking about their American tour. I was only half listening, half zoned out, feeling the peace of being away from my mind for a night. As I looked around the venue at the different faces and colorful art plastered on the wall, a familiar voice shook me from my silent observations.

"Hey, Venn."

I closed my eyes and turned around, stunned by fear.

It was her voice. The voice I'd heard a million times before, the voice I had fallen in love with from the first moment I'd heard it. The voice I cried with, laughed with, argued with, the voice that screamed in my throat as we came in bed together, the voice of my sorrow, my contentment, my persistent infatuation, the voice of my darling Vivienne.

I turned around, unsure if I had heard her correctly, feeling like I was going to be sick on the floor. My heartrate quickened and pulsed loudly in my ears to a deafening, dizzying volume. My hands shakily held my empty drink as I looked at her. She looked healthy, happy. She was wearing a simple, dark red dress and long navy coat, holding what looked like soda or maybe a gin and tonic. Her makeup was light and natural, with a small red outline, the same color as her dress, flushed around her lips. Her skin was glowing with a subtle dew, her perfect nose jutting out, her slightly crooked teeth showing from behind their red curtains.

I stared at her in shock, feeling suffocated, as I always had been, by her effortless beauty. The face that had caused a million births and deaths within my soul, the face of an angel and an executioner. Her hair was longer, dropping in small, delicate waves against her breasts as she stood before me in small heeled wooden clogs.

"Hello, Vivienne," was all I could muster. I continued to stare at her, jaw dropped, eyes wide, not knowing if she was real or if I had gone completely insane and conjured up a physical manifestation of her before me. And where the fuck was Will? I stood with my mouth open, not wanting her to be there, melting before her, not wanting her to leave.

"How are you doing? I'm so sorry about your mother, I heard about it from Violet, she was such a beautiful person, it's so horrible." she said eventually, looking at me like she felt sorry for me, like she pitied me, which made me feel even sicker.

"Oh, thanks. Yeah, it's been *really hard*." I looked into her eyes, emphasizing the words.

I'd known my mother was dying, Vivienne had known

she was dying, but she was the one who made me suffer, not my mother. She was the one who left me on my own to bury her. Left me to figure out who I was is the ashes of both their absences.

I saw Will walking back through the crowd towards me, totally oblivious to who I was talking to until he reached me, and his face turned pale in shock.

"Oh…hey, Viv, how's it going?" he said in a friendly, protective tone, looking quickly back at me, trying to gauge my reaction. I was still staring at her, in a pathetic, silent stupor.

"Hey, Will. So nice to see you, I'm really well. Say hi to Agnes for me, won't you?" she said in her charming, sweet way. I wanted to scream, disruptively drawing all and any attention away from her. But before I could she was joined by a tall, objectively attractive figure toting two drinks. He handed one to her and put his arm around her. I felt like I was suddenly covered in gasoline and lit on fire.

"Here's your sparkling water, this time with lime, babe," he said, smiling. He was mocking me with his smugness, looking at me and Will with a cocked head, then back to Vivienne, who spoke with confidence and grace.

"Guys, this is Andre, Andre, Will, and my friend Venn." She smiled at me, a wicked, smug smile.

Friend? Friend! The words instantly pelleted me with pain I tried in vain to conceal. Who the fuck was she to call me her friend. We weren't friends, we were cemented in love, entwined from the most minute fibers of our being for years.

How fucking dare she call me just her 'friend.' We didn't even talk anymore, she was as good as dead to me now, as dead as my mother. And had she not told this new important person in her life about me? About all we had endured together? A thick lump was beginning to swell in my throat.

"Nice to meet you," the tall figure said to me, with a big smile, shaking my dead, mechanical hand. I couldn't even say his name. My lips soured into a deep grimace, before he added cheerfully, "You guys here to see the Oats? They're very good, kind of like jazz and blues mixed with some kind of old Appalachian folk." He looked at Vivienne and smiled, totally enamored with her. She smiled back, looking disgustingly content. Were they on some kind of first date? How long had they known each other?

I downed my drink and nodded, not wanting to fully process what was happening before me.

"Yeah, they're pretty good," Will spoke for me, looking at me again with worried eyes. He knew I had just taken ten huge steps back in my mourning process.

"So, it was nice to see you, Venn, Will. Enjoy the show, yeah?" she said kindly. I frowned at her. I didn't want her to leave, I wanted her to come home with me.

"Well, as much as we can, anyway! Trying to get as many outings in as we can before the baby comes, right, babe?" Tall Man said, smiling widely before putting his hand over Vivienne's perfect stomach. I hadn't realized her coat was covering her stomach, but upon closer inspection I saw a curvature, a bump, a baby growing inside of her perfect

form. The baby I had denied her, and this guy had apparently delivered. A child we would never share together. A life we
would never have, not in this world at least. Now I really felt
like I was going to throw up.

"I've got to go. See you both around," I said, leaving
them standing there as the music played on.

Will ran after me and grabbed me by the shoulder,
looking me in the eyes. "I'm sorry, man, I'm so fucking sorry.
I didn't know she was back here, I thought she was still in
Berkeley, I didn't know…"

I looked over his shoulder at Vivienne, dancing lightly
with her new partner, floating sweetly in a safe bubble of
joy and new love and expectancy. A laugh broke out of her
mouth, and she flung her arms across his shoulders. I tensed
up and held my throat to stop it from closing entirely. That
used to be us, she used to look at me like that, she used to
love me. It was like watching an actor in a film move on from
one person to the next, seamlessly, without remorse or regret.
She had looked at me like I was an old acquaintance from
her childhood, a nobody, a loser.

"I've got to go, I'll call you later," I said in a curled, cutting tone before nearly running out of the venue, leaving Will
standing on the curb outside, watching me go, a dark, queasy
look on his face as I looked back in dismay and turned the
corner, leaving Vivienne dancing with her new lover.

On my way home I ducked into a liquor store and
bought a liter of whiskey. I was seeing red, everything was
blurry. I cracked open the bottle outside and sat down on

the curb beneath the streetlight. I chugged a huge gulp of harsh alcohol and choked as I swallowed it down, begging it to rob me of the memory of what I had just seen. Vivienne, with another person. Vivienne, pregnant. Vivienne, dancing without me at a show. She didn't even like folk shows. She never went to folk shows with me. Who was this new person? Was she just using me the entire time? Was I nothing to her? Were her words as shallow and hollow as her stare had been just then?

I lit a cigarette and tried to calm myself down. I couldn't stop seeing her face, that guy's face. I didn't want to think about them having sex, the way she had made love to me. I didn't want to think about their potentially perfect life and her transposing her specific love for me onto him. I didn't want to think about her being a mother to his child. I was so upset I couldn't do anything but chain smoke and drink on that curb. Multiple people went in and out of the liquor store, shooting me concerned looks as they drove away. I couldn't care less. She was really fucking gone.

I eventually peeled my drunken body from the curb around 1 am, my throat dry and burning. I walked home slowly, holding my whiskey bottle at my side, feeling too emotional to cry, too upset to sleep, too weak to do anything reckless.

The beginning of this week was such a revelation, a marvel. I had felt a genuine breakthrough in my grief and heartache, and now I was here, drunk on the street, wailing internally over the love of my life who was now with another. I hobbled up the stairs to my apartment and let myself in, sitting on the floor with my head in my hands, smoking, drinking, writhing in pain.

I looked up in the silver light and saw her boxes again. Boxes I had kept in the vain hope that perhaps she would someday return to me, want to try again, want to be with me. Now I knew, with absolute certainty, that she was never coming back. That any potential reconciliation between us was a pipe dream. She had moved on, truly moved on, while I stayed here amongst the ruins of our relationship and pretended to.

I got up and tossed her things into the boxes. Every little thing I could find. Her makeup, her perfume, her clothing, her knick-knacks and napkins and everything else she had left behind, throwing them all angrily into her boxes before closing them and stacking them up. One by one I took them outside to the dumpsters behind the apartment building, tossing them over the bin and into the dark cavern of trash. A lifetime of love dwindled down to six boxes. A lifetime of love that was long gone in her mind. I stared at the contents of her spilling out onto the stained, metal floor of the bin, before closing the lid and walking back up to my house. I looked around, inebriated, heavily choked up and full of sorrow, as I realized I had extricated every final piece of her from our once shared home.

I sat on the floor and drank more whiskey, lighting up more cigarettes as the minutes, then hours passed. I stared blankly at the wall and replayed her smile and teeth and her dancing with him. Then, finally, my eyelids went dark and all I could see was nothingness.

23. Vivienne

The last time I saw Vivienne was almost over a year ago. My mother had been diagnosed with lung cancer and I was spending more and more time away from home, going up to be with her in the hospital. She was fading quickly, and my brother and I were suffering the fallout of trying to both be there for her in equal measure, in addition to comforting our father, who was a complete wreck. They had been together for over thirty years, and she was too young to die.

Vivienne and I weren't in a good place when I first received the news. We weren't in a healthy place by any means, but it was a place I thought we could eventually recover from. She was spending more and more evenings away, with her friends and coworkers, working on art projects, at least that's what she had told me at the time. I was caught up in trying to be present for my dying mother and depressed partner and it was all too heavy on me.

I turned cold towards Vivienne. I lacked the necessary warmth and comfort a decent partner should have provided, and perhaps even grew a little resentful of her freedom and carelessness. Her parents were still healthy and alive, she had family money she could fall back on if she needed. I felt like my whole universe was crashing onto my shoulders and I began to calcify. I didn't ask her for emotional support or help, I didn't talk to anyone. I was callous, cruel toward her advances and attempts to mend me.

We argued more than ever, occasionally erupting into volatile verbal spats, causing her to flee our home for the evening, slamming the door behind her, staying God knows where. I would spend the night calling her dead phone, pacing back and forth along the wooden floorboards, worried sick about where she had ended up this time. Occasionally I'd find her sleeping on the sofa, even locked in the bathroom, having fallen asleep in the tub to avoid looking at me. Other times, when she returned in the morning, to my dismay she would ignore me, and I would ignore her, telling myself this was a temporary lull in our otherwise unbreakable union.

Until one day, after an all-night boxing match of verbal atrocities, she never returned home. Never answered my phone calls, never came back to collect her things. She just disappeared completely from my life. She had finally had enough, enough of the arguing, the petty disagreements over money and her life choices, the absence of my kindness while I tended to my ill mother, the aloof shadow I had become with her. Still, I didn't think she would ever leave. We had promised to be together until the end, through it all. She had promised to marry me.

I found out through mutual friends that she had driven up to Berkeley to stay with her parents while she looked for work. When she finally wrote to me, a short note telling me to donate her things, I didn't believe her. I chalked it up to anger, or some dramatic stunt she was pulling in order to hurt me or gather my attention. Still, I waited, and still she never returned. When six months passed and she hadn't come back, I fell into a deep layer of darkness and depression I couldn't attempt to describe. I continued visiting my mother until she died in the hospital. A cutting, life shattering event that worsened my already fragile condition. I needed Vivienne back. I continued to write and call her, to no response, eventually she changed her phone number, and I was calling a ghost. In one small year, I had lost the two most important women in my life, and I was completely broken.

I pretended she had died, too. Somehow it was easier for me to accept that she was dead than gone and moving on happily without me. I couldn't imagine existing without her, even with the arguments, the disagreements, the dysfunctional pain. I saw her everywhere, in every face, in every voice, in every movement past me, and I ached for her presence, in any capacity. I listened for her key to return to the doorknob, for her to come dancing back into my arms, but that day never came.

24. Venn

I woke up on my apartment floor, covered in drool and ash and booze sweat. My aching head was throbbing harder than a jackhammer. As I stood up, acrid bile rose in my throat, and I ran to the bathroom and threw up in the sink. Harsh, chemical flavored liquid spewed down the drain and splashed over the sides of the sink. When the last of the vomit slowed to a dry heave, I washed my face and drank water from the tap before drying my mouth off roughly with a towel.

I looked in the mirror. My face, swollen and red, was beaded with sweat and floor marks. I sighed heavily, feeling the weight of my decisions on my shaky body. I walked to the kitchen and made myself a coffee, sitting at my table while I waited for it to brew. Then I remembered. I remembered everything. The venue, the band, her pregnant stomach, her new partner, her happiness. I laid my head on the table and tried to forget it, with no success. My coffee hissed and I got up to pour myself a cup, clumsily spilling boiling liquid over the counter.

Then, a realization came. I abruptly felt a dense cloud lifting from my darkness. She was gone, she was really gone.

I looked back into the hall where her things were formerly boxed up, waiting patiently for her to come home, unpack them and continue her life with me. They were gone. Everything was gone. I poured my coffee down the sink and went to the bedroom to lay down, covering my eyes with the blankets and curling up into a ball beneath them. I swallowed bile and cried over her, over the final severance of our relationship, from the first sight of her in her green dress to the last sight of her, swollen and happy in love with another person.

I woke up at 7 am on Sunday morning. I'd slept for longer than I had in two years. A long, dreamless, dead night's sleep. Surprisingly, I felt physically rested. Although my body groaned and ached with hunger and thirst. A light headache dully pulsed down the back nape of my neck.

I flimsily shuffled to the bathroom and turned the shower on, taking a longer shower than normal, washing my oily hair and face, letting the water cleanse me of my painful realizations.

I stepped out and looked in the mirror, really taking a good look at myself, at my eyes, my sunken bags, my skin. I took out a razor and shaved my stubble and rough patches, cleaning them up around the cheeks and ears. I subtly recognized this person, even if the reflection was fragmented and a bit too thin for my liking.

Then I made my way to the bedroom and mechanically made my bed. The way I always used to make it, properly, not cutting any corners. Making sure to tuck in the sheets and pillowcases. I dressed in a simple shirt and trousers and combed my hair, the way I used to, focusing on taming my wavy, occasionally wayward hair into place.

I sauntered casually into the kitchen and put the coffee pot on to boil, before cleaning up the overflowing ashtray and cigarette butts. I took the leftover whiskey and poured it down the sink, watching the last of the brown liquid bubble as it left its bottle. I took the cigarette box and crushed it in my hands, throwing it into the trashcan and cleaning up the fallen ashes from the floor with a wet tea towel.

Taking two brown eggs out of the fridge and cracking them into a bowl, I added a smooth sliced red chili and cracked black pepper while I whisked them together, forming a gloopy, bright yellow liquid. I heated up a frying pan and placed it over the flames, before pouring myself a cup of steaming hot coffee. I moved the eggs around in the pan, watching them bubble and solidify as I scrambled them together with a wooden spatula. I plated them up on a clean plate before turning on the radio to my favorite station. Soothing music wafted slowly into the room and mingled with the enticing scent of Sunday breakfast.

I placed the eggs and coffee down on my dining room table, opened the blinds and windows, and sat down before my simple meal. I stared down, stabbing my dull fork at the coagulated mass of yellow protein. As I ate and drank, I thought of nothing. Nothing but quiet thoughts, passing thoughts. For the first time in years, I didn't think about her coming back. I didn't hear her voice calling to me from the far side of the kitchen. I didn't notice her absence beside me, and I didn't crave her touch. I suddenly realized, putting my fork down in shock and gazing forward, that today I didn't miss her. For the first time since I had met her, I felt like I was finally alone in my home, and in my mind. I felt like I was going to survive without her.

I could, indeed, live without the person I felt I couldn't possibly live without.

I stared down at my nearly empty plate and laughed.

Printed in Great Britain
by Amazon

36463514R00179